DEADLY DRUNK

"You're a brazen bastard. I'll give you that, Burrack," Stone said, the gun level and steady in spite of the whiskey goading his thoughts, his rationality.

Sam offered no reply. He stopped and gazed at the sheriff, letting his hands lower a little.

"The judge said you kept Dexter Benson from killing him midtrial, over in Merit," Sam said, wanting to cool the tension.

Stone stared at him. Sam saw the sheriff appear to replay the scene in his whiskey-pinched mind.

"Long time ago," Stone said finally. Sam noted the Colt never lowered an inch. Drunk or sober, this lawman was no easy call. "I did shoot ol' Dexter the Snake. Somebody had slipped him a gun. He jumped up with it from his chair and flipped a table over—I put three rounds through the table before he could get a shot off."

"Judge said your shots fit in a circle no bigger around than a tin top," Sam said to Stone.

"My shots always did," Stone said, still with the stare, the leveled Colt.

SHOWDOWN AT GUN HILL

—

Ralph Cotton

A SIGNET BOOK

SIGNET
Published by the Penguin Group
Penguin Group (USA) LLC, 375 Hudson Street,
New York, New York 10014

USA | Canada | UK | Ireland | Australia | New Zealand | India | South Africa | China
penguin.com
A Penguin Random House Company

First published by Signet, an imprint of New American Library,
a division of Penguin Group (USA) LLC

First Printing, July 2015

Copyright © Ralph Cotton, 2015

Ⓣ REGISTERED TRADEMARK—MARCA REGISTRADA

ISBN 978-0-451-47158-1

Printed in the United States of America
10 9 8 7 6 5 4 3 2 1

For Mary Lynn, of course . . .

Part 1

Chapter 1

Big Silver, the Arizona Badlands

At first light, Arizona Territory Ranger Sam Burrack followed a series of pistol shots the last mile into town. The shots came spaced apart, as if offered by some wild-eyed orator who used a gun to drive home the points of his raging soliloquy. Sensing no great urgency in the shots, Sam had circled wide of the town limits and ridden in from the south, keeping his copper black-point dun at an easy gallop. At his side he led a spare horse on a short rope.

Being familiar with the position of the town, he knew if he'd followed the main trail into Big Silver at this time of morning he would have ridden face-first into the rising sunlight—not a wise move under the circumstances. Never a wise move, he reminded himself, given his line of work.

His line of work . . .

A Winchester repeating rifle stood in its saddle boot; his bone-handled Colt stood holstered on his hip, hidden by his duster but close to his right hand. Necessary tools for *his line of work* . . .

A block ahead of him another pistol shot rang out in the still air—the *fourth*, he noted to himself. Along the street townsfolk who had scrambled for cover a few minutes earlier when the shooting began now looked out at the Ranger from behind shipping crates, firewood and anything else sufficient to stop a bullet.

"He's in his office, Ranger!" a nervous townsman's voice called out from a recessed doorway.

"Thank God you're here!" a woman's voice put in. "Please don't hurt him."

"Hurt him, *ha*!" another voice shouted. "Shoot that drunken son of a—" His words stopped short under the roar of a fifth gunshot.

"Everybody keep back out of sight," the Ranger called out.

He veered his dun into the mouth of an alleyway for safety's sake and stepped down from his saddle. The big dun grumbled and pawed its hoof at the dirt, yet Sam noted that the animal showed no signs of being spooked or otherwise thrown off by the sound of gunfire.

"Good boy," he said to the dun, rubbing its muzzle. The spare horse sidled close to the dun. As Sam spun the dun's reins and the spare's lead rope around a post, a townsman dressed in a clerk's apron hurried into the alley and collapsed back against the wall of a building.

"Man, are we glad to see you, Ranger!" he said. "Didn't expect anybody to show up so soon."

"Glad I can help," was all Sam replied. He didn't

bother explaining that he'd been headed to Big Silver to begin with, or that he'd ridden all night from Dunston, another hillside mining town some thirty miles back along the Mexican border. As soon as the telegram arrived, Sam had gathered his dun and the spare horse and headed out. He'd made sure both horses were well grained and watered. He'd eaten his dinner in the saddle, from a small canvas bag made up at Dunston's only restaurant. "Good eten," he could still hear the old Dutch cook say, handing him the bag.

He drew the Winchester from its boot and checked it. Hopefully he wouldn't need it. *But you never know*, he told himself.

"Say, Ranger," said the man in the clerk's apron, eyeing the Winchester, "you're not going in there alone, are you?"

"Yep," Sam said. He started to take a step out onto the empty street.

"Because I can get half the men in this town to arm up and go with you," the man said.

Sam just looked at him; the man looked embarrassed.

"All right," he said, red-faced, "why didn't we do that to begin with? is what you're wondering. The fact is, we didn't know what to do, a situation like this." He gestured a nervous hand in the direction of the gunfire. "He claimed he's a wolf! Threatened to rip somebody's heart out if we didn't all do like he told us!"

"A wolf . . . ," the Ranger said flatly, looking off along the street. He took a breath.

"That's right, a *wolf*," the man said even though Sam

hadn't posed his words as a question. "Can you beat that?"

"It wasn't their hearts he said he'd rip out," another townsman said, cowering back into the alley. "It was their *throats*!" He gripped a hand beneath his bearded chin and stared at Sam wide-eyed with fear.

"It was their *heart*, Oscar," the man in the clerk's apron said. "I ought to know what I heard."

"*Throat*," the old man insisted in a lowered voice as he cowered farther back.

Sam looked all around. The alley had started to fill with people pouring into it from behind the row of buildings along the main street. Another shot rang out; people ducked instinctively.

Number six, Sam told himself.

"All of you stay back," he said calmly.

As he stepped out and walked along the street, he knew that he only had a few seconds during reload to make whatever gains he could for himself. He pictured the loading gate of a smoking revolver opening, an empty shell falling from its smoking chamber to the floor. Another shell dropped, and another. . . .

As he walked forward he gauged his pace, keeping it deliberately slow, steady, trying to time everything just right. Now he saw the fresh rounds appear, being thumbed into the gun one at a time by a hand that was anxious, unsteady, in a boiling rage. Then, with the scene playing itself out in his mind, as if signaled by some unseen clock ingrained in his instincts, Sam stopped in the middle of the street—it was time—and faced a faded wooden sign that read in bold letters above a closed door: SHERIFF'S OFFICE & TOWN JAIL.

Here goes. . . .

"Sheriff Sheppard Stone," he called out loud enough to be heard through the closed door, above an angry rant of curses and threats toward the world at large. "It's Ranger Sam Burrack. Lay your gun down, come out here and talk to me." Looking around, he saw empty whiskey bottles littering the ground and boardwalk out in front of the building. Broken bottle necks lay strewn where bullets had blasted their fragile bodies into shards.

"Well, well, well," a whiskey-slurred voice called out through a half-open front window, *"Saint* Samuel Burrack. To what do I owe the honor of your visit?"

Saint Samuel Burrack . . . ? He hadn't heard that one before. Just whiskey talking, he decided.

"Territory judge Albert Long sent me, Sheriff," he said. "He wants to see you in Yuma." He wasn't going to mention that the judge had heard outrageous complaints about Stone's drunkenness and had sent Sam to persuade the sheriff to step down from office. A year earlier, *drunk*, Stone had accidentally shot two of his toes off.

"Oh . . . what about?" Stone asked in a wary tone. "Is he wanting my badge?" He paused, but only for a moment. "If he is, tell him to come take it himself. Don't send some *upstart do-gooder* to take on the job."

Upstart do-gooder? A couple more names Sam hadn't heard himself called before—although he'd heard himself called worse.

He took a breath. All right, this wasn't going to be easy, he told himself, but at least there were no bullets flying through the air. Not yet anyway.

So far so good.

"The judge said you and he were old friends," he replied, ignoring the drunken threat, the name-calling. "Said you once saved his life. Now he wants you to come visit him . . . spend some time on his ranch outside Yuma, I understand."

"Ha!" Stone said in more of a jeer than a laugh. "Spend some time on the judge's ranch. . . ." His words trailed into inaudible cursing and slurred mumbling. Then he called out, "Let me ask you something, Ranger. Does anybody ever fall for these yarns you pull out of your hat?"

Sam let it go. But he couldn't stand out here much longer. He had to get the gun out of the sheriff's hand. Whiskey was too unpredictable to reason with.

"I'm coming in, Sheriff Stone," he said. "Don't shoot."

"You ain't coming in! Take one step, you're dead!" Stone shouted, the whiskey suddenly boiling up again.

"I've got to. It's too hot out here," Sam called out, calmly, taking a step forward. He ignored a gunshot when it erupted through the half-open window and kicked up dirt only inches from the toe of his boot.

"The next one won't be aimed at the dirt!" the drunken sheriff shouted.

"I'm coming in," Sam said in a steady tone. He knew a warning shot when he saw one. Whiskey or no whiskey, he had to gain all the space he could, get in closer.

It was a dangerous gamble, but he took it. Another bullet erupted. More dirt kicked up at his feet. Realizing Stone had not made good on his threat, Sam took another step, then another.

"Hold it, damn it!" Stone shouted. "Come on in, then, but first lay that rifle on the ground! Don't test me on this."

All right . . . Sam let out a tense breath, calming himself.

"Sheriff, look," he said, "I'm laying it down right here." He stooped, laid the Winchester on the dirt, then straightened and walked forward, his hands chest high.

When he stepped through crunching broken glass onto the boardwalk, the door swung open before he reached for the handle. In the shade of the office, Sheriff Stone stepped back five feet, a big Colt cocked in his hand. He weaved drunkenly. His eyes were red-rimmed and staring through a veil of rage. Sam glanced past him through a cloud of burnt gunpowder and saw two frightened eyes staring at him from the jail's only cell.

"You're a brazen bastard. I'll give you that, Burrack," Stone said, the gun level and steady in spite of the whiskey goading his thoughts, his rationality.

Sam offered no reply. He stopped and gazed at the sheriff, letting his hands lower a little.

"The judge said you kept Dexter Benson from killing him midtrial, over in Merit," Sam said, wanting to cool the tension.

Stone stared at him. Sam saw the sheriff appear to replay the scene in his whiskey-pinched mind.

"Long time ago," Stone said finally. Sam noted the Colt never lowered an inch. Drunk or sober, this lawman was no easy call. "I did shoot ol' Dexter the Snake. Somebody had slipped him a gun. He jumped up with it from his chair and flipped a table over—I put three rounds through the table before he could get a shot off."

He was talking, which was good, Sam noted to himself. Inside the cell behind the sheriff, the two frightened eyes had moved sidelong to the farthest corner and sunk back into the striped shadows.

"Judge said your shots fit in a circle no bigger around than a tin top," Sam said to Stone.

"My shots always did," Stone said, still with the stare, the leveled Colt.

Always *did* . . . not always *do*, Sam noted, trying to get an idea of what was going on in the man's mind.

"What happened here?" Sam asked bluntly, gesturing a nod toward the bottle-littered street.

"I've been drunk longer than I've ever been sober," Stone said in a defiant tone. "That's what *happened here*. Think the judge will want me to *visit* him, the shape I'm in?" He emphasized the word *visit* with a wry twist.

"If he doesn't, he can send you home," Sam replied. "He said to bring you, so that's what I'm doing." He lowered his hands a little more. Watching for any change in the way the drunken sheriff kept his Colt level and steady, he took another step closer.

"Huh-uh, Ranger," said Stone, "not so fast. You're not taking me anywhere."

Sam stopped. He needed an edge, something to tip the scales in his favor, but so far he saw no sign of one.

"Lift that Colt off your hip easy-like and pitch it away," Stone ordered. "I've heard too many stories of how you trick a man and get the drop on him. It ain't going to happen here." As he spoke he swayed on his feet, dangerously close to falling. He batted his eyes to keep them open; still the sheriff's Colt stayed leveled and steady in his hand.

Sam just stared at him for a second. Finally he eased his right hand toward the butt of his holster Colt.

"You're the law here," he said humbly. "You're the one holding the gun."

"You're well told I am," said Stone, swaying even more on his feet.

Sam reached down and lifted his Colt calmly from its holster and raised it slowly, his hand around the butt.

Stone noted that instead of using two fingers to raise the Colt, Sam used his whole hand. But before he could say anything about it, Stone saw the Colt level and cocked in the Ranger's hand. The sheriff had just witnessed his best advantage turn into an equal standoff.

"Damn you, Burrack," he growled, realizing his was no longer the only cocked gun in play. "I told you, you're not pulling that trick on me."

"What trick?" Sam said quietly, stepping closer as he spoke, getting arm's length from Stone before the drunken sheriff seemed to realize it.

"That trick!" Stone said, incensed, knowing he'd just been had, knowing he'd even asked for it. His face reddened with humiliation.

"Turn the gun away from me and uncock it, Sheriff,"

Sam said with more authority in his voice. "You've taken this as far as it's going." He'd moved in, the situation turning better for him.

"Why, you—" Stone's words stopped short as Sam's big Colt swung around in a flash, his thumb clamping down in front of the cocked hammer for safety. The long barrel made the hard, sharp sound of steel on bone and sent the sheriff backward to the floor, knocked out cold. Stone's own cocked pistol flew from his hand and went off as it slid away across the plank floor.

The Ranger stepped over and picked up the smoking Colt and laid it on the sheriff's battered oak desk.

"Everything all right in there?" a voice called out from the street.

"Yep, we've worked it out," Sam called back in reply. He looked into the cell and saw the frightened prisoner spring from the shadowed corner with a cry of relief.

"My God, Ranger! Let me *out of here*!" the prisoner shrieked, grabbing the bars with both hands as if to pull them down. Sam noted his ragged work clothes and mining boots. A week's worth of dark beard stubble shone on his face.

Sam picked up the key to the cell from atop the sheriff's desk. "What's your name? What are you in for?" he asked quietly as he walked over to the cell door, staring at the disheveled hair and the terrified eyes.

"Caywood Bratcher . . . in for drunk and rowdy," the prisoner said hastily. "I might have also been a little disrespectful to some passing townsfolk."

Sam started to stick the key in the door lock. But he

hesitated. "You don't want me finding out you're lying," he warned.

"I'm not! I'm not! I swear I'm not," the miner said rapidly. "I was drunk and rowdy, is all. I'll pay my fine, whatever you say. Please let me out!" As the Ranger pushed the key in the lock and turned it, the prisoner glanced fearfully toward the knocked-out sheriff. "Although three days locked in here with that lunatic ought to be punishment enough. I might never drink again."

Sam glanced all around the small office, seeing bullet holes in the walls, ricochet dings on the iron bars.

"I'm letting you go, Caywood Bratcher," he said. "Get on back to your mining."

"I'm gone," the prisoner said over his shoulder, already headed for the door. "No disrespect for the law, Ranger, but that crazy sumbitch turns himself into a wolf, a bear, a bat . . . all kinds of things—gave me the willies just hearing about it."

"Get on out of here, Caywood," Sam said.

"No offense, Ranger, there's plenty of crazy drunks in Big Silver without the sheriff being one," the miner said on his way out the door. "Something ought to be done."

"That's why I'm here," Sam said quietly as the miner's boots stomped hurriedly across the boardwalk.

Chapter 2

———

Sheriff Stone awakened inside the cell, sprawled on one of the four cots set up along the walls. Outside the cell, the Ranger stood holding two steaming mugs of coffee in his hands. He watched as the waking sheriff moaned and raised a hand to the dark bruise reaching up along his left jawline. Early sunlight streamed through the front window and partially open door.

"Morning, Sheriff," Sam said, moving forward to the cell.

Stone pushed himself up onto the side of the cot with shaky hands and stared out at him with a puzzled expression. He looked over at the sunlight; he rubbed a hand on his sore beard-stubbled jaw. Then he looked back at the Ranger.

"Ranger Burrack . . . ?" he said with uncertainty. "Is that . . . *you*?"

"It's me, Sheriff," Sam said. "Can you use some hot coffee?"

"Oh yes," the sheriff said without hesitation. He made a failed attempt to rise from the cot, then sank back down, looking as if the room had started to tilt around him.

"Easy does it, Sheriff," Sam cautioned. "You've been in and out for a while. Careful getting your legs back."

"In and out for *a while*?" said Stone, confused, looking all around the cell, seeing early sunlight shine through a small barred window. "The sun's still coming up."

"Yep, but you haven't seen it do that the past two days," Sam replied. "Get up slow and easy."

"*Two days?*" the sheriff said, this time making it to his feet unsteadily when he pushed himself up and swayed forward.

"Two days," Sam repeated. He stepped over and set the sheriff's coffee mug on the battered desk and picked up the key to the cell.

The sheriff managed to stagger forward and grab the bars to steady himself.

"I've been out for *two days*. . . ." He pondered it for a moment, trying to pull up any memory of the time he'd lost. He looked up and all around. "Why am I locked in my own jail?" he asked. "Who hit me in the jaw?"

"I locked you up for your own good," Sam said. "I hit you in the jaw because I didn't want to shoot you. Sound fair?" he asked in a quiet tone.

Stone only stared, rubbing his sore jaw.

"Where's Caywood, my prisoner?" he asked.

"I let him go," said Sam, unlocking the cell door. "I needed the room."

Stone sniffed the air.

"It smells something awful in here," he said.

"Yep, it does," Sam agreed.

Stone looked around at the bullet holes and ricochet nicks all over his office, a pile of empty whiskey bottles in a garbage crate.

"Jesus, I did all this?" he said.

"Yep," Sam said again. He swung the cell door open and stepped back for the sheriff to walk out of the cell. Stone made his way around behind his desk and hung on to its edge. He reached a shaky hand down and pulled open a bottom drawer.

"I—I don't remember much," he said. His trembling fingers searched all around in the open drawer. "I've got to pull myself together . . . get to work."

"I threw it out, Sheriff," Sam said. "The drinking's over."

"I always have a little bracer this time of morning," Stone said. "It steadies my hand the whole day."

"Not this morning, Sheriff," Sam said. "We've got a long ride ahead of us."

The sheriff looked at him through bloodshot eyes, his mood turning ugly at the prospect of not having a drink to calm his shakes and tremors.

"The hell you say," he replied, straightening. "Who do you think you are, Ranger, coming in here, giving orders, making me look like a fool in my own town—"

"You've been telling townsfolk that you turn into a wolf, Sheriff," Sam said, cutting him off. "It's time to get off the whiskey."

"A *wolf*?" Stone said. That stopped him. "Jesus . . ." He squinted and dug deep for any remembrance of the past few days. Things were starting to come back to him, but his mind was working slowly, still under the effects of alcohol. He straightened again and ran his trembling fingers back through his graying hair. "So what? Lakota medicine men claim to do that all the time."

"You're not a medicine man," Sam said flatly. "You're a lawman. A lawman who's been drunk a long time. Now it's time to get sober."

"Don't preach," the sheriff said in a warning tone. He glanced down into the empty drawer again, and an angry look appeared on his face when he still couldn't find his hidden bottle.

Sam just watched.

"You've no right coming here sounding off to me, sticking me in a cell, shaming me," Stone said, needing a drink more and more with every passing minute.

"You shame yourself, Sheriff," Sam said. "If I wanted to make you look bad, I'd lead you out of here in hand-cuffs."

"Lead me out of here?" Stone said. "Lead me where?"

Sam let out a patient breath. "You're riding with me to Yuma, to Judge Long's ranch, remember? We talked about it." He wasn't going to mention that when they'd talked about it, Stone had refused to go.

Stone tried hard to remember. He only managed to pull up parts of the conversation they'd had.

"Yeah, sort of," he said. As he spoke he reached down and felt his Colt in its holster. He looked back up at the Ranger.

"I holstered it for you," Sam said. "I didn't want you

seen leaving here unarmed either. That would have been as bad as handcuffed."

Stone took a deep breath, realizing how tough the Ranger could have played this if he'd had a mind to.

"Obliged, Ranger," he said, trying to calm his shaking hands. "I didn't mean to get mouthy with you. It was the whiskey talking. It's been doing my thinking for me lately."

"I know it," Sam said. "As long you say you've been drunk, it's going to try to keep doing your thinking for you. You've got to leave it in the bottle."

"I'll get sober," Stone said. "Only, it would help to have just one drink—just a shot, enough to get myself untangled—"

"No drink," Sam said. "I told you we've got a long ride ahead. You're going to make it there sober."

Anger flared again on Stone's brow. His hand dropped over his gun butt.

"I need a drink bad, Ranger, damn it! You do not want to cross me on this."

"It's not loaded," Sam said calmly, nodding at the holstered Colt standing beneath the sheriff's trembling palm. "I didn't want them seeing you unarmed, but there's no way I'd trust you with a loaded gun."

The sheriff stared at him, his hands and face trembling like those of a man with a bad fever. Finally he managed to get himself back under control. He eased down into his desk chair and gripped his shaky hands around the hot coffee mug. Then he raised his hands and swabbed them over his sweaty face. "I don't know how I ever got in this shape, Ranger," he said.

"Think about it later," Sam said. "First thing to do is get yourself out of it."

"You're right," Stone said humbly. "I've got to get myself sobered and cleaned up." He raised the coffee mug to his lips with both hands and sipped it down carefully. "First thing I'm going to get is a hot bath."

Sam only watched and listened, the sheriff sounding a little inauthentic to him.

"It's going to take me a while," Stone continued. "I'll tell you what, Ranger, why don't you ride on ahead? I'll just get cleaned up some and join you along—"

"We're ready to ride, Sheriff," Sam said, cutting him off.

Again the whiskey flared in Stone's head. "Damn it, Ranger, I can't just haul up at the last minute and ride off to Yuma with you! I've got to get my horse ready, load my saddlebags—"

"I've had two days to prepare," Sam said. "I boarded my spare horse at the livery. Your horse and mine are ready, standing at the hitch rail. Your saddlebags are packed. The blacksmith is going to serve as deputy while you're gone."

"Elmore Frazer can't handle my job," Stone said. "Law work ain't like shoeing a horse. A man has to be ready for anything, at all times."

Sam gave him a look; Stone's face reddened in shame.

"There's a water hole seven miles out," Sam said, letting the matter drop. "You can get cleaned up there."

The sheriff wrung his shaking hands together, all out of excuses.

"I see you've thought of every damn thing, Burrack,"

he said with sarcasm. "You going to crack me in the head again if I say I ain't going?"

Sam didn't reply; he only stared, leaving the sheriff's question hanging between them.

"Damn this all to hell," Stone growled, pushing himself up from his chair. "I don't even remember saying I'd go to Yuma with you."

"There must be a lot you don't remember, Sheriff," Sam said, stepping over and opening the front door for them. "Maybe some of it will come back to you along the trail."

Stone reached over and took down his hat and riding duster from a wall peg and put them on. He started toward the door. Then he stopped.

"I need to tell you, Ranger, there might be some saddle tramps wanting to kill me," he said.

"Might be?" Sam said.

"Yeah, there will be. I'm sure of it," said Stone. "They work for a rancher named Edsel Centrila. Ever heard of him?"

"I've heard of him," Sam said. "Why does he want you killed?"

"He claims I owe him money," Stone said.

"Do you?" Sam asked.

"Yeah, sort of," said Stone, getting edgy again just talking about it.

"Nobody *sort of* owes somebody money," Sam said. "Either you do or you don't."

"I *do*, then, if you put it that way," said Stone. "Anyway, we could run into them out there. They could be waiting anywhere along the trail to Yuma."

The Ranger gestured him toward the open door.

"I'm glad you told me before we got under way," he said wryly.

"It just came back to me. I figured you ought to know," said Stone. "These gunmen are the Cady brothers, Lyle and Ignacio. They're dangerous hombres—especially Ignacio." He walked out the door, across the boardwalk and down to the waiting horses.

"Obliged for you telling me," Sam said in the same tone as they unhitched their mounts and swung up into their saddles. "If anything else comes back to you, be sure to let me know."

"I will," Stone said flatly, his hands trembling on the reins as they both turned their animals to the street.

At the water hole seven miles outside Big Silver, Sam sat with a telescope to his eye. He watched the trail snake south along the hill lines and desert flats. Behind him, Sheriff Stone walked up barefoot, wearing his frayed long johns, carrying his boots and wet clothes under his arm. His graying hair dripped water under the edge of his hat brim. His gun belt hung over his shoulder, carrying his unloaded Colt.

"I have to admit, I feel a little better after that," he said. He wiped a hand over his wet face. "What are you watching out there?"

Without turning, Sam held the telescope up to him.

"Are they the Cady brothers?" he asked.

Stone took the telescope and dropped his boots and clothes in a pile. He raised the lens to his eye and searched out through the glaring sunlight until he spotted rising streams of trail dust following two riders toward the water hole.

"That's them all right," he said. "They had to be watching the town, to show up this quick."

Sam just looked at him.

"They're coming from the opposite direction," he said.

"You're right. They are," said Stone, getting defensive, lowering the lens. "So I should have caught that, so what? I would have caught it, had I gotten my eye-opener before we left."

Sam wasn't going to waste time arguing the point.

"Get yourself dressed," he said. "They'll be riding in here soon enough."

"But maybe they're not looking for me," Stone said, sounding shaky and cross all over again. "Maybe they're just riding to town for a drink, some faro. They both like faro."

Sam stared at him.

"Even so," he said. "Don't you think we ought to be ready for them, just in case?"

Stone rubbed a trembling hand across his forehead. He looked troubled, confused and agitated.

"Of course we should, Ranger. I know that. I'm just trying to get my thoughts collected." He wiped his whole face as if clearing off cobwebs. "All right . . . first thing, I need some bullets." He held a shaky hand out toward the Ranger.

Sam looked him up and down, judging his condition, seeing his trembling hands, his sweaty face.

"Huh-uh," he said, "no bullets for you—not the shape

you're in. When they get here you stand back, let me handle them."

"Ranger, nobody has to do my fighting for me," Stone said in an anger-proud tone. "I was handling tramps like this, drunk or sober, when you was just a—"

"But you're not going to today," Sam said sternly, cutting him off. "Every time I see you flare up, it tells me you're still too shaky to be handling a gun. The best thing you can do is get yourself settled down and get the whiskey out of your head."

"And meanwhile I have to stand here with an unloaded gun?" said Stone. "Let another man do my fighting for me? I can't do that, Ranger. You should know I can't. I'm a lawman just like you—"

"No, you're not," Sam said, again cutting him off. "You've been a whiskey drunk. I haven't. I'm not doing another lawman's fighting. I'm doing what I have to do for both our good. Now stand down and try to keep your shaking under control."

Stone bristled, but he shut up and stood rigid, his feet shoulder-width apart.

After a moment of silence, Sam said quietly, "Are you going to get your clothes and boots on before they get here?" He looked Stone up and down as he spoke.

Stone glanced down, then looked up in surprise, realizing his clothes and boots were still on the ground where he'd piled them a moment ago.

Sam shook his head and walked to where the horses stood at the water's edge. He drew his Winchester from his saddle boot and walked out of sight behind an eight-foot boulder on the side of the trail. Stone stepped over to his boots and clothes and dressed quickly as the sound of hooves grew clearer on the last thirty yards of trail leading up to the water hole. The Ranger stayed out of sight as the two riders brought their horses down to a walk, then stopped ten feet from where Stone stood staring at them.

"Well, well, what have we here?" said Ignacio Cady, a tall, swarthy gunman with a long scar on his right cheek.

"We've got a drunk who don't pay his debts, Iggy," said Lyle Cady, a heavier version of his brother, Ignacio, only with a wide waxed handlebar mustache.

"Are you boys dogging me?" Stone said, playing his part pretty well, Sam thought, watching from the cover of the boulder. Stone managed to keep his hands steadier, his face still sweaty, but with a dark determination. *Real good*, Sam thought, *for a man with an unloaded gun on his hip*.

"Oh, yes, we're *dogging you*," Ignacio said. "We'll dog you until you make good on your word." He looked all around. "Where is the Ranger traveling with you?"

"Right here," Sam said, stepping out from behind the boulder, walking forward as the two turned their horses to face him.

"Ranger, you need to know you're traveling with a man who takes money to perform a service, then crawfishes on the deal."

"Oh? Is that so?" Sam said, stepping closer, sounding interested. "You rode all this way just to tell me that?"

"Yes, we did." Ignacio grinned. "Just so you'll know,

we'll be showing up every now and then, reminding the sheriff here what happens when a man doesn't stick to his word."

"All right, I understand," Sam said, standing close now, but looking relieved, letting his rifle slump a little in his hands. He turned toward Stone. "See? I told you they might not be hard to get along with."

"Hard to *get along with*?" said Ignacio. He grinned sidelong at his brother, the two also looking relieved, letting their guard down a little. He started to say more, but before he could, the Ranger's rifle butt struck hard, sideways into his shin, knocking his boot from his stirrup. Ignacio let out a yell in pain. His horse spooked. Before the horse could bolt, Sam grabbed the sole of Ignacio's boot and heaved him upward out of his saddle. Then he grabbed the horse's reins and held firm.

The frightened animal spun but settled under the Ranger's grip. Ignacio, whose other foot had stuck in his stirrup, slung around and slid to a dusty stop right under the tip of Sam's rifle barrel. His brother, Lyle, started to draw his gun, but froze at the sight of Sheriff Stone's Colt up and cocked and aimed at him.

"Just so you know," Sam said, repeating Ignacio's words down to him. "Every time you show up *dogging us*, you'll get this kind of welcome. Only it'll get a little worse each time." As he spoke he grabbed the stunned gunman's shirt and yanked him to his feet.

"I—I think you've splintered my shinbone," Ignacio said, staggering under the pain.

"Good, now get out of here," Sam said in a low warning tone. "Don't stop until I see you're across the flats."

"All right, we're going," said Ignacio, crawling up his horse's side into his saddle. "But you need to know what this is all about. Your sheriff pal there took money to get a man out of going to prison. Then he crawfished."

"You want to make it two cracked shins?" Sam said.

"You saddle tramp son of a bitch," Stone shouted, walking forward, his Colt up and aimed. Sam wondered if he'd forgotten the gun wasn't loaded. But before Stone could get any closer, the two gunmen spun their horses and gigged them into a run back down onto the trail. Sam and the sheriff stood watching until the horses headed out across the flats the way they'd come.

"Here's the deal," Stone said in a calmer voice. "I was drunk. I took money from Centrila to bribe the judge with, to get Centrila's son, Harper, out of going to prison. I was going to present the money and the deal to the judge and tell him everything, see if he could charge Centrila for trying to bribe a territory judge."

"Where's the money?" Sam asked, still watching the two gunmen ride away, dust roiling up behind their horses.

"It's in a strongbox where I hid it under the floor of my office," said Stone. "I put it there as evidence, until I had all this ready to present to the judge."

"When were you going to present it?" Sam asked.

"Three months ago," said Stone.

"Three months ago?" Sam said. "What happened? Why didn't you do it?"

A tense pause set in. Finally Stone let out a breath and said in a tone of regret, "I was drunk, Ranger . . .

and I kept forgetting to." He jammed his Colt down into his holster angrily, as if all of it was the gun's fault.

"You kept forgetting to . . . ," the Ranger said in a lowered tone.

"It's the truth," said Stone. "I meant to turn in the money and tell the judge all about it. You've got to believe me."

"I believe you, Sheriff Stone, for what it's worth," said Sam. He looked him up and down, then turned his eyes back out at the two riders. "But this is all something you and Judge Long need to square up between you."

"I'm getting sober, Ranger," Stone said with more determination than Sam had heard so far. "I'm not the kind of man you're seeing. But I'm going to show you, I'm still the lawman I always was—" His words stopped short. He swung away suddenly and ran off a few feet and heaved and gagged, bowed at the waist. The Ranger looked at him, then turned and gathered the horses. It was going to be a long ride to Yuma, he reminded himself again.

Chapter 3

———

Gun Hill, the Arizona Badlands

At daylight eleven gunmen reined their horses to a halt behind a rise of sand and rock. Three other riders booted their horses up a path and stopped atop the rise. The three pulled their horses abreast and sat looking out across the sand flats, getting a view of the town and the long stretch of hills standing a few miles behind it to the northwest. On the trail leading into the town, they saw two ore wagons moving along slowly. Four sorrel mules pulled each lumbering high-sided wagon. On the other end of the desert town, a locomotive sat idling. Puffs of black smoke belched from its stack like the breath of a sleeping dragon.

Their horses settled atop the rise, a thin hard-faced Georgian gunman named Holbert Lee Cross, aka Crosscut, stared at the scene in the near distance and gave a trace of a sneering half grin beneath a fine mustache. He wore a dusty pin-striped suit beneath a ragged yellow rain slicker. The slicker lay too wide across his narrow shoulders and caused his sleeves to droop low on the backs of his hands. A bandanna circled his neck atop a black string tie.

"There it is, boys," he said to his cohorts. "Pretty as a painted picture for you."

In the middle of the three, their leader, a Missourian gunman named Max Bard, rested his crossed wrists on his saddle horn and studied the town with a look of approval on his face.

"Good reconnaissance, Crosscut," he said to the Georgian gunman after a moment of scrutiny.

Cross gave a single nod of his head, letting the compliment pass.

"Siedell building all these rail spurs is going to be the best thing ever happened to us," he said.

"What *was* the man thinking?" said Bard, staring out at the bleak, weathered badlands town.

"Must be thinking he wants to make us all rich," the third rider, Pete "Kid Domino" Worley said on Bard's left.

"As rich as he is, Kid?" Bard asked idly.

"Well . . . maybe not that rich," said Worley, the youngest of the three. He gave a short grin. "Maybe just rich enough to go away and leave him alone."

Bard and Cross looked at each other.

"Is that ever going to happen, Crosscut?" Bard said.

"Not that I can rightly foresee." Cross shook his head. "He owes us far too much for us to stop robbing his vast enterprise." As he spoke he pulled the drooping bandanna up over the bridge of his nose and smoothed the tail down, covering the lower half of his face.

"Consider this just *one more* payment, Kid," Bard said to Worley, also pulling his bandanna up over his face. "We've still got a lot more due us."

"Let's get collecting," Worley said, following suit. As he adjusted the dusty bandanna over his face, he backed his horse into sight of the riders waiting below for a signal.

"All right, Dewey, sound a charge," he called down, his voice muffled by the dusty mask.

"Ready, Kid!" Dewey Lucas, who'd been with the Bard Gang since the war, raised his fisted hand to his lips as if blowing a bugle, took lead of the riders as they turned in unison and rode around the rise onto the flatlands where Bard, Cross and Worley had ridden down to meet them.

The fourteen men rode single file at an easy gallop toward the rail siding where the big steam locomotive sat idling. The deep pulsing sound of the engine seemed to mark time steadily to the rise and fall of the horses' hooves. Yet they started fanning out abreast and speeding up as they drew closer. Seeing express clerks stop in their tracks and look out toward them, Bard called out, "They've spotted us, men! *Give 'em hell— get that money!*" He booted his horse into a hard run as all around him his men's rifles and handguns erupted, their voices rising amid the pounding gunfire.

On the long wooden freight platform, an old freight hand named Cleveland Ballard stopped pulling his freight wagon when he first saw the riders' rise of dust moving toward town. Behind him his coworker Dan Jennings stopped too. He squinted and looked out through the wavering heat at the curtain of dust spreading wide on the desert floor.

"The hell's this?" Jennings asked Ballard. "A dust devil kicking up?"

"I *wish* it was," said Ballard, dropping the freight wagon tongue to the wooden dock. Then he raised his voice and shouted loud and long for the entire rail station to hear, *"Riders coming! Riders coming fast!"*

As pistol shots fell short of the platform and kicked up dust thirty yards out, rifle shots whistled past the workers and hammered and ricocheted off the idling locomotive and the iron-trimmed rail cars.

"We're in a bad place, Dan!" Ballard called out, crouching, scanning all along the wooden platform for safe cover. He grabbed Jennings's arm and said, "Come on, let's hightail!"

Stunned, Dan Jennings would have none of it. He stood staring squinty-eyed at the advancing riders, hearing their loud, seamless war cry.

"Listen at 'em! They's heathen Injuns!" he shouted. Squinting harder, he added, "Injuns wearing white man's clothes!"

"That's a rebel yell! They're rebels, you fool!" shouted Ballard, pulling him along harder. "Don't make me knock you in the head!"

"Rebels? Rebelling against what?" Jennings shouted in disbelief above the hammer of bullets against wood and iron.

"Take your pick!" Ballard shouted in reply. "And I don't want to get gut-shot wondering about it!" He jerked harder on Jennings's arm. "Come on!"

Jennings gave in and ran alongside his coworker in earnest when a bullet whizzed past his nose. The two hurried for cover behind a stack of whiskey barrels that stood on the platform bound for Gun Hill's saloons. Amber streams of rye arched out of bullet holes and splattered on the platform. The two rail workers began to slip and slide in the spilled whiskey. But they scrambled on until they flung themselves safely behind the leaking kegs.

From their cover the two peeped out and saw the riders drawing near, in full view now even with dust swirling around them. Ballard saw bullets pounding the express car where just inside the open door a clerk in a long leather apron stood crouched in fear.

"Close the doors, Charlie!" Ballard shouted at the clerk.

"I can't!" the clerk shouted in reply.

"What's he mean, *he can't*?" Ballard shouted to Jennings huddled beside him.

But before Jennings could offer an answer, armed railroad guards began spilling out of the express car onto the platform, rifles blazing in their hands.

"Holy Joseph, Dan! We've got us a battle now for sure!" Ballard shouted.

"I'm going to get a gun and shoot me a couple of these yammering idiots!" Jennings shouted, looking all around as the marauders flew from their saddles and got swallowed up by the looming dust. He tried to rise, but Ballard grabbed his arm and yanked him down.

"You stay down and keep out of it! These rail guards know what they're doing," he said.

They stayed low and watched the battle from behind the rounded bellies of the whiskey kegs. The armed guards had caught the bandits by surprise with more than a dozen well-armed riflemen running out of the express car onto the platform. At several points surrounding the station, other riflemen rose from cover and slammed the riders with gunfire. Even as bullets cut and sliced and punched through the bandits, they fought back like trapped wildcats. A rail guard flew backward into the express car as a bullet from Max Bard ripped through his heart and left a mist of blood swirling on the air behind him. At the same instant, a bandit's horse reared as its rider fired upon the rail guards. Then both horse and rider were felled by a deadly barrage of rifle fire.

"*Whooiee*, Dan! It looks like these boys' robbing days are done for," Ballard shouted with joy. They watched as man and horse alike fell beneath the heavy rifle fire. Those men who were not shot from their horses threw themselves to the ground willingly and scrambled in every direction to find cover, firing as they went. Guards fell on the platform under the bandits' fierce return fire. Thick black smoke and red-brown dust spun and loomed and drifted above the embattled rail yard like some scene from a raging day in hell.

For a moment Max Bard and Holbert Lee Cross were the only two bandits left mounted. When a lull in the guards' firing ensued, the two reined their horses back and forth, looking all round for a way out. While their frightened horses reared and spun, Bard scanned along the sitting train until he spotted a stock car with the doors wide open on both sides. He could see straight through it.

"Grab Worley and follow me, Crosscut!" he shouted. On the ground Worley fumbled all around at his horse's side, unable to see, blood filling his eyes. A bullet wound bled freely on his forehead at his hairline. As Bard turned his horse toward the stock car door, Cross jerked his horse over to Worley and grabbed the reins from his bloody hands.

"Come on, Kid," he said.

With Worley's horse secured, he reached down and pulled the bleeding bandit up by his shoulders. Firing grew heavier; the remaining bandits raced and stumbled about, grabbing for any horses left standing.

"You all get the hell out of here!" shouted Cross. He turned his big roan sharply. Pulling Worley's horse by its reins behind him, he gigged his frantic horse hard and raced off behind Bard toward the open stock car. Bard only glanced back once, making sure the other two were coming. Then he faced the platform sidelong and fired his big Starr repeatedly as he raced toward the stock car.

Looking forward at the car, Cross saw the stock ramp reaching down from the edge of the door to the ground. Salvation! *All right, Max, I see it!* he said to himself. Behind him, Worley held on to his saddle horn and tried to wipe blood from his eyes with the sleeve of his riding duster.

"Hang on, Kid!" shouted Cross. "We're going *up and down* real fast!"

"I'm *held on!*" Worley shouted, struggling unsuccessfully to see through his pouring blood.

He batted his bloody eyes and wiped them clear long enough to catch sight of the looming stock car and its ramp jarring and bouncing beneath the hooves of Bard's horse racing ahead of them. He caught a blood-smeared glimpse of Bard and his horse streaking up into the car and dropping immediately out of sight on the other side.

Gripping his saddle horn, tightening his legs on his horse's sides to brace himself, he felt and heard the creaking of the stock ramp threatening to break under the weight of his horse's hooves at any second. But then the bouncing stopped; hooves rumbled loud and hard across the width of the wooden floor of the car. The world beneath him felt smooth and easy as his and Cross's horse took flight out the opposite car door. Then he felt the hard slam of hooves meeting ground and he gripped his horse tighter to keep from being thrown forward over its head as they raced on.

Bullets still exploded behind them on the other side of the stock car, but the three had escaped out of the brunt of the ambush. Ahead of Holbert Lee and Worley, Bard rode hard across a wide corral filled with horses. A rifleman sprang up among a row of horses standing saddled and ready for the trail. But before the rail guard could get a shot off at the three riders pounding toward him, Bard raised his big Starr revolver and sent a bullet through the man's shoulder, spinning him like a top.

Seeing Bard slide his horse sidelong to a halt at the corral gate, Cross did the same. So did Worley.

Without leaving his saddle, Bard grabbed the loop of chain holding two wide corral gates closed at their middle. He raised the chain and flipped it aside.

"Get them out of here, Crosscut!" he shouted as he swung the gates open.

Seeing what Bard was up to, Cross circled back among the corral horses, firing his gun in the air, shooing them through the open gates. In his saddle, Worley managed to get his bandanna raised and drawn firm around his forehead. Batting his eyes, he raised and fired his pistol, sending all the spooked horses galloping out of the corral. Bard pulled the knot out of the rope line and freed the saddled horses to join the fleeing herd.

"What about the others?" Cross jerked his head toward the battle still raging on the other side of the train.

"Leave them or die with them," Bard said harshly without looking toward the gunfire. He jerked his horse around and pounded away among the corral horses.

Seeing that Worley was back in the game, Cross pitched him his reins.

"Keep up, Kid," he warned, even as he turned his horse to ride away.

"You got it," said Worley. The two gigged their horses into the fleeing herd and followed Bard toward the distant hill line. As their horses galloped away, to their left Bard saw two of their men, Dewey Lucas and Russell Gant, hightailing it away in the opposite direction. Bullets from rail guards struck the ground behind their horses' hooves. At the platform the fighting raged.

That's it, Dewey. Get the hell out of there, Bard told himself, riding on.

Chapter 4

—————

Seeing their panicked horses running freely out across the desert floor, Detective Colonel Cooper Hinler, who was following the three bandits, stopped in the middle of the dirt street. Standing among the dead and wounded, smoking rifle in hand, he lifted a bandolier of ammunition from around his shoulder and slung it to the dirt at his feet.

"Damn it! Damn it all to hell!" he raged. "There go our horses! What fool left a loading ramp in the stock car door?"

"Leon Foley?" said Duke Patterson, one of his black-suited detectives, standing beside him. "Where's Foley?" he shouted over his shoulder at the rail guards following him and Hinler. The rail guards stopped and gathered and looked out at the fleeing bandits, the detectives' own personal mounts following their lead.

"He's supposed to be at the corral," a rail guard said.

"Exactly," said Patterson. He gave Hinler a look. "And that explains the ramp, Colonel. No doubt he put it there. Foley's an idiot. I should have said something."

"But you didn't, did you, Duke?" Hinler said venomously.

"There's Foley," said a guard, pointing toward a staggering man who walked out of a thick swirl of dust inside the empty corral. His hand clutched a bleeding shoulder wound. "He's shot!"

"It's a damn good thing he's shot," Hinler said under his breath to Patterson. "I would wear out a gun barrel over his head."

"We can anyway, Colonel," Patterson offered.

"Somebody go help the fool," Hinler called out, ignoring Patterson's remark. "Get him over here." He looked around at the rail guards, all of them in everyday work clothes, distinguishing them from Hinler's detectives in their black dusty suits. "Some of you ride out and round up our horses. We're going to dog them all the way to hell if we have to."

"Round them up on what?" a rail guard asked.

"*Jesus*," Hinler growled, "what a mess." He looked all around at the dead bandits on the ground, at the dead and dying horses, at wounded rail guards and freight handlers. "Get some of the wagon horses!" Across the street a dog and a rooster lay sprawled in blood. A block away an onlooker lay dead in the dust. Townsfolk had gathered around him. "Let's get organized here!" Some of the rail guards and detectives hurried toward three freight wagons sitting at the far end of the station, each with a team of horses hitched to it. As they unhitched the horses, three other detectives dragged two bandits to their feet, both of them wounded, one with a forearm bone sticking out through his skin. The man with the broken arm cried out in pain. Hinler only gave him a sore look, then turned to the wounded Leon Foley, who'd arrived from the corral with the help of a young detective named Thurman Bain.

"Here he is, Colonel," Bain said, steadying Foley.

Hinler glared fiercely at the wounded man.

"I'm—I'm bleeding *real* bad," Foley said. He staggered in place; Bain steadied him.

"Not yet, you're not," Duke Patterson cut in, stepping forward, his long-barreled Colt like a club. "But I'll see if I can—"

"Hold it, Duke," shouted Hinler, stopping the enraged detective.

Patterson stepped back and took a deep breath. Hinler stared back at Foley.

"What in God's earth did you mean sticking that ramp in the car door, Foley?" he demanded. "Are you an idiot?"

Foley shook his lowered head.

"I don't know, Colonel," he said. "I swear I don't know."

"Don't know what, Foley?" Patterson cut in again. "Why you did it, or if *you're an idiot*?"

Foley raised his eyes and stared at Patterson.

"That's enough, Duke," Hinler said to his angry detective. He looked back at Foley and said, "I want an answer."

"I told you, Colonel, I don't know why I put the ramp there," Foley said. "I expect I must've thought it would make it easier for you and the men to get to the horses if any of these bandits tried to get away. I'm not cut out to be a detective. I wish I was still just a rail guard."

Hinler glared at the man, as if at a loss for words.

"Get this pathetic fool out of my sight, Bain," he finally said to the young detective standing beside Foley. "Get his shoulder patched up and don't let him out of *your* sight."

"Righto, Colonel," Bain said. "Come on, Foley." He led the wounded guard away by his arm. Two recently hired gunmen, Bo Anson and Quinton Carlson, stood watching with amused looks on their faces. Anson carried a big rifle with a long brass scope along its barrel.

Duke Patterson stared at Bain as he and Foley walked.

"Did he just say 'Righto,' Colonel?" Patterson asked.

"Yes, he did," said Hinler. "I'll have to correct him," he added, dismissing the matter for that moment.

Patterson shook his head. He and the colonel turned away and looked at the two wounded bandits his men had dragged to their feet.

"Get those two patched up and ready for a hanging," Hinler ordered his men.

"Hang them like they are, if you ask me," Patterson grumbled half-aloud.

"I didn't ask you, though, did I, *Duke*?" Hinler said sharply.

"No, you didn't, Colonel," Patterson said. He braced himself upright as if called to attention.

"For your information, I want to question them both before we drop the earth from under them," said Hinler. He gave a smug little grin. "I want to know where Bard and his gang hide out. If we knew that we could stop waiting around, hat in hand, to see where they strike next—we could kill them in their sleep."

Patterson nodded vigorously. "Right you are, Colonel."

"Even if they don't tell us anything," said Hinler, "I take satisfaction they have a little time to think about that rope snapping tight right beside their ear, eh?"

Patterson returned Hinler's grin.

"I fully agree, Colonel," he said.

"I'm *real* glad you agree with me, Duke," Hinler said with restrained sarcasm. "Go help round up our horses. We'll take these two with us and hang them whenever it suits me." He nodded at the distant rise of dust lying in the wake of the fleeing riders and corral horses. "That was Max Bard and Holbert Lee Cross. I want to be on their tails before they have time to catch their breath."

"Uh-oh," Duke Patterson said under his breath. He stepped back as he watched an irate town councilman elbow his way through the rail guards and detectives toward the colonel.

"Where is he?" the councilman demanded from the men as they moved aside for him.

"Here I am, Fairchild," Hinler said, taking a rigid stand facing the red-faced councilman. "What do you want?" He hooked a thumb in his belt near a white ivory-handled Remington. Sunlight sparkled on the gun's nickel finish.

Noting the Remington, the irate councilman stopped

in his tracks at a respectable distance. But he wasn't going to be put off. He glared at Hinler.

"*What do I want . . . ?*" he said. "Colonel, we have dead bystanders on our streets. I want to know what the blazes you—"

"Move them," the colonel said bluntly, cutting him off. He turned away. "I have dead of my own."

"Now, see here, Colonel," said Fairchild. "We're not going to stand by quietly and allow the railroad to cause this sort of violence in our town."

"Then wire Chicago, Fairchild," the colonel said. "Tell our home office you want this forty-mile rail spur taken up—stop this whole endeavor. Is that what you want?"

The councilman cowed a little.

"Well, no, of course not," the councilman said, relenting. "But we're not going to allow the railroad, or any big business, to come into our town and shove us aside—"

"How many dead?" the colonel asked, again cutting him off, making no effort to mask his impatience.

"Four dead, sir," said the councilman, "an elderly widow, two townsmen and a Piute Indian."

"Workingmen, family men, those two townsmen?" Hinler asked.

"Why, yes, working, *family* men indeed," the councilman responded, "even the Indian."

"One hundred for the widow's burial," said Hinler, "three hundred each for the workingmen's families. That'll feed them awhile." He paused and stared as if awaiting an acceptance of his offer.

"My God, sir!" said Councilman Fairchild. "This is outrageous! There's even been a dog and a rooster killed here! You can't buy your way out of this." But he paused and took a settling breath and said, "What about the Indian? What about *his* family? Who feeds them?"

Hinler shook his head, let out a breath and pulled a folded stack of cash from inside his dusty black suit coat.

"Here," he said. He licked his thumb and peeled off a ten-dollar bill and tossed it at the councilman, who caught it expertly midair. "Give them this. Tell them a dead dog and a chicken come with it—good stewing meat."

Duke Patterson stifled a laugh under his breath as the colonel turned from the councilman and walked away.

"Duke," Hinler called out over his shoulder. "Make certain my stallion wasn't among the horses those poltroons ran away."

Duke gave Leon Foley a questioning look.

"Well, was it?" he asked Foley.

Foley looked pale and ill.

"Oh *my* . . . ," Foley said under his breath.

"Much obliged, idiot," Patterson growled. "I'm the one who has to tell him."

At a small water hole two miles back up into the hills, the three bandits pushed themselves up from the tepid water on their elbows while their horses drank their fill beside them. Cross wiped his face and looked at Worley, whose blood-crusted face had smeared in long black-red streaks. The wet bandanna around Worley's forehead allowed fresh blood to ooze freely down from under its edge.

Cross chuckled and gigged Bard beside him.

"Look at this," he said under his breath.

Seeing Worley's red-striped face, Bard and Cross both let out a short laugh.

"What's so funny?" Worley asked, pushing himself farther up from the water.

"You are, Kid." Bard chuckled. "You ought to see yourself."

"What . . . ?" said Worley, not getting it. He looked all around himself as if searching for an answer.

"Wash your face," Cross said. "You look like a village weeper at a Mexican funeral."

The two laughed again. Worley shook his head and cursed and stuck his face back in the water, scrubbing it with a hand. The horses inched away from him and kept drinking. When he raised his face, he looked at the two older gunmen again.

"How's that? Is that clean enough to suit you?" he said. Stifling a laugh himself, he looked at their shied-away horses. His horse nickered a little. "Oh, so you think it's funny too?" he said.

The three stopped laughing suddenly and swung around, guns drawn, at the sound of a hoof scraping flat rock behind them. Then they all three relaxed, seeing four of the corral horses slowly walking to the water hole.

"You cayuses still with us?" Bard said laughingly to

the horses as they eased forward to the water's edge. One of the dusty animals was a well-groomed dapple gray stallion that had been among the horses saddled and ready for the trail. Its reins dangled to the ground.

The three men laughed as the thirsty animals helped themselves to water.

"Looks like we must've made a good impression on them," Cross said.

Eyeing the dapple gray closer, Bard stood up and walked over to the horse and placed a hand on an expensive tooled saddle.

"This fine fella looks like he's been living better than the three of us," he said. He looked at the saddle closer, held up a flap on the saddlebags and read the initials CH tooled expertly in the leather. "I believe we're being visited by Colonel Hinler's personal mount."

"Hey, let me see that," said Worley, rising to his feet, pressing the bandanna to his bullet graze. Cross rose also. The two walked toward the dapple gray.

"Easy, boy," Bard murmured as the horse sidestepped away from them. "Nobody here's out to harm you." He rubbed the horse's side gently, settling him.

"I bet the colonel's having a conniption about now." Cross chuckled, also rubbing the horse's side.

"If he's not, he will be next time he sees this stud," Bard said, looking the stallion over good.

Holbert Lee and Worley gave him a curious look. Bard stooped and ran his hands down the horse's foreleg, inspecting it.

"That's right," he said quietly, "because I'll be riding this fella."

"That's a *great idea*!" said Cross with feigned enthusiasm. "The colonel doesn't hate us enough as it is."

But Bard didn't seem to hear him. He stood and ran a hand down the horse's short-cropped mane. "Give him some time, let his mane grow out. This fella is going to be a real huckleberry."

Cross shook his head and gave a shrug.

"I'm not saying anything," he said to Bard.

"What should I do?" Bard said. "Turn this fella loose? Let the wolves have at him?" He watched the stallion raise his head and belch, water running from his lips. "The colonel ought to be grateful I'm keeping him instead of leaving him out here for feed." The big stallion tossed his head and took a step back from the water. Bard rubbed his wet muzzle.

"He might *ought to be* grateful, but he won't be, I'll wager you," Cross said. "Anyway, this one looks capable of fending off wolves for himself."

"I'm keeping him," Bard said with finality. "The colonel wants to kill us anyway. I might as well ride in style."

"Suit yourself," said Cross. Dismissing the matter, he turned to Worley, who stood with fresh blood running from under the bandanna on his forehead. "Let's look at that graze, Kid. Might be I'll have to sew it closed for you once we're out of here." He raised a hand to lift the bandanna for a look. But Worley stepped back from him.

"*Might be* you can keep your hands to yourself, Crosscut," he said. "It'll heal up on its own."

"All right, but we still need to bandage it nice and tight for now," said Cross.

"I don't think so," said Worley. "It'll stop soon enough."

"You got it, hombre," Cross said. "Don't bellyache to me when you've got your eyes full of blood again."

"I don't bellyache," Worley said.

"If it heals bad you'll have a scar makes you look like you were smacked with an ax," Cross warned.

"Let him bandage it, Kid," said Bard. "If you don't you'll be bleeding like a stuck pig the rest of the day. Nothing bleeds worse than a head graze."

Worley considered it, then let out a breath and touched the wet, bloody bandanna.

"All right," he said to Cross, "Bandage it up. But don't go saying it needs sewing if it don't."

"Would I do a thing like that?" Cross said. He pointed at a rock and said, "Sit down. Let's get it taken care of."

As the two spoke, Bard took the stallion's dangling reins, inspected the frayed ends and led the animal away from the water so he could look him over. The other horses stood blowing and resting.

"I saw Lucas and Gant getting away," he said as he continued examining the stallion, raising each of his hooves in turn.

"I saw them too," said Cross. Turning from Worley, he walked to his horse and took a flat leather medical kit from inside his saddlebags. "Figure we'll meet up on the trail?" He opened the kit on his way back to Worley and pulled out a package of gauze bandaging.

"Yep, that's what I figure," Bard said. A moment of silence ensued. Then he said, "I didn't see nobody else."

"Neither did I," Cross said solemnly. He paused, then said, "The colonel and his detectives will be on our trail as soon as they get horses under them. Are we going to circle back and take a look?"

"I am," Bard said.

"I figure if one goes back, we all three go back," said Cross, lifting the wet bandanna from Worley's bullet graze.

"You figured wrong," said Bard. "It's easier if one of us slips in and out of there."

Cross knew better than to argue.

"All right, then, where's the two of us going to be waiting for you?" he said.

"I don't want you out on the open flats," said Bard. "We'll find a spot along the way in. I want you in the rocks where you can give me some good cover fire if I need it."

"Understood," said Cross. "I wish we'd get closer to town, though, in case somebody spots you before you get—"

"And that's the plan," Bard said matter-of-factly, cutting him off. "Nobody's going to *spot* me. . . . They'll all be out here trying to trail us—more apt to spot you two than me."

Cross nodded, busily finishing with Worley's bloody forehead.

"We will need to sew this up first chance we get," he said to the wounded young gunman.

Bard cut in, saying in a stern tone, "Crosscut, are you with me on this?"

Cross looked around at him as if surprised they were still talking about it.

"I'm with you, Max." He looked down at Worley.

"What about you, Kid? You've lost enough blood to make you weak. Are you up to all this?"

"That's a hell of a thing to ask me," said the younger gunman. He half rose as if to show that he was strong enough to do whatever he needed to. But Cross held him down with a hand on his shoulder.

"Easy, Kid. Just checking is all," he said. "A graze like this can take some men off their feet for a day or two."

"Not this man, though," Bard put in. "Right, Kid Domino?"

"Damn right," Worley said confidently. He gave an upward look at Cross standing over him and added, "With all that blood out of my eyes, I'm right as rain."

"Let's see if you are," said Holbert Lee. He held his left hand up, his bloody fingers spread wide. "How many fingers am I holding up?"

Worley's jaw tightened in defiance.

"Seventeen," he said flatly.

"Yep, he's doing fine," Cross said with a wry grin. "Let's get riding."

Chapter 5

Three days had passed since the Ranger and Sheriff Stone met the Cady brothers and sent them away, Ignacio with a fracture up his shin from the hard butt of the Ranger's Winchester. Staying up above the desert sand flats, Sam had kept watch on their back trail, but he'd seen no sign of the two brothers, although he was certain they would return once they got their courage back. But so far so good, he told himself as he and the sheriff rode toward Gun Hill, the next in a string of mining towns along the badland border.

They had spent the night outside the small town of Ripley and started early and ridden all day. The ride seemed to do the sheriff some good. His hands appeared steadier, his eyes clearing some, his attention more focused, the Ranger noted. He had talked a lot about the bribery money and the situation of Edsel Centrila and his son, Harper. The Ranger had heard as much about it as he cared to. As far as he was concerned, it was between the sheriff and the judge. But Stone, still nervous, still fighting off the whiskey heaves and tremors, seemed unable to talk about much else.

When they first heard the sound of distant gunfire coming from the direction of Gun Hill, they'd quickened their horses' pace and ridden nonstop until they spotted a group of riders appear on the flatlands below them.

"Any of them look familiar?" Stone asked, watching him observe the riders through his battered telescope.

"I've seen them before," Sam replied sidelong. "I'm sure you have too. It's the railroad detectives who've been patrolling the new rail spurs."

"The colonel and his men . . . ," Stone said, squinting out with his naked eyes but seeing only rising dust and tiny figures loping along in front of it. "They were coming to Big Silver a lot, but lately I haven't been seeing them sneaking around much."

Sam heard a suspicious tone.

"You figure they're up to something?" Sam asked. He lowered the lens and looked at Stone.

"They always are," Stone said. "They protect those new rail spurs like the tracks are made of gold." He paused, then added, "I don't mind telling you I have a low opinion of the rail barons and the kind of people they hire to protect their interests." He stared at Sam. "What about you?"

"I'm used to them," Sam said quietly. "The rail guards are all right—just workingmen. But if you're talking about the detectives, Curtis Siedell in particular, I agree."

"Siedell is a snake," said Stone, "and so are his detectives."

Sam raised the lens back up to his eye.

Stone gave a little chuckle.

"I see you don't like name-calling, Ranger," said Stone. He gave a shrug. "Ordinarily I don't either. But *snake* is one of the better names I can think of for Siedell. I've heard many stories of how he's robbed and cheated people—"

"Stories don't count. Unless a court finds him guilty of something, my job is to— *Whoa*," Sam said, cutting himself off. "They've stopped. One of them just knocked a man from his saddle."

Stone stared out, still unable to see anything with his naked eye.

"Looks like the man on the ground is wearing handcuffs," Sam said, watching closely. He scanned the other riders and saw one of them with a bloody chest, swaying back and forth in his saddle. As he watched, Sam saw the man get shoved from his saddle by a rider who'd sidled up to him. Watching, Sam noted two coiled ropes hanging from the shover's saddle horn. Each rope had a noose dangling from its end.

"What's going on now?" Stone asked, still squinting, still seeing nothing clearly.

"I think we've got a hanging getting ready to take place," Sam said, lowering the lens again.

"A hanging?" said Stone. He looked all around the wide desert flatlands. Far to the east he spotted a hillside strewn with up-reaching saguaro. "I'm out of my jurisdiction or I'd be given to know why."

"I'm not out of my jurisdiction," Sam said. "It's my

duty to ask what it's about." He lowered the lens and closed the telescope between his palms. Looking Stone up and down, he asked, "Are you up for a hard ride?"

The sheriff, feeling better, straightened in his saddle and gathered his reins.

"You bet I'm up for it," he said.

Before he turned his dun to the trail, Sam reached out a closed gloved hand and said, "Here, in case you need them."

Stone held his open hand out; Sam dropped six bullets into his palm.

"Obliged, Ranger," he said, a little surprised.

"I figured if you're going to be pointing that shooter, you need something in the chamber," Sam said. "Let's hope you don't have to draw it."

He spun his dun away from Stone and batted it forward into a gallop across the loose sand. Stone drew his horse in alongside him and loaded his Colt as they rode.

On the desert flatlands halfway up the tall saguaro-clad hillside, Colonel Hinler, his black-suited detectives and the lesser dressed rail guards stood circled around the two wounded, handcuffed prisoners lying in the sand.

Hinler and Duke Patterson stood crouched over the two. When one of the wounded prisoners moaned and gripped his bloody chest, Patterson punched both him and the other man in the face. Blood flew.

"Shut up and pay attention here, outlaws," he said. "You don't want to miss your own hanging."

One prisoner defiantly spat blood at Patterson. The second prisoner clawed a bloody hand up at him. Patterson ran a forearm across his blood-splattered face and cursed. He drew back his fist, but before he could punch either of the men again, Hinler leaned in and nudged him aside.

"Have yourself a smoke, Duke," he said to Patterson. "I want to speak to these fellas one last time. Maybe they've changed their minds." He patted the burly detective's shoulder as he ushered him out of his way.

"Yes, sir, Colonel," Patterson said, wiping his face again.

"Let me explain what's going to happen here," Hinler said, leaning down closer to the two prisoners. He gave the two a cruel grin as he studied their black swollen eyes. "You're going to die here, what we call a horizontal hanging. Meaning we tie your neck to this cactus"—he nodded at a tall saguaro cactus standing beside them—"and your feet to your horses' saddle horns. Can you see how that works?" He grinned and looked closer at them for any sign of fear or regret, but he saw none.

The two only stared, ready for whatever fate had planned.

"If you want to die really slow, feel your bones pull apart as we draw these horses away," the colonel continued, "we can see to it that's the way you go." He studied each one's eyes in turn. "Or, if you want to clear the slate before you leave here, tell me where your pards hide out these days, we can smack these horses with a quirt and make them dig in quick." His grin widened. "Pop your heads off. You'll be dead before God gets his boots on, so to speak."

One of the prisoners, an older outlaw named Parker Fish, who had spat blood in Patterson's face, gestured the colonel down closer.

"Watch him, Colonel. He's a spitter," Patterson cautioned.

"Speak up, Fish," the colonel said, leaning only inches from the bloody swollen face.

Fish coughed and gathered the breath to speak.

"We been . . . hiding out . . . ," he said haltingly, "down in . . . your aunt Lucy's undergarments. . . ."

A muffled laugh rippled across the rail guards. The black-suited detectives gave them a hard, sharp stare.

"Oh, that's *real funny*, Fish," said Hinler, straightening, adjusting his dusty vest over his stomach paunch. "Be sure and tell it to the devil when he's got you both turning on the spit." He ended his words with a kick to Fish's shoulder. Fish only grunted and rolled onto his side.

"Get the nooses around their necks!" Hinler shouted. "Get their horses ready. Let's see what these game birds look like when their bellies burst open." He kicked at Parker Fish again, but missed, almost fell. Then he stepped back angrily as two detectives stepped forward and twisted the nooses around the men's necks.

"I've been *sugary-kind* up until now," Hinler said down to the prisoners. "Now you'll see my *dark-ugly* side." As he spoke, two rail guards tied the other ends of the ropes to the saddle horns on the outlaws' horses. He turned to the two guards as they stepped forward and took the horses by their reins. "Remember, men, slow and steady, like mules pulling cedar stumps."

From among the detectives and rail guards, Leon Foley looked away as the ropes drew tighter around the cactus, around the two men's necks. As the two men rose slightly off the ground, their hands still cuffed behind them, Foley closed his eyes tight.

"I can't watch this," he said under his breath. "I ain't cut out for this kind of work."

"Keep the horses moving slow, men," Hinler called out to the two rail guards. "We don't want these thieving saddle tramps to miss a thing."

The cactus made a creaking sound as the two ropes tightened.

The colonel stood with his feet spread, his hand clasped behind his back, as if at parade rest. He smiled with satisfaction as the horses took another slow, measured step. But then his smile vanished quickly as he heard the rifle shot behind him. He felt a blast of air streak between his knees from behind and saw a puff of dust rise in front of him. He spun toward the sound of the shot and grasped the ivory-handled butt of his shiny Remington. But he froze when he saw the Ranger and Sheriff Stone sitting atop their horses on a slope above him. The Ranger's Winchester was at his shoulder, cocked and ready. Aimed at the colonel's chest.

"Back those horses off *now*, Colonel," he demanded, thirty feet away, "else the next bullet takes an eye out."

The detectives and rail guards alike froze, seeing the rifle aimed at Hinler. The two guards stopped the outlaws' horses before the colonel told them to. Feeling the

tension on their saddle horns, the horses stepped back
instinctively; the two stretched-out outlaws lowered to
the dirt, gasping.

"How dare you even *threaten* me, let alone fire a
weapon at me, Ranger!" the colonel shouted, enraged.
His hand kept a tight grip on his shiny pistol butt, but
he made no attempt to raise the big Remington from
his holster. "I will have your hide for this, so help me,
God!"

"Shut up, Hinler," said Sheriff Stone. "Do like he
says or I'll settle your hash myself." He held his Colt
leveled and cocked toward the colonel. "I've wanted to
shoot you more than I've wanted goose for Christmas."

The rail guards stood in rapt silence, but the detectives started to make the slightest move. Stone swung
his Colt toward them. "I'll settle for a couple of you
black-suit *plugs*, though," he said. The detectives froze
again and stared.

The bloody prisoners gagged and coughed and
wrung their heads back and forth, trying to loosen the
nooses around their necks.

"Get the nooses off those men, pronto," Sam called
out to the two rail guards.

Leading the horses around by their reins, the two
guards hurriedly stooped and took the nooses off the
prisoners and tossed the ropes aside. They loosened the
other ends from the saddle horns and pitched them
away.

Seeing the Ranger lower the cocked Winchester an
inch from his shoulder, the enraged colonel took a step

toward him, shaking his finger in the air. His other hand still gripped his ivory-handled Remington.

"This is a justifiable hanging, Ranger," he shouted. "You and this whiskey sop have no right interfering here!"

Before the Ranger could stop him, Stone swung his Colt around and fired two rapid shots. The first shot kicked up dirt and stopped the advancing colonel in his tracks. The second bullet hit the spot where the colonel's next step would have been had he not jerked his foot back a split second sooner.

Sam gave Stone a sidelong glance, holding his Winchester ready.

"Easy, Sheriff," he whispered.

"Easy, my ass," Stone whispered in reply. Then he called out, "Colonel, if you think I won't kill you pinebox dead, take another step. I dare you."

The colonel stood where the two bullets marked the dirt in front of him. He raised his hands chest high; the detectives did the same, amazed at the sheriff's gun handling. "Raise that Remmy with two fingertips." He shot the Ranger a knowing glance and said under his breath, "The way you're *supposed to*—and pitch it away," he added, raising his voice again.

"I thought you couldn't remember anything," Sam said between the two of them.

"It's coming back to me," Stone said sidelong. Then he said to the detectives, "All of you do the same— pitch them away."

"That's good to hear," Sam said, swinging down

from his saddle, lowering the rifle as he drew his Colt and walked forward as the detectives raised their side-arms and did as Stone told them to.

As Sam passed the colonel, he picked up the big Remington and unloaded it, walking toward the prisoners and motioning the colonel to walk in front of him. With his hands up, the colonel walked along, cursing and grumbling as he went.

"You're making a big mistake, Ranger," he said. "These men tried to rob the express car at the new rail station in Gun Hill. They killed innocent bystanders! Wait until those people hear that you stopped this."

"Bet they didn't get any money, though, did they?" Sam said knowingly.

"Fortunately, no," the colonel said.

"Because there was no money to be had, was there?" Sam said.

The colonel fell silent.

"You've been baiting these rail spurs with empty strongboxes and letting the word out that there's big money being shipped to the mines." He paused, then said, "Wait until those townsfolk hear what *you've* been doing."

"This is railroad business, Ranger," said the colonel. "Mr. Siedell has a right to do what needs to be done to protect his interests."

Sam stopped him a few feet back from the two prisoners. Looking down at the outlaws' battered faces, the bloody untreated bullet wounds, he shook his head.

"Let me remind you that hanging is not an illegal

act, if justified, Ranger. The territory law is clear enough on that."

"Here's another law, Colonel," Sam replied. "If I happen upon a hanging in progress, I'm sworn to stop it and make an inquiry. If I feel it necessary, I'm obligated to take the accused to a place where charges will be filed and a territorial judge will preside over the case."

"There . . . you son . . . of a bitch," Parker Fish wheezed, and chuckled in a weak voice.

"Give it . . . to him, Ranger," the other prisoner said in a broken voice.

"Shut up, both of you," Sam said. He turned and stared at the two rail guards holding the outlaws' horses.

"Are we in trouble?" one guard asked.

"No," Sam said. "Not if you get these men some water and get them washed. I'm taking them into custody. I'm sure that's what an upstanding man like Curtis Siedell would want." He gave the colonel a flat stare. "Come to Yuma and make your charges, Colonel. That's how the law works."

"The law, *ha*," Hinler returned with sarcasm, his tone growing louder with his rage. "All the law does is mollycoddle these thieving reprobates!"

"Everything all right over there, Ranger?" Sheriff Stone called out, keeping his Colt aimed at the detectives. "If not, let me know. I'll clip an ear off from here."

The colonel stiffened at the sound of the sheriff's voice.

"I don't think he likes you, Colonel," Sam said, seeing the fear in Hinler's eyes. "You might want to keep your mouth shut while we get these men ready to ride."

Hinler backed up a step. He stood watching as the Ranger and Stone prepared the two prisoners for the trail.

"Are we going to stand here and let them take these prisoners from us, Colonel?" Patterson asked quietly at Hinler's side.

"Yes, we're going to abide by the law for now," Hinler said in the same guarded tone, "but taking them doesn't mean they're going to keep them." The two gave each other knowing looks. "It's a big, mean desert out there, Duke. A lot can happen." He paused, then said, "Take Anson along with you. It's time he showed me something."

Chapter 6

It was afternoon when the Ranger and Sheriff Stone rode away from Colonel Hinler and his band of railroad detectives and rail guards. The prisoners' wounds had been attended to and bandaged. Their hands were uncuffed from behind their backs and recuffed in front of them, making it easier for them to negotiate the dips and rises of the sloping sand hills as they crossed the desert flats. On the far side of the flats they stopped to rest their horses at a stone-lined water hole bedded in a hillside thirty yards up a rocky trail.

The Ranger sank a row of canteens into the water to let them fill and stood back and watched as man and horse quenched their thirst. The first to finish drinking was the younger of the two prisoners, a wiry Texan named Rudy Bowlinger. The Ranger had seen his face on Texas wanted posters for the past two years. But the face looking up at him from the water's edge was battered, swollen and barely recognizable.

"Ain't you drinking, Ranger?" Bowlinger asked, his wet hair clinging to his forehead. "It's a long hot ride to Yuma."

Sam only stared at him, not liking the sudden familiarity the wounded outlaw tried to establish. He knew that in spite of his saving the two men from the slow death the colonel had bequeathed them, they would kill him and Stone without batting an eye if the opportunity presented itself.

"Sounds like you're feeling better, Bowlinger," said Sam, with no attempt at masking his distrust of the wanted man.

"Call me Rudy, Ranger," Bowlinger said with a swollen, twisted grin. He raised a careful hand and cupped his bruised jaw. "All us ol' boys heal fast. You know that." He paused, then added, "What's the chance they won't hang us once we get to Yuma?"

Sam considered it as Parker Fish and the sheriff pushed up from the water. Fish spat a stream of water and wiped some from his face. Having heard Bowlinger's question, he lay anticipating the Ranger's answer. Stone rose to his feet and stood listening too.

"Hard to say," Sam replied to Bowlinger. "I know the judge is not real happy with how Siedell has been letting the colonel set up these fake cash shipments. He feels like it has drawn unnecessary violence from robbers like yourselves—gotten lots of innocent people killed."

"I couldn't agree more," Bowlinger said with his swollen, twisted grin. "There's something don't seem right about it, baiting us that way." He looked at Parker Fish.

"I've never gone on a robbery in my life that I thought didn't have any money to it," Fish said.

"I see the judge's point," Sam said, looking back and

forth between the two outlaws. "If the railroad didn't put the rumor of big cash shipments out there, nobody would try to rob it."

Stone, who'd been listening closely to the Ranger, took the opportunity to cut in when Sam paused.

"Maybe if their inside man did a better job, he wouldn't send them riding into a trap," he said to Sam, knowing he had the outlaws' full attention.

"I see your point too, Sheriff," Sam said.

Fish gave Bowlinger a look that stopped him nodding at the two lawmen's conversation.

"Who said we've even got an inside man?" Fish said in a wary tone. "Could be the information just gets out there on its own somehow."

Sam just stared at him.

"I see," he said, "sort of the way cattle round themselves up and do their own branding?"

Fish cursed under his breath.

"I ought to know better than try to converse with a lawman," he grumbled.

"That's right," Sam said. "We're not here to *converse*. Our only interest is taking you both to Yuma—let the court deal with you." He turned toward his bay as the horse raised its dripping muzzle from the water.

"Oh . . . ?" Fish said, as if surprised. "You mean you don't want to try making us tell where the Bard Gang hides out?"

"I already know," Sam said. "Close enough anyway." He reached out and rubbed the dun's wet nose as he spoke. The horse twisted its lip back and forth, liking it.

"Ha! You're wishing that was true, Ranger," Fish said. "You don't know anything. If you did you'd be spurring that hammerhead right now, trying to get there."

Stone caught the thread of what the Ranger was doing; he stood still, listening, watching.

"If I were a betting man," Sam said, "I'd wager I could leave here right now and be there in four days, five at the most." He studied the two swollen faces as he spoke, checking their reactions.

The two looked stunned, but just for a second, just long enough that the Ranger knew he'd struck a nerve. But Fish wasn't to be bluffed. He chuckled as he gripped his bandaged wound.

"And I would take that bet, Ranger," he said. "Good try, but you're a long ways off target. Besides, leaving some men behind like they did, Max Bard and Holbert Lee Cross won't take any chance on one of us talking. They'll pull stakes and go looking for a new place to hole up. I wouldn't know where to find them now myself. The colonel's too damn stuck on himself to figure that out."

"Maybe he figured that's so," Stone cut in. "Maybe he just wanted to see you two die real slow-like."

"That's more how I see it," Fish agreed. He directed his attention to the sheriff. "Say . . . didn't I hear somewhere that you've been turning yourself into a bear or coyote or something?"

Stone gave the Ranger an embarrassed look.

"I might have thought that," he murmured, humiliation lowering his voice.

Fish chuckled and said, "Hellfire, Sheriff, it ain't nothing to be ashamed of if you did. I've been that loco drunk myself, on mescal and peyote and the like."

"Mescal and peyote . . ." Bowlinger shook his head, thinking about it. "I once thought I was somebody else for going on a week," he put in. "I couldn't find my horse or nothing else." He looked back and forth between the two lawmen.

Sheriff Stone looked away, not wanting to say he only drank rye, albeit lots of it. Seeing the conversation unravel, Sam took his dun by its reins and led it toward the filled canteens on the edge of the water. He cupped his hands and washed his face and spat a stream of water. Then he raised a cupped handful of water and drank it down without letting the two outlaws out of his sight.

"Time to go," he said, standing, lifting the canteens by their straps. He handed two canteens to Stone and hung the other two on his saddle horn. Watching the prisoners, he swung up into his saddle, his rifle still in hand. "Fish," he said, "we both know Bard's not going to change his hideout. He's got too nice a setup over in the hill country." He nodded toward the border. He watched Fish's expression tighten.

Bowlinger said without thinking, "There's plenty of other good hiding places. He don't have to—" His words halted as he saw the scorching look in Fish's eyes.

Fish looked back at the Ranger. Sam gave a faint, wry smile.

"Like I said, Fish," he repeated, "four days, five at the most." He backed his dun and watched the two handcuffed, wounded outlaws struggle up onto their horses. Stone gave him a nod of approval and swung up himself.

"Get in front," Stone said to Fish and Bowlinger. Then he backed his horse a step and motioned them forward.

Holbert Lee Cross and Pete "Kid Domino" Worley had spotted Max Bard's rise of trail dust as soon as horse and rider wound into sight on the desert floor. At least they thought it was Bard. Their leader had started out as a black dot at the head of the rising dust. It took a while longer before he grew into a recognizable form against the harsh glare of sand and wavering sunlight. Neither man commented upon seeing him. They sat their horses in the cover of rock and watched him ride.

When Bard drew close enough for the two to be certain it was him, they both relaxed a little and stayed out of sight up on a rocky hillside.

As the rider drew nearer, Cross stepped his horse to the edge of the sandy trail and looked all around. Then he raised his rifle sidelong and adjusted it back and forth until sunlight reflected sharply off the shiny steel chamber. He counted three flashes and lowered the rifle.

"Think he saw it, Holbert Lee?" Worley asked.

Cross looked at the younger outlaw but didn't answer at first. Instead they sat and watched as their leader veered the colonel's stallion and a spare horse on a lead rope beside him in their direction.

"Yeah, Kid," Cross finally said, "he saw it." They

turned their horses and rode down at a walk to meet Bard on the hill trail. Cross led Bard's other horse beside him.

Near the bottom of the hill, they found Bard sitting on a rock, the reins of the colonel's stallion and lead rope to the spare horse, a blaze-faced chestnut, in hand. In his other hand he held his rifle and an open canteen of water he'd been sipping from.

"We've had no shortage of riding stock this time out," Cross commented, looking the spare horse up and down. A canvas bag lay tied down on the chestnut's back.

"These corral horses are scattered everywhere," said Bard, capping the canteen. "I figured it was a good idea to bring him along. He was following us anyway." As he spoke, he walked over to the canvas bag on the chestnut's back.

"How'd it go, Max?" Cross asked, watching him rummage down into the bag.

Bard pulled up a bottle of whiskey and a package of medical gauze and supplies.

"It went like I expected," he replied. He walked over, pitched the bottle up to Cross and the medical supplies to Worley. "The whole town's shook up. The colonel and his men are on our trail."

"You took a hell of a chance riding in on that stallion," Cross said.

Bard gave him a short grin.

"I had to see how it rides," he said. He watched Cross shake his head, raise the bottle and take a deep swig. He continued. "We've got dead there. They've got Fish and Rudy. The colonel took them along with him, following our trail."

"Damn it," Cross said under his breath. He sidled his horse over beside Worley and handed him the bottle. "Fish won't tell them nothing. Rudy might."

"The colonel took them along so he can hang them out here, keep from too many townsfolk seeing it," Bard said.

"Since when did townsfolk start caring about watching outlaws hang?" said Cross.

"The colonel likes to play it safe, I suppose," said Bard. He looked back across the stretch of desert he'd just crossed. "For two cents I'd stick here and pick their eyes out when they get here."

"I've got that two cents," Cross said.

Bard looked at Worley.

"What about you, Kid Domino? You up for it?" he asked. He looked at the dark dried blood on the young outlaw's shirt, his neck, down his ear. Worley wiped a hand across his lips, following a deep drink of whiskey.

"I've got nothing planned that can't wait," he said with a weak grin. He handed the whiskey down to Bard, who took it, swirled it in the bottle and took a drink.

Corking the bottle, Bard studied the settling whiskey as he considered the matter. He knew the colonel and his men were on their trail; he knew they would be showing up here, either on the hill trails or on the desert flats he'd just crossed.

This is perfect ambush country.

"Well, what do you say, Max?" Cross finally asked.

Bard let out a tight breath. "No, we're going on. I hate to start out doing one thing and end up doing something else."

"Hell, Max, we got ambushed ourselves," said Cross. "We didn't ask to get skunked out on this job."

"It makes no difference if we kill the colonel or he and his men kill us," said Bard. "It's no skin off Siedell's rump. He still gets no sting from it."

"Likely he never will," Cross said in a weary voice. He rested his gloved hands on his saddle horn and let out a breath. "So, you call it. Stick here and shoot who we can, or cut out of here and get ready for what comes next?"

"I'm still out for King Curtis Siedell," said Bard. "I want him to pay for what he done."

"So do I," Cross said stoically.

Worley sat watching, listening, knowing that this was all about things that had happened before his time, all the way back during the last days of the civil conflict.

Finally Bard said again, "No, we're going on. We'll circle wide of Gun Hill and try to find Dewey Lucas and Russell Gant."

"What about Fish and Rudy?" Worley cut in.

Bard and Cross gave each other a look.

"Forget them, Kid," Bard said. "They were as good as dead the minute the colonel sank his claws in them." He turned to the stallion and rubbed its hot, sweaty muzzle. The spare horse stood beside it. "One good thing," he continued, "all these loose horses running around out here is making it tougher for the colonel to figure which prints belong to us."

"Aw, ain't that too bad?" Cross said with a wry grin. "I hate putting the man to all this trouble."

"I still want to kill him," Bard said seriously. He swung up atop the stallion and took the spare horse's lead rope from the saddle horn.

"There's plenty of *colonels* just like him waiting to take his place," Cross said. "Siedell knows that." The three of them turned their horses to the high trail, headed back into the cover of rock and scattered pine woodlands. "He runs out of retired *colonels*, there's always majors, captains and so on, down the line." He gave a wry grin. "We can't kill them all."

Bard looked back at Worley and Cross.

"Who says we can't?" he said over his shoulder.

Chapter 7

In the evening sunlight, Sheriff Stone led the prisoners up a narrow path to the crest of a hill line. Sam brought up the rear and kept an eye on the prisoners and their back trail. The sheriff realized the Ranger still didn't trust him a hundred percent, but the more sober he became, the better he understood. He would not have come on this trip on his own, yet regardless, he had to admit that the longer his sobriety held out, the better he was starting to feel. Being back on the job, gun in hand, helped, he reminded himself. It helped a lot.

There were still twinges and shakes in his hands and chest. Dark, destructive thoughts still set upon him once in a while, like some ugly spirit that followed him until it found an opportune time to strike. At those times, he believed he would have traded his soul to the devil for just one long pull on a bottle of rye.

"We'll stay up here overnight, Sheriff," the Ranger called out as the four of them topped the hill. As Stone reined his horse down and turned it to face the prisoners, he looked all around for a sheltered place to make a camp amid a sparse scattering of pine woods.

"Think you can uncuff us long enough to relieve ourselves, Ranger?" Rudy Bowlinger asked, shifting uncomfortably in his saddle, gesturing toward the sparse woods. "You can keep an eye on us from here. We won't go nowhere. You've got our word."

"You're not talking about a one-hander?" Stone asked, studying the outlaw suspiciously.

"No, sir, Sheriff," Rudy said. "This is a two-hander if I ever had one—unless you want to stay a good distance from me the rest of the trip."

"Kind of you to give us your word, Rudy," Sam said before Stone answered. "But we'll just cuff one hand to a pine sapling. You'll do okay."

"I don't get a very good feeling for that, Ranger," Rudy replied. He shifted uncomfortably again. "But I've got no time to jaw over it." He looked serious. "I've got to go."

"All right, Sheriff," Sam said to Stone, "let's get over into the shade."

Stone led the three forward, keeping his horse to the edge of a clearing so they wouldn't be exposed in the open sunlight. When they were inside the shelter of tall older-growth pines, they stopped the tired horses and stepped down from their saddles.

"I've got these two," Stone said as Sam pulled out the key to the handcuffs. Sam only looked at him and laid the key in his outstretched hand. He could tell the sheriff was feeling better. He saw fewer tremors in his hands, less stress pain around his eyes.

"Let's go," Stone said to the prisoners, stepping back, keeping his hand on his holstered Colt.

Sam took down his canteen and watched, rifle in hand, as the three walked away along the edge of the clearing toward a stand of rock and brush. As he raised the canteen to his lips, he saw a quick flash of sunlight among the taller hillsides to their right and instinctively called out Stone's name in warning. But his warning came too late. He saw the first rifle shot hit Rudy Bowlinger and send him staggering sidelong in a broken, twisted waltz. Blood flew before the sound of the distant shot resounded on the towering hillsides.

"Get down!" the Ranger shouted in reflex. He dropped the canteen and raised the Winchester to his shoulder. As he took cover behind a thick pine, he returned fire. With no target other than the direction of the flash of sunlight among the higher rocks, he knew he needed to offer some defense, anything to deflect the shooter while the sheriff and Parker Fish scrambled across the rocky ground for cover.

Another rifle shot reached down, then another. Sam didn't take time to see what damage the shots might have caused. He levered and fired round after round into the high stony hillside. Two more shots pounded down as the sheriff and Fish hurried out of sight behind a large boulder. Sam heard one of the shots ping and ricochet away. He leaned back against the pine, his smoking rifle levered and ready. He looked over at the horses, seeing their position was safe enough unless someone was deeply committed to killing them.

He waited in a tense ringing silence for a few seconds, realizing the shooters had run out of targets now that the sheriff and Fish were out of sight. Then he ran to the horses, grabbed his telescope from under his bedroll and hurried to a spot behind a rock where he could scan the upper hillside. As he stretched out the telescope and raised it, he called out toward where the sheriff and Fish had taken cover.

"Stone? Are you two all right?" He started scanning the lens among the rocks. He caught sight of three figures running through a stand of brush toward waiting horses. One carried a rifle with a long brass scope atop its barrel. All three wore long dusters and their heads were topped with black cavalry-style hats. Within the flapping lapels of the riding dusters he saw the black suits.

Hinler's rail detectives . . .

When Sheriff Stone didn't reply, Sam lowered the lens for a moment and called out again. Still no reply. He closed the lens and shoved it down in the back of his belt, looking all around warily. Without another word, he inched his way around the perimeter of the clearing and stopped when he got to the boulder he'd seen Fish and the sheriff crawl behind.

When he eased a look around the edge of the boulder, he saw Sheriff Stone lying facedown in the dirt, a wide circle of blood on his back, more blood in the dirt beside him and a bullet wound in Stone's back. As the wounded sheriff tried to push himself up, Sam looked around and hurried to him in a crouch. He saw no sign of Fish. When he stooped down to help the wounded lawman, he noted the discarded handcuffs lying in the dirt; he also noted Stone's empty holster.

"Watch yourself . . . Ranger," Stone said in a strained voice, struggling up from the dirt.

"I'm watching for him," Sam said in a lowered tone, looping his arm around the sheriff's shoulder. "Are you able to get up?" Blood ran down the sheriff's back.

"I'm doing it," Stone said with pained determination. He hobbled along beside the Ranger, leaning against him. "Get us . . . to the horses . . . before he makes a run for it," he warned in a weakening voice.

But even as they struggled forward, Sam and the wounded sheriff heard Fish shouting at the horses, trying to shoo them away. They heard the sound of a horse's hooves as the fleeing outlaw batted his boots to the horse's sides and sent it galloping away along the rocky hill trail.

"I—I lost a prisoner," Stone said in a struggling voice.

"You've been ambushed and back-shot, Sheriff," Sam said, helping him get to the place where they had left their horses. He helped Stone lie down onto his side. Looking around, he saw the sheriff's claybank barb and his own copper dun standing only a few feet away. Fish hadn't been able to spook the animals. The outlaw had raced away with Bowlinger's horse beside him, Stone's loaded Colt in his hand.

"Still . . . I lost one," Stone said in a pained voice. "No need . . . softening it any."

"Whatever you say, Sheriff," said Sam. "Lie easy here." He walked over to the horses, gathered their reins and led them back. Stone raised his head and looked at him almost in surprise.

"Aren't you going . . . after him?"

"He'll keep," Sam replied; he took down his saddle-bags and tossed them on the ground beside Stone. "First, we get your bleeding stopped, see what kind of shape you're in." He pitched a canteen down beside him.

"I'm in good enough shape, Ranger," Stone said, sounding strengthened by having a point of contention. "I'm still . . . kicking, ain't I?"

Sam only looked at him.

"I mean it, Ranger," said Stone. "Get on after him. I'll tend to myself." He gripped the canteen and pulled it to him.

"Soon enough, Sheriff," Sam said. "Keep quiet for now, help me get the bleeding stopped." He pulled out a clean cloth bandage and folded it to a size that would cover the bullet wound. He reached to place the bandage on the sheriff's back.

"Wait, what's that?" Stone said, stopping him.

The two froze and listened close until they heard a weakened voice call out from where the bullet had dropped Rudy Bowlinger to the dirt.

"It's Bowlinger. He's alive," Sam said in surprise. "Here, hold this." He pressed the bandage to the sheriff's back, drew Stone's hand around and pressed it firmly over the wound. Then he rushed out into the clearing to where Rudy Bowlinger had pushed himself up with his cuffed hands and sat swaying back and forth unsteadily. His bloody hands gripped a bullet hole high in his shoulder.

"Ranger . . . who shot me?" Bowlinger asked, his voice sounding stunned, half-conscious.

"It looked like the colonel's men," Sam said. "Let's get you on your feet, get you behind cover."

"Is—is Parker . . . shot?" he asked, making no attempt to rise even with the Ranger trying to help him.

"No, he's not shot," Sam said.

"Where . . . is he?" Bowlinger asked, looking around aimlessly.

"He's gone," Sam said. "He lit out of here."

"Left . . . me?" said Bowlinger. "That lousy bastard . . ."

Sam looked at him, seeing from the look in his eyes, the amount of blood all around him, that it wasn't going to help trying to get him onto his feet. He would likely pass out from the loss of so much blood.

"Stay down," Sam said. He stepped behind him, hooked his hands under his arms and dragged him over to where Stone lay watching.

"How bad a shape . . . is he in, Ranger?" he asked, his voice still weak and halting.

"You're both alive, Sheriff. Let's see if we can keep you that way," Sam said, reaching out for the canteen Sheriff Stone held in his hand.

In the late afternoon the Ranger was sitting sipping a cup of coffee when he heard the sheriff moan and begin to stir from his deep sleep. As Stone raised his head, Sam lifted a small pot of jerked elk he'd heated into a broth over the small fire. He poured the simmered broth into a tin cup and stooped down beside the waking lawman.

"Seems I'm spending a lot of time waking up lately,

Ranger," he said, his voice sounding a little stronger. He noted the cup in Sam's hand.

"Waking up is good for you," Sam said wryly. He held the cup out to Stone's mouth. "Drink this. It'll help you get some of your blood back."

Stone propped himself up on an elbow and sipped the broth. He looked over at Bowlinger.

"Is he alive?" he asked.

"He is," Sam said. "I don't know for how long if the colonel's men keep dogging us."

Both lawmen turned when they heard Bowlinger's raspy voice.

"I can . . . still fight, Ranger," he said weakly. "Get me on . . . my horse."

Sam looked at the cup of broth and at the sheriff. Stone nodded him toward the wounded outlaw.

"Go on, give him some," he said. "He needs it lots worse than I do."

"You both need it," Sam said. He handed Stone the cup; he stood and walked back to the low-burning fire. He emptied his remaining coffee from his cup, filled it with broth and carried it to where Bowlinger lay with his eyes half-closed. He stooped down and raised Bowlinger's head.

When the outlaw had taken two sips of the broth, Sam eased his damp head down onto the blanket. Bowlinger coughed and stirred and kept his eyes open.

"I'm . . . going to die here, ain't I, Ranger?" Bowlinger asked as if having already resolved himself to his fate.

"You've got a chance, Bowlinger," the Ranger replied. "The bullet nicked a vein, but it went through your shoulder clean. You've lost a lot of blood."

"More than that one?" Bowlinger asked, gesturing his head toward the sheriff.

"Yes, more than him," Sam said.

"Just my damn luck," Bowlinger said, his strength seeming to surge a little. "A lawman lives . . . a man like me dies. What's the use? If I don't die now, I'll dance on a hangman's rope."

"A man *like you*?" Stone called out from his blanket ten feet away. "You mean a *thief* and a low-handed *poltroon*?"

Bowlinger ignored the sheriff, batted his eyes and raised himself onto his elbows. He looked all around at the waiting animals and asked, "Where's my cayuse?"

"Fish took him," Sam said.

"That rotten . . . no-good bastard," said Bowlinger. "He cut out on me . . . took my horse?"

"He did at that," the Ranger said.

Bowlinger fell silent, but only for a moment.

"You want to know where . . . they hide out? All right, Ranger, I'll show you where—those dirty sons a' bitches. I don't owe none of them nothing."

Sam didn't reply. He heard the outlaw talking himself into betraying his gang; he wasn't going to say anything and take a chance on stopping him.

Bowlinger seemed to consider the matter a moment longer as if trying to figure how he might gain something for himself in exchange for the information.

"You keep me alive, Ranger . . . and let me go free," Bowlinger threw in as an afterthought, "I'll tell you everything you want to know about where they hole up over there." He gestured a weak nod toward the Mexican border. "I give you my word on it."

"His word, ha!" Stone called out.

Sam didn't bother replying. Instead he half stood up, as if to cut the conversation short. But Bowlinger stopped him.

"Wait, Ranger," the wounded outlaw said, his strength appearing to wane as quickly as it had surged. He dropped onto his back and coughed and settled himself. "All right . . . will you tell the judge to go easy on me?" He paused, then said, "I had a terrible time growing up. You wouldn't believe—"

"I'm done with you," Sam said, cutting him off. He stood the rest of the way up. "I'll tell the judge you cooperated—gave us valuable information about the Bard Gang. That's all you'll get from me."

Bowlinger sighed and closed his eyes.

"That don't sound like much," he said.

"Then how about this?" Sam said. "I'll keep the colonel's men from killing you all the way to Yuma."

"And I'll help him do it," Stone put in, his strength also starting to wane.

Bowlinger kept his eyes closed. The wounded sheriff and the Ranger only stared at him.

"So what? That's your job. . . . You've got to do that anyway. . . . ," Rudy said, his voice trailing, slurring as he drifted back to sleep.

"Wake that bummer up—wear his head out with a

gun barrel, Ranger," Stone said, still up on his elbows, but starting to look a little shaky again. "Help me up. I'll do it."

Sam watched the sheriff melt back onto his blanket, his voice trailing away into a low grumble.

With both wounded men back to sleep, the Ranger emptied broth from his coffee cup, refilled it with strong black coffee and sat watching the sun drop low on the jagged western hill line. He wasn't going anywhere tonight. Three men on two horses, two of the men wounded, traveling at night with the smell of blood on them.

Huh-uh . . . too risky, he warned himself. His best move would be to ride to the nearest mining town or Mexican hill village and get whatever help was available there for these two. Whatever reckoning was to come between him and the colonel's men would have to wait for now. The main thing now was to keep both the sheriff and the outlaw alive, if it was within his power to do so.

He sipped the coffee and watched the red fiery sky fade under a cloak of darkness. But the reckoning was coming, he reminded himself, as surely as the coming dawn. Colonel Hinler and his men were not above the law. They had shot a lawman. Whether the act was intentional or by slip of chance in the heat of battle, that would not stand, he told himself, staring out at the far edge of the darkening sky.

No, that would not stand.

Chapter 8

When the four black-suited detectives left the spot over-looking the ambush site, they rode three miles without stopping, hoping to catch up to Parker Fish, whom they'd seen ride away. When they gave up on catching the fleeing outlaw, the fourth detective, Bo Anson, stopped his tired horse beside Duke Patterson and looked out over a rugged rock valley.

"I say let the fool go," he said. "Like as not a rattle-snake will spike him before nightfall." He crossed his wrists on his saddle horn and spat a stream of tobacco. Dust covered his long, drooping mustache.

But Duke Patterson was having none of it.

"Like hell we'll let him go," he said angrily. "The col-onel said kill them both. That's what we're going to do."

"Then you go on and chase him through there, Duke," Anson said with a dark chuckle. "I'll have my-self a nice dinner of jackrabbit, ride back come morning and tell the colonel what a fine job you done out here." He nodded at the jackrabbit hanging down the side of his horse by a strip of rawhide. Then he turned and looked at the two detectives behind them with a flat grin. "What about you fellas? How does some rabbit on a spit sound to you?"

"I could eat my saddle," said Thurman Bain in a serious tone.

The other recently hired detective, Quinton Carlson, nodded in agreement.

"We come to kill two thieves," he said. "One out of two ain't so bad."

"Not for you maybe," said Patterson, "but I've got to answer to the colonel, tell him why one of them got away." He looked at the rifle lying across Anson's lap, a long brass scope running the length of the barrel. "I'll also have to explain how the sheriff got shot."

Anson gave a dark chuckle and spat again.

"I'd like to hear that myself," he said. He and Carlson both laughed. Bain sat watching.

"I see nothing funny about it," Patterson said angrily.

"I can see how you wouldn't," Anson said, "you being the one who shot him."

"In all that shooting how can you say *I* shot him?" said Patterson. He nodded at the rifle with its long scope. "How do you know it wasn't your bullet that hit him?"

"Because I didn't *aim* at him," Anson said, stifling a laugh. He gave Carlson a look; Carlson grinned and looked away.

"Neither did I!" Patterson raged.

"That's even worse," Anson said coolly. Again he grinned, the lump of tobacco in his cheek twisting his face sideways. "Maybe he'd been safer if you had."

"I've had enough of this," said Patterson. "I'm in charge, and I say we're going in there after him." He gestured toward the endless tangle of brush and up-reaching stone.

Anson and Carlson only stared at him with grins frozen on their faces. Patterson looked away from them, at Thurman Bain.

"What about you, Bain? Are you coming?" he barked.

"Righto," Bain replied, putting his horse a step forward.

Righto . . . ?

Anson and Carlson gave a chuckle at Bain's snappy reply.

"Then let's go," said Patterson, jerking his horse around toward the trail. But he hesitated for a moment, then slumped a little in his saddle. Anson and Carlson gave Bain a look that stopped him.

"All right . . . ," Patterson said. "Maybe it would be a good idea to rest these horses overnight—get a fresh start come morning." He backed his horse a step and looked at the three men. "I expect what the colonel don't know won't hurt him."

Bo Anson spat tobacco and grinned as he raised a black-handled Colt from the holster on his side.

"You should have said something sooner, amigo," he said. He fanned three shots into the detective's chest. Patterson, wide-eyed, flipped out of his saddle and landed facedown on the rocky ground.

Thurman Bain started to swing his horse around and make a run for it, afraid he was next. But Carlson's big Smith & Wesson slid free of its holster, cocked and aimed at his belly.

"Not so fast, *Righto*," Carlson said. "When the colonel asks how this fool died, what's your answer?"

Bain looked back and forth at the two in terror.

"We—we got caught up in a shooting with the lawmen and their prisoners! A wild shot killed him?" he offered quickly.

"Did you believe that, Bo?" Carlson asked Anson.

"Not for a minute," Anson replied. He turned his horse as he spoke. "Go on and shoot him. I'll go skin this rabbit and rustle us up a cook fire."

"Wait!" Bain pleaded as Anson rode away at a walk. "I can say something else. Tell me what to say—!"

Anson grinned to himself, hearing the young detective's voice cut short beneath two rapid gunshots.

"Want me to tie them over their saddles, Bo?" Carlson called out, seeing that Anson wasn't going to slow his horse a step.

"Naw, leave them where they're lying," Anson called back. "All that shooting, dry-gulching and carrying on, we were lucky to get out of here with our lives—don't you see?"

Carlson watched as he stopped his horse a few yards away before riding out of sight around a boulder.

"Yeah, I see. But do you think the colonel will believe us?" he called out.

"That's hard to say, Quinton," Anson replied with a slight chuckle. He picked the rifle up from across his lap and propped it on his knee. "I might have to wing you a little just to make it look real. Sit real still now."

Carlson stared, stunned for a moment.

"That's not a damn bit funny, Bo," he called out. "Don't fool around!" He fidgeted in his saddle seeing the rifle come up in Anson's hands.

"You're right, Quinton, ol' pal," he said, taking aim through the long brass scope. "The colonel's too smart to fall for a *winging* story."

"Jesus, Bo!" said Carlson. "Stop joshing me. This ain't the least bit fun—" His words stopped as the rifle bucked in Anson's hands and smoke billowed up around the barrel. Anson lowered the smoking rifle. He stared at where Carlson lay limp in the dirt, his horse shying back a few feet in confusion. He studied the area, then spat tobacco and smiled in satisfaction. "Yeah, that looks about right," he said. Then he turned his horse and rode away, the dead rabbit flapping at his horse's side.

Dewey Lucas and Russell Gant, the two outlaws who'd managed to escape the battle at the rail siding, lay high on a rock ledge watching the four detectives on the trail below. They both looked at each other in surprise when they saw the familiar face of Bo Anson. Their surprise heightened when they saw him raise a gun from its holster and shoot the lead detective out of his saddle. From their rocky, lofty perch they lay in rapt silence as he rode off a few yards and blew Quinton Carlson from his saddle with his big scoped rifle.

"Holy thunder!" Russell Gant said after a moment, watching Anson ride away with his rabbit swinging at his knee. "What the blazes are Anson and Carlson doing riding for the railroad?"

Lucas scratched his scraggly gray beard stubble, contemplating what they'd just seen.

"Beats the devil out of me," he said, still staring at the bodies on the trail below. "I'm stuck at seeing Bo kill ol' Quinton. They was best of pals, I always thought."

"Ol' Quinton must have aggravated him about something," said Gant, rising from his stomach onto his knees, dusting the front of his shirt and his brush-scarred jacket. "Bo could never stand much aggravation, as I recall."

"Well," Lucas said, standing, dusting himself off and adjusting his battered gray cavalry hat, "whatever that was, we'll have to jaw about it on the trail. I'm just glad this bunch won't be dogging us all the way home."

"I expect somebody will be dogging us, though," said Gant, the two of them walking back a few steps to where their tired horses waited. "Colonel Hinler only does the bidding of Curtis Siedell——King Curtis we call him. Siedell ain't giving up until we're all lying dead somewhere. The colonel is just his striking rod."

As the two stepped into their saddles, he turned and looked at Lucas. "I'm new here, Dewey," said Gant. "You've been with this bunch from the start. I've heard stories, but just how strong is this grudge between Bard and Curtis Siedell?"

"It's as strong as it is long," said the older gunman. "It started when we all rid guerrilla for the Galveston Raiders back in the war. The colonel was no different than the rest of us then. He was a guerrilla to the core, same as us. We robbed Northern trains, payrolls, gold shipments and whatnot together," he explained. "But then the colonel got himself captured and got himself converted, turned into a Yankee. I can't blame him none, sitting there in Andersonville, waiting to hang— eating rats when he could catch one. It turned him into a galvanized Yankee."

"A galvanized Yankee from the Galveston Raiders . . ." Gant pondered the coincidence, then said, "That would have sure converted me if they offered it."

"Me too." Lucas nodded and went on. "Siedell became the North's highest-ranking *galvanized* officer at that time. It was quite a feather in Abe Lincoln's hat, bringing a Southern regular colonel over to his side. When the war started swinging toward the Yankees' favor, Grant commissioned Siedell as a colonel in the army of the North. Hearing about it nearly killed all of us ol' rebel freebooters—him and Max Bard was best of pals until then. We'd been looking for a chance to bust him out of prison."

They turned their horses and rode along at a walk; Gant listened closely and shook his head as Lucas continued.

"Imagine," he said, "switching over and becoming a Yankee officer."

"I know," said Lucas, "but switch over he did, and he never looked back. At the end of the war, one word from him and Bard and all of us would have been pardoned. But Siedell wouldn't lift a finger. He was busy building himself a fortune by then."

"Did you want to be pardoned?" Gant asked.

"Hell no," said Lucas, "but that ain't the point. Everything else Siedell done could have been overlooked as trying to stay alive. But when he turned his back and was willing to let us all hang when he could have cleaned the slate, so to speak, it was all that Max and Holbert Lee and the rest of us ol' boys could take."

"The son of a bitch," Gant said in a lowered tone. "Nobody does his friends that way."

"We was the only friends King Curtis Siedell ever had that he could trust," said Lucas. "Maybe that's why it suited him to see us all dead—figured whatever we knew about him would die right along with us. He made himself rich. They say a man gets rich enough he don't have friends he can trust anymore. He's just sitting on a mountain of riches that he thinks will be taken from him at every turn."

Gant rode along in silence, letting it all sink in.

Lucas paused and let out a breath.

"Anyway . . . that's where it started between us and Curtis Siedell. The War of Northern Aggression ended and our own private war began. Siedell and us have been out to kill each other ever since."

"And nothing's ever going to make things right?" Gant said.

Lucas just looked at him.

"Have you not been listening to me?" he said. "We're making it right. We're killing each other at every chance. These are matters of *wronged* honor. Killing and dying is the only things that ever settles *wronged* honor." He gazed at Gant. "You ever heard of any other way?"

Gant shook his head, not even having to consider the question.

"No, I expect I haven't," he said.

The two turned forward in their saddles, but before going three more yards, they stopped abruptly, seeing the three figures on horseback spring into the trail facing them. Both men grabbed for their holstered revolvers, then caught themselves and eased down when they recognized Max Bard, Holbert Lee Cross and Worley staring at them from ten yards away.

"Damn it to *bloody hell*!" said Dewey Lucas to the three. "I wish you wouldn't do that—jump out and spook a man that way."

"We heard gunfire, Dewey. Besides, you're too old to be spooked by anything," Cross said, smiling, nudging his horse closer.

"The gunfire wasn't us," Lucas said.

"But we didn't know that, did we?" said Cross. "What if it was the colonel's men, instead of us, catching you unawares?"

"Then I expect you'd be dead instead of sitting there grinning like a possum on a pine nut," said Lucas. As he spoke he and Gant noted the dried blood down the front of Pete Worley riding toward them. "What happened to Kid Domino?" he asked.

"Scalp graze," Cross said matter-of-factly.

"Ouch," said Lucas. He and Gant put their horses forward again as Cross sidled up to them. After they met Bard and Worley, all five of them rode on as if nothing had ever happened to scatter them all over the desert hill country.

"What's next for us, Max?" Lucas asked, not wasting

any time. The four of them gazed ahead as Cross lagged his horse back a few yards to check their back trail.

"Another one of Siedell's rail spurs," Bard said without looking at the graying gunman. "Only this time we get paid for our trouble. Any objections?"

"No, I'm just asking," said Lucas. "But I've got to say, my poke is getting light. I need to fill it before it flies away—before all those *señoras calientes* along the border forget my name."

"Those hot ladies won't forget you, Dewey," Worley put in, riding beside him. "You've got too much invested in them. They might build a statue of you."

"It'll be different next time, Dewey," said Bard. "I've put a fresh dog in the ring."

Lucas gave Gant a knowing look, then turned to Bard.

"Is that dog's name Bo Anson?" he asked. "Because if it is, that's all the *barking* you heard a while ago."

Bard gave him a surprised look.

"Suppose it is?" he said, trying not to look caught off guard.

"Yep, that's what I thought," said Lucas. "Ol' Bo just shot the colonel's right-hand man and some other fool down there because they wanted to chase Parker Fish into the rock valley." He gestured toward the rugged valley land below them. "Then he shot his pal Carlson, *balooie!* Left them all lying where they fell."

"You don't say . . . ?" said Bard. He kept his horse moving forward.

"I do say *indeed*," said Lucas with the trace of a grin

through his gray beard stubble. "If Bo Anson is your *fresh dog in the ring*, I just hope you've got a powerful leash on him. That's one dog that needs lots of room to prowl."

Max Bard shook his head.

"Anybody ever tell you that you talk too much, Dewey?" he said, riding on at a walk.

"Oh yes, all the time," Lucas said. "Usually when they know I'm right and don't want to admit it."

Behind them, having found their back trail to be clear, Cross rode forward at an easy clip and fell in beside Worley and Bard. He eased his horse down to a walk and gave Bard a slight nod. And they rode on.

Part 2

Chapter 9

Colonel Cooper Hinler and Bo Anson stood over the scattered bone-picked remains of Duke Patterson, Thurman Bain and Quinton Carlson. A few yards away the colonel's mounted detectives sat wrapped in their riding dusters, watching with sour expressions. A week of exposure to the desert heat and wildlife had taken a drastic toll on the three scattered corpses. A dead black buzzard whose fate was indiscernible lay dust-covered near Patterson's chewed-upon head. A feathered wing stirred on a hot breeze.

"No decent man deserves this," the colonel said, clenching his fists at his sides. He looked all around at layer upon layer of paw prints and buzzard tracks left in the darkened sand surrounding the bodies. "These scurvy desert beggars—" He kicked at a pile of dried coyote droppings.

Anson eyed him, finding it curious that a man would vent such anger at ignorant creatures of the wild.

"These critters got to eat too," he said in a mild tone. "Take it easy, Colonel."

Take it easy, did he say?

The colonel just scowled at him, not liking the man's coolness, his apparent indifference to the colonel's authority, at anything and everything around him. But he reined in his temper and kept it in check, knowing Bo Anson's reputation as a gunman and paid assassin. Besides, with Duke Patterson dead, who did he really have here that could step in and fill his boots? He eyed Anson up and down, noting the scoped rifle over his shoulder, the holstered Colt on his right hip, the second Colt hanging up under his left arm in a shoulder rig.

"You're right, Bo," the colonel said. "I realize that you yourself have lost a friend here." He gestured a nod toward the loose pile of blood-darkened rags and bones that had been Quinton Carlson.

"Not just a friend, Colonel," said Anson, calmly chewing a fresh wad of tobacco. "My very *best* friend." He spat a stream, nodded and said, "Don't even wonder what I'm going to do when I get my scope set on Bard or any of his freebooters."

The colonel nodded.

"I'm going to be depending on you a lot, Bo," the colonel said, using the same tone and manner that he found worked well on men like Duke Patterson and the rest of his detectives.

"That's good to hear, Colonel," said Anson. "I shouldn't tell you this, but the last thing Duke said before he died was for me to promise him I'd stay after Max Bard and his gang and see they get what's coming to them."

"On the contrary, Bo," said the colonel, "I'm glad you told me. It helps me see clearly what kind of man you are, that Duke would say such a thing. You see, speaking bluntly, Duke wasn't too keen on me hiring you. The fact that your merit impressed him before he died speaks well for you."

"I'm honored, Colonel," Anson said in a tone that was hard to describe as sincere. "Not to disparage the man's memory, but *speaking bluntly*," he added, "had Duke listened to me, he and the other two would most likely be alive today."

The colonel just looked at him.

"It's true, Colonel," said Anson. He spat a stream. "I said we needed to go right on after Parker Fish into the rock valley, but Duke wouldn't hear of it. He finally agreed for me to ride on out and see if I could flush him out. I was on his trail when I heard the ambush and hurried back." He shook his head as if to free himself of some bloody death scene. "It was terrible," he continued. "I got here just as Duke was breathing his last. That's when he made me promise." He breathed deep and added in a determined tone, "I'll keep that promise as God's my witness."

"So you shall, Bo," the colonel said. He patted Anson on his broad shoulder. "I want you to lead these men for me. Don't stop until the Bard Gang is dead." He flagged the detectives forward, then asked Anson, "Do you know some good men like yourself who are looking for gun work? The attack in Gun Hill, and now this, has left me shorthanded." He motioned at the three bodies on the ground.

"It just happens that I do, Colonel," said Anson. "In a town right over the hills there, across the border—"

He caught himself and stopped and said, "These men have had run-ins with the law. Is that going to cut them out?"

"Not if you vouch for them, Bo," the colonel said. "This is no church group, and I'm not looking for deacons."

Bo gave a crooked tobacco-lumpy smile behind his drooping mustache. "In that case, yes, sir, I'll vouch for them. They're a tough lot, but it'll be my job to keep them in line. Deal, eh?" He spat on his palm and held it out to shake hands.

The colonel looked at the brown tobacco-stained palm, but he masked his distaste, spat lightly in his own hand and reached out.

"Yes, deal," he said. "I say we leave right away, gather these new men and get after Bard."

But Anson hesitated, considering the matter. "Wouldn't it be faster, Colonel, if I went after these new men alone, took a spare horse with me? I could ride all night, get them and catch up with you and the detectives across the rock valley."

The colonel didn't like his orders overridden, yet upon thinking about it, he saw Anson's point. It made no sense giving up a set of fresh tracks while all of them rode to bring back the new men.

"Yes, I agree," the colonel said. "Take a spare horse and get going. I'll lead the men from here until you catch up to us."

"Aye-aye, Colonel," Anson said. "When I bring these new men onto Max Bard's trail, you're going to see some changes in how these outlaws are handled. You'll soon be taking Bard's head to Curtis Siedell on a stick."

The colonel gave him a stiff look, not liking the aye-aye response, which he considered flippant at best.

"It's *Mr.* Siedell to you, Bo," he said. Raising a cautioning finger, he said, "Don't take liberties with your superiors." He lowered his voice just between the two of them. "Keep this to yourself, Bo. Mr. Siedell is coming to inspect his new rail spurs personally. I expect him in Gun Hill any day. I shan't have to correct your manners again."

"No, sir-ree, Colonel," said Anson. "You certainly *shan't* have to." He spat a stream of tobacco juice and turned toward the horse and the mounted detectives. A faint smile of satisfaction went unnoticed on his face.

While the lawman and the wounded outlaw lay healing from their fight in Resting, the Ranger met with the lady sheriff of the small badlands mining town. Sheriff Colleen Deluna stood six feet in her sock feet, taller still in her Mexican knee-high riding boots. She wore a gingham dress beneath a brush-scarred denim waist jacket. On her left hip she wore a holstered Colt, butt forward in a cross-draw slim-jim holster. A wide dusty sombrero mantled her clear yet sun-darkened face. Her dark hair hung the length of her back in a single braid that swayed easily when she walked.

Sam watched her as she turned from gazing out the window of her small plank-and-adobe office and walked behind her desk to sit down facing him. Sam realized she had a barred cell in which to billet a prisoner, but he saw on the stone-tiled floor a heavy blacksmith's anvil with a six-foot shackle and chain attached to it.

The sheriff noticed his gaze. "If carrying an eighty-pound anvil isn't enough to make a prisoner behave himself, I have the old territory jail wagon sitting out back," she said. "Even rowdy prisoners settle right down when they see it." She smiled. "Your prisoner is safe with me."

"I never doubted it, Sheriff Colleen Deluna," Sam said. "This one belongs to the Max Bard Gang, and he's got Colonel Hinler's detectives out to kill him. I just wanted to make sure I gave you the whole story before I left him here—not leave you with any surprises in store."

"Obliged for that, Ranger," said Sheriff Deluna. "I've heard you're a lawman who can be trusted." She paused and gave a slight shrug, seeing the look on his face. "I'm sorry I can't say that about all lawmen," she added. "But I'm just being honest." She kept a level gaze on him and asked, "What about Sheriff Stone?"

"I trust him," the Ranger said. "He's had some problems lately, but I think he's got things settled."

"Whiskey problems, is what I've heard," the woman sheriff said bluntly. "I've heard he's had them for a while. Heard he thinks he turns into a bear, a wolf or something . . . ?"

"Yes, ma'am," Sam said. "He admits he thinks he's done some shape-shifting—like some of the Plains Indians claim to do."

"No surprise, but most of their shape-shifting comes

out of a whiskey bottle too," she said. "Some, not all," she added in a quiet tone. "Were you going to tell me about Stone?"

"Yes," Sam said. "I was waiting to see if I'd be leaving him here to recuperate first. I didn't want to say something that didn't need saying."

"Then you're thinking of taking him with you?" said Sheriff Deluna.

"I'm thinking of taking them both with me," Sam said. Seeing her expression change, he said before she could respond, "I know how bad the colonel's detectives can be when they don't get their way. Not to mention what lengths this prisoner, Rudy Bowlinger, will go to—"

"Ask yourself this, Ranger Burrack," Sheriff Deluna said, cutting him off. "If I were Sheriff Stone sitting here, would you be having these same concerns about leaving your prisoner here with me, or your wounded lawman for that matter?"

The Ranger thought about it for only a second.

"Yes, I would," he said. "I would still have to weigh what's best for keeping us all alive, same as you would, *sitting here.*"

"All right." Sheriff Deluna nodded, letting him know she'd resolved the matter. She redirected the conversation as she took a short stack of wanted posters from a drawer and laid them across her desk in front of the Ranger. "Here's something I think you'll find interesting— maybe more than a coincidence."

Sam leafed through the posters, calling the names printed below each of the pictures.

"Roland Crispe, Mexican Charlie Summez, Hugh Kirchdorf, Buford 'Bo' Anson, Quinton Carlson, Ape Boyd and Dawg Merril," he said. He read the attached telegram with the names also handwritten on it: "All reportedly seen in the town of Bexnar, Mexico." He shook his head a little and looked at two more pictures that had no names below the faces. One of them he recognized as Doyle Hickey, an outlaw with a vicious scar under his left eye. "Bexnar's right across the border," he added.

"Yes, just over that line of hills to be exact," said Colleen Deluna, gesturing a nod toward the distance beyond the front window. "I got the telegram, thought I'd do some desk work and dig up their wanted posters."

"Quinton Carlson and Bo Anson both rode with Max Bard under other names, back after the war," Sam said, summoning up the information from memory. "I see what you mean about coincidence, all of them showing up this close at the same time." He paused, considering the matter. Then he put it aside. "There might be some connection, but I don't see it yet. Obliged, but for now I'm headed back to Gun Hill. The colonel has to answer for his detectives ambushing us." He started to slide the posters back across the sheriff's desk, but she stopped him with an outreached hand.

"You keep them. I can ask for more if I need to," she said.

Sam took the posters, folded them and stuck them inside the bib of his shirt.

"Obliged," he said again. Considering the dangerous closeness of the gunmen on the wanted posters, he said, "I'm thinking I might travel faster on my own—leave Sheriff Stone to heal up here a few days." He gave her a questioning look.

"He's welcome here. Whether he's a white man or a Plains Indian, I believe a man changes into something else when he's unhappy with what he *is*, his conditions and circumstances in life," she said. She paused and studied the Ranger's face as if awaiting his opinion.

Sam picked up his rifle leaning against the desk and his sombrero lying atop it. "I knew an old prisoner who spent his life behind bars. He told me that he kept from losing his mind by making up a life for himself outside the walls. Over the years he put himself somewhere on a little spread in New Mexico—made himself up a wife, children, everything he ever wanted in his real life but knew he'd never have." He paused in reflection, then said, "They found him dead one morning inside his cell. Said he had a peaceful smile on his face. I think about him. I always wonder where he really died. In that cell, or somewhere in New Mexico with his wife and family gathered round him."

Sheriff Deluna watched him shake his head slightly.

The Ranger straightened and leveled his sombrero across his brow.

"My point is, I don't judge who turns into what, or who goes where when they die." He nodded toward a gun rack where a few shotguns and rifles stood in a row. "Keep Sheriff Stone sober. If Max Bard or the colonel's men come around causing trouble, Stone will do his part. He's good with a gun."

"Don't worry, Ranger," said Sheriff Deluna. "You leave him here, I'll keep him sober if I have to break his drinking arm."

"I don't know if he'd be happy to hear that," Sam said, turning to the door, "but I am."

Bexnar, the Mexican badlands

Dawg Merril flew through the dusty blanket that draped the doorway of the town's Riendo Gato—Laughing Cat— Cantina. The blanket wrapped around him as he hit the hitch rail between two resting horses, bounced high and landed in the dirt street. The horses shied against their tied reins. Dust billowed. Dawg lay thrashing and wallowing, trying to get untangled from the heavy clinging wool as Ape Boyd stepped out of the Laughing Cat. A bottle of mescal hung from his left hand. In his right hand he held a big Starr revolver leveled toward the blanketed man. His bare head was shaved bald save for a foot-long braid hanging from above his left ear. The music and voices fell silent behind him.

Boyd's fellow gunmen, Roland Crispe and Mexican Charlie Summez, who were drinking outside the cantina, stepped back to give him a clear target.

"Kill him quick, Ape," said Crispe. "We're having a conversation here."

Ape Boyd snarled as he stepped away from the hitched horses and cocked and pointed the big Starr.

"Nobody calls me April and lives," he shouted at the frantically struggling gunman.

In spite of Dawg Merril's best efforts, the blanket refused to free its grip around his head and shoulders.

"Damn it, Ape!" shouted Dawg. "I wasn't trying to goad you. I was just saying with a name like *April*, no wonder you sooner go by *Ape*!" He ripped and clawed and pulled at the blanket. The blanket seemed to have a mind of its own. It appeared to only cling tighter as he tried to force himself free.

Ape snarled even louder and looked in disbelief at the two drinking gunmen.

"You believe this? He's already said it again!" he bellowed, enraged.

"We heard it this time, Ape," Mexican Charlie said. "It's his own damn fault."

"Yeah," said Crispe, "and we are talking here."

"You *sons a' bitches!*" Dawg shouted, thrashing more intently until he heard the sound of the big Starr cocking and realized the blanket would never turn him loose in time. "Damn this to hell," he bellowed. He grabbed his Colt from its holster under the blanket and began firing blindly at the sound of Ape's voice. Ape grinned venomously and took a side step. He fired shot after shot into the blanket at Dawg's chest, each shot causing Dawg to falter back another step. When the fifth shot raised another puff of dust on the blanket, Dawg staggered in place. His Colt fell to the dirt at his feet. As if adding insult to injury, the blanket slid freely down off his face, his bloody chest, and fell in a pile at his feet.

Dawg stood wide-eyed as the blanket fell and the life spilled out of him.

"I'll be . . . gawddamned," he said, not believing his dose of foul luck.

As he crumpled to the dirt, Ape Boyd blew smoke from the tip of his gun barrel and holstered it. To the side, Crispe and Mexican Charlie both nodded, then turned away and went back to their conversation. Crispe rounded a finger back and forth in his ear as the shots still echoed out across the Mexican hill line.

Stepping out of the Laughing Cat into the harsh smell of burnt powder, Hugh Kirchdorf looked all around and fanned the smoke with his hand.

"Did you have to shoot him from right here, Ape?" he said, gesturing all around the endless badlands. "We're not cramped for space."

Before Ape Boyd could answer, Mexican Charlie said quietly, "Hold on, pards, looks like we've got company coming." He nodded at a single figure riding out of the wavering desert heat into the far end of town at a gallop, leading a bareback spare horse beside him.

"Reload, Ape," said Kirchdorf. "Might be some more shooting for you."

"Me?" said Ape. "Why me?"

"Because your gun's already dirty," said Kirchdorf, giving the big man a look. "Is that asking too damn much?"

"Huh-uh, fellas," said Roland Crispe. "Don't nobody shoot this one. It's Bo Anson himself, just who we've been waiting for."

Chapter 10

More gunmen filed out of the Laughing Cat and stood watching as Bo Anson kept his horse at a walk the last few yards, then stopped and looked down at the body of Dawg Merril lying bloody in the dirt, the blanket in a pile at his feet.

"I heard shooting," Anson said in an offhand tone. "I expect this was it."

"Howdy, Bo," Crispe said, stepping over quickly and taking the lead rope to the spare horse from Anson's hand. "Yeah, that was it all right. Ape warned him not to call him by his full name. You know Dawg. He always was thicker than molasses."

"And Ape thinned him," said Anson, swinging down from his saddle, taking a closer look at Dawg's body.

"That's pretty much the gist of it," said Crispe. "Ape's real sensitive about his name. Hell, everybody knows it. I figured Dawg knew it too."

"If he didn't, he does now," said Anson. "Get him drug out of here," he said to Mexican Charlie. As he spoke he led his tired horse to the hitch rail that had launched Dawg Merril out to his hapless fate. "Everybody gather up, I've got news for you."

Crispe tied the spare horse to the rail and stood by, waiting to hear what Anson had to say. The others drew in closer around them.

"Things are starting to move a little faster than I thought they would," Anson said. "I left the colonel at the rock valley. We're going to catch up with him and his detectives along the border. They've got Parker Fish on the run—wants as many guns as he can get, hoping Fish might lead him to Max Bard."

"Ha, that's not likely," said Crispe.

"But it suits our purpose, Roland," said Anson, "so we play this thing the way we find it. Colonel wants top guns, we've got him covered."

"You mean the colonel's hiring *all of us*, Bo?" Crispe asked, appearing surprised at their good fortune.

"That's right, Roland," said Anson, eyeing him sharply. "Just like I told you he would. Have you got any more doubts?"

"I never doubted you, Bo," said Crispe. "I was just curious is all." He grinned beneath a finely trimmed mustache. "I knew you were good for what you said."

Anson looked at the body in the dirt.

"Looks like we'll be a man short now," he said.

"Not hardly," Hugh Kirchdorf cut in. "The Cady brothers rode in here last night looking for gun work. I always said they're dumb enough to tattoo a rose on a grizzly's ass if somebody held its head. We told them to stick around, just in case somebody fell out on us, like this." He cut his eyes toward Dawg's body as Mexican Charlie dragged it from the street. Then he jerked his head toward the inside of the Laughing Cat. "I told them to wait for us at the bar while we palaver out here."

"Well, then," said Anson, "let's not keep these *tattoo artists* waiting."

Kirchdorf lowered his voice as he glanced toward the open cantina door. "I might ought to tell you one thing, Bo. They had a run-in with Ranger Burrack and that sheriff who thinks he's a wolf. Ignacio is still limping smartly from it."

Anson looked at him coolly.

"A wolf, you say?" Anson replied. "Now I'm intrigued."

Anson walked into the cantina and over to the tile-topped bar, the rest of the men following him. Seeing him approach them, the Cady brothers, Lyle and Ignacio, straightened and faced him, whiskey glasses in hand. In the front corner of the Laughing Cat, the band stopped playing again. The accordion player sighed and waited with restraint.

Anson motioned for the bartender to set up fresh bottles of rye and mescal. Then he tilted his head and eyed the Cady brothers.

"Howdy, Lyle . . . Ignacio," he said. "Roland says you two are looking for gun work."

"Howdy, Bo," said Lyle.

"We are," Ignacio said, coming right to the point. He tossed back the rye from the glass in his hand and set the shot glass on the bar for a refill. "Whatever you've got going, either side of the border, we're up for it."

"What's Edsel Centrila going to say about you two cutting out on him?" Anson asked.

"We didn't cut out on him. He cut out on us," said Ignacio. "We went after the sheriff over in Big Silver for crawfishing on a deal they had going. The sheriff had been drunk so long he didn't know his name from a bean label. But he was riding with that damn Ranger, Sam Burrack."

"The Ranger got the drop on Iggy here," Lyle put in. "Cracked his shin with a rifle butt. Threatened to crack his other one."

Ignacio just looked at his brother stiffly.

"The Ranger's bad about that," said Anson.

"He truly is," Ignacio confirmed. "Anyway, we spotted the two of them across the hill line in Resting. They brought in one of Max Bard's men, Rudy Bowlinger, in handcuffs. I figure the woman sheriff there has him sweating his liver out in that jail wagon she keeps out back."

"This is all interesting, but what's your point, Iggy?" Anson said.

"I don't know what you're up to, Bo," said Ignacio, "but if you're riding for Max Bard, I figure it might be mine and Lyle's interest to tell you about it."

"Riding for Max Bard . . ." Anson seemed to ponder the matter for a moment. "The thing is we're not riding for Bard, Iggy," he said. He grinned. "Fact is, we're heading over to ride for the colonel, see how he is to work for."

Ignacio and Lyle both looked stunned.

"Riding for the railroad, for the colonel?" Lyle said. "Wearing a detective badge?"

Anson only smiled, watching their reaction.

"There it is, boys," he said. "You want to throw in with us, you're both welcome. You never know what strange twists and turns my trail might take. I've got two men out rounding us up some fresh Mexican horses. You can fill their places till they catch up to us."

The brothers gave each other a puzzled look. Yet as they considered it, it came to them that Bo Anson had to have something up his sleeve.

"I don't know what you're up to, Bo," Ignacio said. "But if it's gun work with money in it, Lyle and I are just your pace."

"Good decision, *Cady brothers*," Anson said in a mocking tone. "Now drink up. We got to hurry and meet up with the colonel." He looked at the band and spun a hand in the air to get them started. Then he said to Lyle and Ignacio, "We've got just one little stop to make on the way there."

"You mean going to Resting, taking Rudy Bowlinger?" said Ignacio.

Bo Anson grinned. "I wouldn't mind him hanging over a saddle, taking him to the colonel when we meet along the trail."

"I hear you," said Ignacio. "Can I ask one favor of you? When you get Bowlinger, will you oblige Lyle and me to kill that Ranger and Sheriff Stone?"

"Kill whoever it suits you, *Cady brothers*," he said to

both of them. "I like seeing men keep their hands in the game."

The Ranger first caught sight of Colonel Hinler and his detectives from a high ridge overlooking the rock valley. He'd spotted them from his lofty perch as they rode through wavering heat and glaring sunlight and moved his dun along at a walk, sticking with them along a stone ridge from above as they crossed a flat rocky stretch and headed up a narrow trail. At a place where he knew their trails would intersect, he sat atop the dun on the shadowy side of a rock wall and waited until the hooves of two horses came forward, their riders scouting the terrain.

As the two detectives rounded the turn, the Ranger stepped the dun out and sat midtrail staring them down, his Winchester rifle leveled at them across the crook in his left arm.

"Wh*oooa* . . . !" shouted a detective named French Devoe, caught off guard, his horse almost rearing with him. Beside him Detective Leon Foley stopped his horse suddenly and threw both hands in the air.

"Both of you gather up and come forward, easy-like," the Ranger said calmly. "Raise your shooting irons and let them fall." He'd made sure his duster lapel was open enough to show the badge on his chest.

"Just a damn minute, Ranger," said Devoe. "We're lawmen, same as you. You've no right telling us—" His words stopped short as he saw the Ranger's hand tense around the rifle—heard the metallic sound of the hammer cock.

"You'd be wrong thinking I'll tell you again, Devoe," Sam said in the same even tone.

French Devoe looked surprised, almost proud that the Ranger knew his name. He sat frozen in place as beside him the younger detective, Foley, lifted his pistol from its holster and dropped it to the ground.

"Do I know you, Ranger?" Devoe said. He formed a cautious half smile. Sam saw trouble with this one.

"Not as well as you're going to," Sam warned.

Devoe gazed off as if something had caught his attention. But Sam knew what that meant. The detective was getting ready to reach for his holstered Colt.

"I'm just thinking—" Devoe said. His hand plunged for his gun butt. He didn't finish his words. Instead he flipped backward in a bloody mist as the Ranger's rifle barked and slammed a bullet through his high right shoulder.

Beside Devoe, Foley's horse sidestepped, spooked. Foley kept his hands high. He swayed in his saddle with a frightened look on his face.

"D-don't *shoot*!" he pleaded even as Devoe landed on the rocky trail in a large puff of dust. "I'm covered here! See?"

"I see," Sam said, a ribbon of smoke curling up from his rifle barrel. "Rein your horse down before you lose him."

The younger detective moved his hands enough to tighten the reins hanging loose in his right hand. Sam cut his eyes from him back to the wounded detective lying in a heap on the ground, his Colt glinting in the dirt three feet away.

"Crawl away from the gun," Sam called out to him.

"Go to hell, Ranger! I'm shot bad!" Devoe shouted, half enraged, half sobbing. He heard the rifle bark again. Dirt and rock kicked up an inch from his knee.

"Jesus, Ranger!" he shouted. He scooted and crawled sideways hard and fast and stopped ten feet away from the Colt lying on the ground. "The hell do you want with us?" he said.

Sam didn't answer right away. He took two fresh cartridges from his duster and replaced the two he'd just fired. He looked over at Leon Foley.

"Step down," he said. "Take a canteen over to him. Check him out."

He watched the young detective step down from his saddle with a pale sickly look on his face and lift a canteen by its strap.

"You all right, young man?" Sam asked. He tilted his head in curiosity. The young detective had tried to step over to Devoe, but halfway there he stopped and weaved, bowed slightly at the waist.

"I'm going . . . to wretch," he said.

"Good Lord, not here, Foley!" Devoe shouted, shying away. But Foley couldn't stop himself.

Sam looked away a little as the young man gagged and heaved and emptied his stomach in the dirt three feet from Devoe. When he'd finished, he wiped his hand across his mouth and stepped forward with the canteen extended toward Devoe.

"For God sakes, Foley, stay where you are," said the wounded detective, scooting farther away, clamping a hand on his bleeding shoulder.

Sam sat watching as he heard hoofbeats coming up the trail at a gallop toward the sound of the rifle shots.

"Take the canteen, Devoe," he said. "Let him stick a bandanna on the wound for you." He leveled the rifle back at French Devoe as he spoke. The wounded man eyed the rifle, then took the canteen from Foley with reluctance.

"Tell your men to take it real easy, Colonel," Sam called out toward the riders, hearing their horses slow to a walk and come up into sight on the rocky trail. "I'm Ranger Sam Burrack. I'm here looking for a man carrying a brass-scoped rifle."

The colonel put his horse forward at a walk, his men spreading out around him on either side. He looked over at French Devoe on the ground, at Foley standing over him. He eyed the sickness in the dirt with a sour expression.

"What is the meaning of this, Ranger Burrack?" he said, stopping his horse fifteen feet from the Ranger. "What gives you the right to shoot a duly appointed rail detective? This man is a lawman the same as you."

"That's something we could jaw about another time, Colonel," Sam said, leveling the rifle toward him. "For now you need to let your men know that I will drop you in the dirt if any of them look like they're reaching for a gun." He cocked the rifle as he spoke.

"All right, men," the colonel said, "stand down. Don't give this man an excuse for killing someone." He said to Sam, "I demand to know why you shot Detective Devoe."

"Call it a misunderstanding, Colonel," Sam said. "I

told him to *drop* his gun. He must've thought I said *draw* it. You can see why it's real important we both listen close to what we're saying." He paused, then said, "Now, about the man with the scoped rifle. He shot a prisoner of mine and a duly sworn lawman. I'm not leaving without him."

"I know who you mean, but I'm afraid he's dead, Ranger," the colonel lied. "I will show you his body, or what's left of it. Max Bard and his saddle trash ambushed him and two other of my men. Their remains are twenty miles back along the main trail."

"Dead, huh?" Sam said.

"Dead indeed," the colonel said.

"Have your men sit real still, Colonel," Sam said, putting the dun forward. He walked the horse slowly among the mounted men, looking in turn at each saddle boot for the scoped rifle. When he finished he rode back and stopped, facing the colonel.

"Satisfied, Ranger?" the colonel asked.

"For now," Sam said quietly. "I will take a look at those three bodies along the trail."

"Be my guest, Ranger," the colonel said. "It may interest you to know that the scoped rifle now belongs to another of my detectives. You *will* see it somewhere along the trail if you're around when he catches up to me. We're headed across the border right now to flush out Max Bard and his guerrillas for once and for all." He looked around at his men, then back to Sam with a smug expression. "I would not welcome a lawman like you coming along to see how we conduct this mission. You might get squeamish."

"Who you hang in Mexico is between you and the Mexican government, Colonel," Sam said. There was more for him to say, but he held it back. It went without saying that if he found out the colonel was lying about the men who ambushed him and the sheriff and their prisoners, he would be back to arrest the colonel himself.

"Oh? So nice of you to say so, Ranger," Colonel Hinler said with sarcasm, his men gathered behind him to back his play.

Sam had seen many men like the colonel, men who professed a love for the law, yet who threw the force of their power and influence into bending or breaking it as it suited their interest. Yet for now he'd said enough. The colonel and his men would keep. He still had Sheriff Stone and his prisoner, Rudy Bowlinger, to consider—not to mention the town of Resting if anyone showed up wanting Bowlinger, either to hang him or to set him free. Without another word he backed his dun a few steps, turned it and rode away.

The colonel only sat staring for a moment. Then he turned to the wounded detective, whom Foley had helped to his feet. The two limped toward Devoe's horse, Devoe sticking his retrieved Colt down into its holster.

"French," he said sternly, "I trust you told this lacklegged lawman nothing about Bo Anson or what happened."

"Colonel, he didn't even ask," said Devoe. "Besides, I couldn't have told him anything anyway."

"Very well," the colonel said. "Foley, dress this man's wound and catch up with us on the trail—"

"Colonel, if it's all the same with you," said Devoe,

cutting in, "I'd sooner have somebody else bandage me. This man can't even hold his biscuits when gunplay is involved. I don't want him around me."

The colonel snapped his eyes to the sickness on the ground, then to Foley.

"Is that true, Detective?" he asked.

"Colonel," Foley said meekly, "I keep saying I ain't cut out to be a detective—"

"Nonsense!" the colonel shouted. "You *will* dress his wound. You *will* keep your food inside your stomach!" He signaled his men with the wave of a hand and swung his horse away from Foley and Devoe.

Devoe and Foley stood watching as the colonel led his column off along the trail.

"You heard him, Foley," said Devoe, cocking his Colt as he drew it and pointed it at the young detective's belly. "Dress this wound and get it right. If you wretch on me again, I'll leave you for the coyotes."

Chapter 11

————

It was in the afternoon when Sheriff Sheppard Stone first put the bottle to his lips. Sheriff Colleen Deluna had been called out of town to help deliver a baby—an additional duty a *woman sheriff* might be called upon to do. She had been gone all day, having left Stone convalescing on a cot in the corner of her office. She'd left Rudy Bowlinger and his anvil shackled to an iron ring sunk deep into the lower wall. A blanket covered a pallet of straw for him to sleep on.

Stone took the bottle away from his lips and handed it back to the old Indian lying sprawled on the ground, leaning against the side of the livery barn, across the alley from the rear of the cantina.

"*Gracias,*" he said, noting that the taste of the liquor was boosted by a mixture of mescal and something else his tongue failed to identify.

The drunken Indian held an open palm toward him, welcoming him to help himself to more. Then he just lay staring at Stone, flat-faced and flat-eyed. Stone drank. And he drank again.

What the hell? I can handle it. . . .

Anyway, he hadn't gone looking for a drink, not really, although admittedly he had awakened with a slight tremor in his gut that he knew a taste of alcohol would wipe away like a soft warm cloth. But drinking was not what he'd set out to do. He'd felt the urge to drink and overcome it most of the morning. It was only when he'd walked into the cantina and limped to the bar for . . . *well, no particular reason,* he told himself. *Just being sociable.* Yet before he could even say *Howdy, bartender*, he was told straightaway that Sheriff Deluna had left strict orders not to sell him anything to drink.

Who does she think she is?

The drinking had leveled him out; he felt better now than he'd felt for days. His mind was sharper, clearer. Was that so bad? *No, not at all*—leastwise not if he kept control of it, which of course he would. He emptied the bottle and let it fall from his hands, sitting beside the old Indian now, leaning back against the livery barn. *And this feels good,* he told himself. He'd come to realize perhaps for the first time that livery barns were made to lean against in the afternoon heat—that drunken old Indians were here for a man to drink with, be *friends with*, he decided, wondering only vaguely why he had never realized any of this before.

He saw the old Indian's weathered hand again. This time it lay palm up toward him. The fingers wiggled a little. Stone glanced at the ground and saw three empty bottles lying at his thigh. He looked back at the up-turned palm. *Oh. . . .* He understood; he reached into his trouser pocket for money as he looked at a bony donkey standing with a bundle on its back less than twenty feet away.

"*Un-kay-cha,*" the old Indian said as Stone dropped the money on his palm. He sat watching as the Indian ambled to the donkey and came back with another dusty bottle and wiped it on his forearm.

"Let me ask you something, while I can," Stone said. "Do you know anybody who changes into creatures, wolves maybe?" He saw interest stir in the old Indian's eyes as the cork pulled up from the bottle. The cork looked long, much longer than usual, he thought— seven, eight inches, *a foot*? He didn't know.

But yes, the old Indian had known men who changed into not only wolves, but owls, coyotes, all sorts of animals. As it turned out, he himself had changed into animals on several occasions, he said at some point in the swirl of conversation.

"Is that a fact?" Stone replied, taking the bottle offered to him. "Let me tell you what happens to me sometimes. . . ."

Afternoon hung on the cusp of darkness when Rudy Bowlinger saw the front door open and a young Mexican boy in yellowed-white peasant clothes walk in carrying a tray of food. The shackled outlaw stood up quickly and stepped out to the end of his anchor chain, waiting eagerly for the food.

"It's about time," he said, his hand cupping his bandaged wounded shoulder. "Where's the sheriff? I mean, the woman sheriff." He looked all around as if noting for the first time that he was alone. "Where's

Stone? Who's going to empty this bucket?" He gestured a nod toward an oak bucket standing in the corner ten feet away. "It smells like hell in here."

The boy laid the tray on the edge of the sheriff's desk and calmly went down the prisoner's list of questions.

"Sheriff Deluna is out helping deliver a baby," he said in mission school English. He pulled the cloth from over a large wooden bowl of beans with chunks of goat meat and peppers in a thick broth. Rolled tortillas lay beside it. A wooden spoon stood up in it. A cup of coffee swirled steam upward to the ceiling.

"The wounded sheriff is gone," he said. "Someone saw him and a donkey walking out toward the flats."

Bowlinger, barely reaching the desk with his leg outstretched on the chain behind him, let go of his wounded shoulder and tore into the food like a rabid dog. The boy watched.

"Ha! Drunk as a one-eyed rooster, I'm betting," he said with his mouth stuffed, broth oozing down his chin and his bare upper chest.

"*Sí*—I mean, yes, I think so," the Mexican boy said. "Why else would any man walk out onto the flats in the heat of the afternoon? The man drinks a lot. Sheriff Deluna told the cantina owner to not sell him whiskey. But perhaps he finds the whiskey anyway, *mi madre* says."

"Yeah, well, good for him," said Bowlinger, hurriedly, not missing a bite. Steam forked at his nostrils and rose as he drank the hot coffee without a flinch. "What about this bucket? I'm going to be needing it again soon."

"I will be back for it when I come for the tray," the boy said.

"What about a key? Who's got a key, in case of emergencies?" he asked, fishing for any information he could get.

"Emergencies . . . ?" the boy repeated.

"Yeah, you know," said Bowlinger, "say a raging fire, something like that?"

"Only Sheriff Deluna has the key, I think," the boy said. He crossed himself as if to ward off something so terrible as a raging fire.

"That's plain loco!" said Bowlinger, getting cross and excited at the dire prospect. "It shows no regard for human life." He stuffed the end of the tortilla in his mouth as he spoke. "You ask around some, see if somebody has an extra key, just for that reason."

The boy backed up a step and said, "Let us hope and pray no such thing as this happens."

"Yeah, well, it could," Bowlinger said. "Somebody else ought to have a key, is what I'm saying here." He chewed and swallowed and took another hurried bite. "Another thing—"

But before he could say anything else, he saw the boy turn and walk out the door.

"Little bastard," he grumbled, unable to find out anything useful from the boy.

As soon as the young Mexican closed the door behind himself, Bowlinger looked all around, searching for anything he could reach that might aid him in making an escape. He saw nothing. There were rifles and shotguns standing in a closed rack across the office, but they appeared to be there only to tease a man—a man dangling on the end of a chain, he thought. He continued eating.

Moments later when the front door swung open again, he started right in.

"Did you ask around?" he said to the open doorway. "I don't mean to sound pushy, but my life is—"

"Your life ain't worth a plug of wet-chewed tobacco, Rudy," said Bo Anson, cutting him off, stepping inside. In his cheek a large plug of tobacco stuck out, a sliver of brown stain streaking down to his chin. Bowlinger looked stunned as Anson's recent recruits stepped inside beside him, spreading out, filling the small office.

"Bo . . . ?" Bowlinger glanced all around. "What—? I mean *who*? I mean *where* . . . ?"

Bo Anson gave a dark chuckle and glanced at the men standing around him.

"I can see the cat's got your tongue, Rudy," he said. "But better the cat than the hatchet, I always say, don't you?"

"Yeah, I suppose," Bowlinger said ponderously, touching on all manner of terrible consequences that might accompany these men facing him. "What brings you here?" he managed to ask, summoning up a casual shrug.

"Business," said Anson bluntly. "I come to kill the Ranger—"

"And Sheppard Stone, in mine and Lyle's case," Ignacio Cady cut in, giving a nod toward his brother beside him.

His words caused a tense silence among the men. Anson turned his head slowly toward him.

"You'll not want to barge in like that again, Iggy," he said in a low warning tone. "Here's a case where rudeness alone will get you straight-up killed."

Both Cadys lowered their eyes in apology. Anson turned back to Bowlinger.

"As I was saying," Anson repeated, giving the Cadys a harsh, glaring look, "we're here to kill the Ranger, Sheriff Sheppard Stone, the woman, Sheriff Deluna, and anybody else who needs killing here tonight."

"They're none of them here, Bo," said Bowlinger. "Leastwise if they are, I'm being told they're not."

"Oh?" Anson eyed him closely. "So you're here all alone, *resting* in *Resting*, I take it?" He smiled at his play on words.

"That's my understanding," said Bowlinger. "The woman is gone to help birth a child. Stone was seen wandering around drunk with some medicine man and a donkey."

The Cadys gave each other a guarded look, taking note of Stone's whereabouts.

"The Ranger left to track down the man who shot me and Sheriff Stone."

"Good luck to him on that." Anson and the men chuckled. "I can't kill them if they're not here," he said, letting out a breath. He shook his head as if disappointed. "Anyway, we're all riding for the colonel now, Rudy," he said with a dark twisted grin. "Never thought you'd hear me say that, did you—any of us ol' boys, for that matter?" He gestured a hand toward the others. Bowlinger swallowed hard, looking from face to face, recognizing the men as rogues and killers all.

"Jesus . . . riding for the colonel?" he said, wondering where that put him.

"No, Rudy, not *Jesus*." Anson chuckled. "Just us ol' boys, is all." His little joke caused a slight ripple of laughter. "But here's what I know you're wondering right now," he added, touching a finger to the side of his head under his hat brim. "You're thinking, 'Oh my goodness, they're riding for the colonel. The colonel wants Max and all of us dead. Does that mean he wants Bo here to kill us?'"

Bowlinger just stared, frozen, stunned, waiting for an answer, knowing Anson was only dragging this out in order to torment him.

"And the fact is he *does* want us to kill all of you, Rudy," Anson said, finally. "Is that the damnedest thing or what?" He grinned and chewed against the lump of tobacco in his cheek. The men stared in silence.

"You shot me, didn't you, Bo?" Bowlinger said, the notion of it just then springing to mind. "You shot me, and you shot Sheriff Stone."

Anson raised a finger for emphasis as he spoke.

"It's true, I did," he said. "But the thing is—"

Without warning Bowlinger leaped over to the slop bucket in the corner, jerked it up with both hands and drew it back, ready to empty it forward on the gunmen.

"Nobody move, Bo," he shouted, "or you'll get it right in the face!"

Bo Anson tilted his head a little to the side and stood giving him a curious stare. The men looked bewildered, waiting for an order from him. Anson ignored the bucket and the threat and went on.

"As I was saying, Rudy, *yes*, I shot you. But note that you're still alive. I needed to make a showing for the colonel's *segundo*. If I wanted to I could have splattered your head all over hell's half acre."

Bowlinger held on to the oak bucket but thought about it, feeling the sloshing weight of the bucket's contents. The smell nearly staggered him.

"Now set the bucket down, Rudy, before I change my mind and take your head to the colonel in a pickle jar."

Rudy considered it some more, then eased the bucket down to the floor and stepped away from it along the wall.

"I've—I've felt like hell all day, Bo, this wound and all," he said.

"Were you really going to throw that mess on me?" Bo asked pointedly. "Because you know if you had I would have killed you boneyard dead."

"I was scared you was here to kill me anyway, Bo," said Bowlinger.

"I can see how you might be," said Anson. He grinned and spat a stream of tobacco juice. "But the fact is, I want you alive. I want you to go tell Max what a good job I'm doing here. Tell him this is what we talked about doing—I'm what you call taking the *initiative*. He'll understand."

"You want me to go . . . ?" Bowlinger said, suspicious to the core.

"Nothing to hold you here, Rudy," said Anson. "Us either if everybody we wanted to kill had previous engagements for the evening."

"Can I say something?" Ignacio asked in a humbled tone.

"Have at it, Iggy," Bo said, "now that you've shown some manners. But if you were going to ask if you and Lyle can go traipsing off after Sheppard Stone, the answer is *no*."

"Can we ask why?" said Lyle Cady.

"Because, *Cady brothers*," said Anson in his mocking tone, "we came all this way to kill somebody. Least we can do is sack this stub of a town and light it up on our way out."

"Whooiee!" Mexican Charlie Summez shouted loudly. "Now you're talking."

"What about this, Bo?" Bowlinger asked. He shook his shackled foot.

"Hold real still," said Anson, drawing his big Colt and cocking it. "Boys, let's set ol' Rudy free."

"Wait, Bo!" Rudy shouted. But he was too late. Rifle and pistol shots resounded. Outside, the darkened building flashed in the night like lightning. Townsmen heard the shooting and began grabbing guns of their own.

Bowlinger had covered his head with both forearms as dirt, splinters and ricochets rose and zipped all around him. When the firing stopped he looked, his ears ringing, and saw the chain had been severed from the wall, but he still remained shackled to the heavy anvil.

Anson and the men stared at the anvil for a moment. Anson shook his head in wonder.

"You might ought to just carry that around for a while, Rudy," he said.

"And do *what* with it?" Bowlinger queried. "I can't even lift it the shape I'm in."

Anson stepped forward and patted his good shoulder.

"But you *will* lift it, Rudy," he said with feigned encouragement. "I just know you will." He held the smoking Colt aimed loosely at Bowlinger's stomach. "Now pick it up. Get yourself on a horse." He spoke slow and distinctly, like a man explaining the use of a spoon to an idiot. "And go tell Max what's happened here. Tell him I am now the man with the biggest stick"—he grinned—"or anything else for that matter." He spat a stream and winked. "Now, don't let me look around and see you still standing here."

Chapter 12

Ten miles from Resting, Sheriff Deluna saw the glow-ing mantle of fire bellow up on the horizon only mo-ments after hearing the barrage of heavy rifle and pistol shots split the night. As soon as she'd heard the gunfire, she stood up crouched from her buggy seat and slapped the reins to the team of horses. Now, as more gunfire echoed out from within the licking flames, she contin-ued slapping the reins steadily but sparingly, knowing the horses were already giving her their all—*had been* giving it, galloping nonstop, the last three miles.

With over six miles left to go, she realized if she didn't slow the hard pace she would at the very least wear the horses out and render them useless. Or, *at the worst*, exhaustion could send one of the tired animals tumbling, snagging its hoof in a rut on the hard trail lying beneath the coating of loose desert sand. If one horse went down, like as not they both would, she warned herself. Ahead of her the shooting from the streets of Resting had died down. Whatever had hap-pened there was now left to smolder in a bed of fire. She was still needed there. But the immediacy of defending the town had passed. Now she was needed to bring order, to bring comfort, to settle her town in the aftermath of whatever terrible storm had struck it.

"Easy, now," she said to the horses, slowing them with her reins taut until their pace fell to a safer, less exhausting level. She continued staring ahead at the wide strip of firelight glittering on what she knew by heart to be the length of Resting. On either side of the trail she noted both small and larger images in the purple darkness—creatures of the desert wilds. The poised images turned beady red eyes toward her as she rode past. Then their eyes turned back in the night toward the glow of fire that assaulted their domain. Black smoke rose like columns of raging apparitions, taking that same assault upward to the purple heavens.

As soon as her team of horses fell into a lighter gallop, she heard the sound of hooves pounding hard along the trail coming toward her. Instinctively she reined the horses down and swung the rig off the trail and out of sight into the darkness. At the same time she reached over and grabbed the rifle leaning against her buggy seat as the buggy rolled on. A mile out, she slid the buggy to a halt, tied off the reins quickly and jumped down. She took cover behind the rig and waited.

Her eyes searched the looming darkness until she saw the riders moving along the trail. They drew their horses to a halt at the place where the buggy wheels had cut off the trail out onto the flats. She held her breath. They saw the tracks. She was sure of it. She watched, barely able to make out the darker images of men against the grainy starlight. The riders were black dots on a pale ribbon of sand that was the trail.

She looked all around. This was no place to stand off against a group of armed riders. She could put up a fight, but in the end the sheer volume of numbers and gunfire would win out. If they came for her, she would be dead staying here. She knew it. As she hurriedly considered her situation, she saw two of the black dots move off that ribbon of sand and come toward her. The others turned and rode on.

She crept away from the buggy, crouched, rifle in hand, knowing that an attempt to move the cross and worn-out horses would cause them to chuff and blow, maybe even whinny aloud. She couldn't have that. Better to leave them standing, she decided. Maybe the two riders would follow the buggy tracks only a short ways and turn back. She hoped so.

She moved as quietly as a ghost, out across the loose sand, through the sparse beginnings of a wide bed of cactus, over the low rise of a dune, praying not to be seen against the starlit sand.

Dropping down onto her stomach on the other side of the rise, she searched back and found the two black dots moving toward her. Had they spotted her boot prints? She didn't know; she wasn't waiting to find out. The others had ridden on. The odds were better now— two to one, she told herself. She cocked the rifle and watched and waited.

The two riders moved closer in silence until at length they heard a long bawling howl rise from the flatlands that drew their attention, Sheriff Deluna's as well.

"What the hell was that, *a wolf*?" said Lyle Cady.

"No," said Ignacio. "That was no wolf like any I ever heard. It's not even a good imitation." He jerked his horse around in the direction of the sound, just in time to hear it again. Lyle jerked his horse around beside him.

"That loco sheriff, Sheppard Stone?" he said.

"Sure it is," said Ignacio. "Who else would be out here howling at the moon like a lunatic?" He gigged his horse. "Come on, Lyle. We've got the son of a bitch now!" he added, excited.

From atop the rising dune, Sheriff Deluna lay quiet, listening, barely making out their words. She stared down her rifle sights, her finger on the trigger. But the shot was too risky, she decided. One miss and the two would be charging her position—her without a horse, here on this barren dune. She lowered the rifle and watched the two black figures ride away toward the howling. She stared in that direction for a moment and decided the two were right. It was a terrible wolf imitation.

Damn him! What's he doing out here? she asked herself, hearing a seemingly endless litany of drunken madness. Then she stood, dusted herself off and hurried down the loose, slippery dune. At least Sheriff Stone had drawn those two off her trail, she told herself, hurrying along. Instead of heading back to her buggy, she ran along the sand trail, her long gingham dress hiked up in one hand, her rifle in the other, following the two riders, keeping a safe distance back. The string on her sombrero loosened and let the big hat fly from her head, but she didn't go back to retrieve it. She'd run almost a mile when she saw the shadowy figures stop their horses and step down from their saddles at a stand of rock that marked a water hole she was familiar with. She stopped for a moment, gasping for breath.

From the water hole came another bellowing howl that reminded her of the urgency and caused her to run on, getting closer now. When she stopped again she staggered to the stand of rock and hung there. The two horses stood only a few feet from her; she saw their curious eyes gleam in the moonlight. She watched the two riders approach the water hole on foot. She listened as they spoke.

"There's that drunken fool," Ignacio Cady said, loud enough for her to hear him. She saw the sheriff squatting at the water's edge. Stone let out another howl, the sound of gunfire and the sight of the town burning on the horizon having stirred him from a drunken stupor only moments earlier. Now he sat staring bleary-eyed, trying to gather his senses. Three empty bottles lay in the rocky dirt beside him. He was naked save for a loincloth, his gun belt, one boot and a flop hat that he'd never seen before.

What in God's name are you doing here? he managed to ask himself through a drunken swirl. He saw the two gunmen walking toward him, one limping. In his unsteady vision they pitched back and forth as if standing on a swaying boat floating toward him.

"There you are, you son of a bitch," said Ignacio, the one walking with the limp; they stopped swaying a little and stood twenty feet away.

"The Cadys . . . ?" Stone managed to ask in a slurred, drunken voice.

"As you live and breathe, it's us," Ignacio confirmed. He leveled his Colt out at arm's length, aimed directly at the drunken sheriff. "You thought you'd seen the last of us, but you were wrong."

Seeing the gun pointed at him, Stone growled and bared his teeth in the shadowy moonlight. The Cadys glanced at each other and chuffed. Lyle chuckled under his breath.

"He's gone crazy as a blind bell ringer," he said.

Blind bell ringer?

Ignacio looked his brother up and down curiously. Then he looked back at Stone.

"I'm not wasting any time on you, Sheriff," he said, "and that two-bit Ranger ain't around swinging his rifle butt." He stepped forward, bolder now, his voice raised in anger. "Where is Edsel Centrila's money, you chiseling crawfish?"

"I got it . . . put up," Stone said in a drunken voice, swaying on his haunches. "You can't . . . have it."

"You shouldn't take money given in good faith to bribe a judge, and not do what you was told with it," Lyle said, stepping forward beside his brother. "Where *is it*?" he demanded.

Hand on his gun butt, Stone howled long and loud in the night.

Both brothers were taken aback, but only for a moment.

"Oh yeah," Lyle said with a dark, quiet laugh, "he's as nuts as a monkey, this one."

Ignacio stared steadily at Stone as he replied to Lyle, "When he yanks that Colt, try not to kill him. I want to cut on him for a while, find out where that bribe money is. Don't forget it's *our money* now—to hell with Centrila."

Lyle said, "I ain't forgot—" He cut his words short as Sheriff Stone's Colt came up from his holster fast, awfully fast for a drunk.

The Cadys fired as one as the sheriff fell over onto his side and blue-orange fire streaked at them from his gun barrel. In the dark their shots went wild; so did Stone's. But one of his bullets managed to stab Ignacio hard in his upper left arm. The hot lead shattered bone and left a large bloody exit wound. Ignacio yelped, yet he continued firing without leaving his feet.

Even as the Cadys fired repeatedly, they heard a woman's voice call out behind them and the pounding of their horses' hooves coming directly for them.

"*Yiiii!*" shouted Sheriff Deluna, charging forward atop one horse, leading the other close beside her.

"What the—?" shouted Lyle, the horse coming so fast that he had to leave his words unfinished and hurl himself out of the animal's path.

"Look *out!*" Ignacio shouted, launching himself away in the opposite direction. He landed on his wounded left arm and let out a scream of pain. His Colt went off in his right hand, but the shot streaked upward into the air like fireworks. At the water's edge he heard Stone let out another howl.

"Die, you crazy bastard!" Ignacio cried out. He tried to raise his gun for another shot at the shadowy figures. Before he could get a round off, he had to roll away to keep from being trampled by the horses that came running through again. This time one of the horses carried both Sheriff Deluna and Sheriff Stone on its back. Stone, almost naked, sat holding on behind the woman sheriff, his head tilted back, bobbing limply, howling straight up at the dark purple sky.

When Sheriff Deluna reached the place where she'd left her buggy, she set the two tired buggy horses free on the sand flats and rode on. She didn't bring the Cady brothers' horses to a halt again until she'd reached the main trail. Then she only stopped long enough to drag the drunken sheriff down from behind her saddle and shove him atop the other horse—Stone howling mindlessly all the while. A dull throb had lodged itself in her head from the sheriff's loud piercing voice so close to her ear.

"You've got to shut up, Stone," she pleaded as she tried to right the limp, wobbling sheriff in the saddle. "Those two heard your voice. So can anybody else." As she spoke, she noted that once atop he was the horse, some inborn sense of horsemanship seemed to stabilize him a little. He sat upright and shook his head.

"I—I will, Sheriff," he said in a blurred tone. "I didn't mean to . . . cause you trouble—" His words ended in an attempted howl that curled up out of his chest. He stopped the sound before it gained its full volume. He clamped a hand over his mouth as if stifling a belch. "Sorry," he said.

Sheriff Deluna shook her head and turned away; she stepped back to the other horse. She raised a foot to the stirrup, rifle in hand, and had started to swing up into the saddle when she froze, hearing the sound of a rifle cock in the darkness. Looking around slowly, she saw four gunmen rise from sagebrush and stone only a few feet off the trail. They held rifles aimed and cocked toward the two sheriffs.

"*Uh-uh-uh,*" said Bo Anson, stopping her from lowering her boot from the stirrup, her long dress hiked up over her knee. "Stay just like you are there," he added, walking forward. When he stood a foot from her he took the rifle from her hand and stepped back. "Do I need to search you for additional firearms? Tell the truth, I don't mind at all."

"That's my only gun," Sheriff Deluna said quietly, ignoring the question of him searching her.

"Go on, search her, Bo. . . . Search her good!" said the excited voice of one of the riflemen.

"Easy, Ape," Anson warned over his shoulder. "I've got this covered." He looked up at Stone, then back at Deluna. "You're right. We could hear *Mr. Wolf* there all the way back at that water hole. Although I have to say, I've heard preachers pass gas that sound more like a wolf howling than he did. You should have knocked the damn fool in the head first—pardon my language." He reached up and took Stone's Colt from his holster. Stone swayed and only stared blank-faced.

"Next time," Sheriff Deluna said, casting a glance up at Sheriff Stone.

"Next time . . . ?" said Anson. He gave a chuckle in the shadowy moonlight. The men followed suit. "I can see you're fun to be around." He looked up at Stone. "I'll go on and shoot this naked fool right now, keep him from spreading fleas." He turned his rifle up toward Stone's bare chest. Stone curled his lip and let out a low growl.

"What about the money?" Deluna asked calmly, seeing this as her only chance to save Stone's life. "He knows where the money's hidden."

Anson spat tobacco, shook his head and turned to face her again. "Am I flattered that I look that young and innocent to you, or just plain offended that you mistake me for a fool?" He started to turn the rifle back to Stone.

"Wait! I'm not lying," said Sheriff Deluna. "I heard your pals the Cady brothers asking him where it's hidden. Don't you know that's why they were after him?"

Anson turned back to her and appeared to consider the matter for a moment. The other three men stared intently until finally he let out a breath.

"Let's say it's true, this hidden money," he said in an offhand manner. "Are we talking a sizable amount? I mean, if it's only a few dollars . . ."

"How much money does it take to bribe a *territory judge*?" the woman sheriff said.

"Is that a riddle?" Anson said.

"No, I'm serious," said Deluna. "He took money to

bribe a judge, they said. Then he didn't do it. They said he has it—I believed them." She gave him a firm, level stare.

"All right, but now the Cadys are dead, so we'll never really know," said Anson.

"They're not dead," said Deluna. "I didn't kill them. One of them is wounded, I think."

"You didn't kill them?" Anson looked at her in disbelief. "I've never seen anybody who wouldn't kill a Cady if they had one in their sights."

"I didn't," said Deluna. "I took their horses, left them stranded. There's a buggy and two loose horses back there. All they've got to do is round them up and they'll be coming out."

Anson spat again, gave a dark grin and said, "You're giving ol' Lyle and Iggy more credit than I ever would." He turned to the other three riflemen. "Couple of you ride out, get them two turds and bring them along the trail. We'll take the two sheriffs here and catch up with the others."

"You mean we're not going to kill Stone?" Ape asked, sounding disappointed.

"Haven't you been listening, Ape?" said Anson.

"What about her, then?" Ape asked, pressing the point.

Anson turned back to Deluna and grinned in contemplation as he chewed his wad of tobacco.

"We'll see," he said. "I've always wanted a *pet sheriff*. Never dreamed I'd have one I'd enjoy bouncing on my lap."

Sheriff Deluna lowered her eyes, hearing the riflemen laugh quietly at Anson's remark. This was not the time to reply. This was the time to stay silent, for both her and Sheriff Stone's sake. She forced herself to look away from Bo Anson, out across the dark purple sand flats. She took a deep breath and let it out slowly, thinking about the short, sharp knife, sheath and all, stuck down deep inside her boot well.

Chapter 13

In the early-morning light, Bo Anson brought his riders to a halt and watched as Leon Foley rode toward them on the trail. Spotting Anson, Foley waved his hat back and forth above his head and kicked his horse up into a gallop. Anson sat his horse at the head of his riders and rested his gloved hands atop his saddle horn.

"Now I suppose I'll be saddled with this idiot all day," he said to Ape Boyd as Boyd sidled his horse on his left.

"I can shoot him, Bo," Ape volunteered.

Anson looked him up and down.

"The colonel sent him, Ape," he said. "Think I ought to first hear what he has to say?"

Ape didn't answer; he just stared ahead as Foley approached. Five minutes later Foley slid his horse to a halt crosswise in front of Anson. Dust rose around the riders.

"Man, am I glad I found you so early!" Foley said to Anson when his horse jolted to a stop. "I was afraid I'd be riding the flats all day." He put his hat back on and pressed it down against a warm morning breeze.

"Lucky me, huh," he said, "finding you already on the trail?"

"Yeah, I'm thrilled for you," Anson said in a flat tone, fanning a gloved hand against the dust. "Why'd the colonel send you looking for us?"

"He wanted me to scout you out and tell you to hurry up. We're headed back to Gun Hill," Foley said.

Hurry up? Anson almost chuffed out loud.

"Headed back to Gun Hill? *Why?*" he asked.

"Because a rider came out from the rail station there and said Mr. Siedell's train is in town—" He caught himself and stopped and said, "Oops, I don't think I was supposed to tell you that part. I was just supposed to tell you the colonel's on his way."

"I won't mention it," Anson said, the wheels already turning in his mind.

"Just how far back is the colonel?" he asked, crossing his wrists again.

"Four or five miles," Foley said, still elated at having found Anson and the new men so close on the low hill trail. "That's what I meant about being lucky that I—"

"I got it," Anson said, cutting him short. "Now shut up and leave it alone." He half turned in his saddle and spoke back to the rest of the men. "We're stopping right here, boys, waiting for the good colonel."

The men relaxed in their saddles, having already heard how close the colonel was to them.

"What's so important the colonel wants us waiting right here? We could ride on and meet him along the trail."

"I have no idea on that matter," Foley said. "I'm always saying I have no business being a detective."

"Nonsense, you don't mean it," Anson said.

"No, I really do," Foley said. He looked back at the dust-streaked buggy sitting close behind Anson, the ragged, bloody Cady brothers sitting in it.

"My goodness, what happed to them?" he asked, seeing only one tired bay pulling the two-horse rig. Lyle had caught the horse and hitched it just before Anson's men had arrived and escorted the brothers back to the trail.

"It's a long story," Anson said grimly, glancing back over his shoulder at the Cadys. Lyle drove the buggy while Ignacio lay sprawled to the side, his bloody bullet-shattered upper arm wrapped in his torn-off shirtsleeve. A foot-long length of iron wagon frame served as a splint. "How many men are riding with the colonel now?"

"Seven, same as when you left," Foley said with a shrug. He gave Anson a questioning look.

Anson returned the shrug.

"I figured he might've got some of them killed since then." He gave Foley a thin, wry smile.

"No, everybody's fine," Foley said, not realizing that Anson was only making a dark joke. That he couldn't care less about the colonel or his men. The naive detective looked back at the woman, her dusty ragged dress, and at the nearly naked man on the horse beside her, his head bowed beneath the floppy hat brim. "Who's that?" he asked Anson.

Anson studied his face for a second with a flat stare as if deciding what to do with the man. Finally he gave out a resolved breath and straightened a little in his saddle.

"She's my sister," he said. "And that's my crazy cousin, Lonzo, beside her. Keep your hands off her—him too, for that matter."

"My goodness," Foley said for the second time. He looked bewildered at the naked Sheriff Stone. Then he looked back at Anson and asked, "Why is your cousin naked?"

"That's a whole other long story," Anson said with the same flat stare. He leaned forward a little, eyed Foley closer and said, "Look at me, fool. I'm obliged you brought us the colonel's message. But ask me one more question and I will leave you lying dead in the dirt."

Foley sat stunned for a moment. But he wasn't able to keep his mouth shut for long.

"What on earth for?" he said. "How else can I know anything without asking—"

The roar of Ape Boyd's big Starr silenced the young detective and sent him flying backward from his saddle. Foley's spooked horse reared and turned on its hind hooves. It touched down and darted back along the trail.

Sheriff Deluna kept herself from gasping and looked away as if not wanting to see anything she shouldn't.

"Jesus, Ape, that was right in my ear!" shouted Anson, rounding a finger deep into his left ear against the loud ringing. "What the hell?"

"Didn't you want me to shoot him?" Ape asked. "You said *one more* question. He already asked *two*." He held up two large grimy fingers. "I just figured . . ."

"All right," Anson said. "It makes no difference. That one was just looking for somebody to kill him every time he opened his mouth." He gazed down at Foley lying in the dust. "Drag him off the trail and throw some sand over him—give him a cat burial, before the colonel gets here."

As Ape stepped down and Roland Crispe joined him to drag the dead detective off the trail, Anson swung his horse around and rode back a few feet to where the woman and Stone sat their horses side by side.

"Get down and give the Cadys their horses back, and both of you get in the buggy," he said to Deluna.

Sheriff Deluna nodded at Sheriff Stone beside her. "Can he have a duster or something? He's burning up alive out here bare-chested."

Anson chewed as he looked Stone up and down. Then he spat and said, "Naw, he's a tough lawman. Sun won't hurt him."

"The sun will kill him," Deluna said.

"So?" said Anson. "It won't kill him before he tells us where the bribe money is." He gave a crooked tobacco-chewing grin. "If it does, just reach over and give him a shove. I've got something bigger on the spit right now. I'll have to deal with him later." He touched his hat brim, backed his horse and turned it away. Hearing the conversation from the buggy seat, Lyle Cady looked up at Anson.

"Can we switch right now?" he asked.

"I don't care," Anson said in passing, nudging his horse forward back to the head of the riders. "Get switched and come up front. Sit beside me."

"Iggy, wake up," said Lyle. "We're getting our horses back."

"Oh, why now?" Ignacio asked in a pained voice.

"I expect Bo must've decided he's tormented us enough," Lyle said. "Says he wants us to come join him up front. Maybe he's giving us our guns back."

"What about the bribe money?" asked Ignacio. "Did Stone tell him anything yet?"

"Not yet," said Lyle. "Anson said he's got something more important going on right now."

"Damn it," Ignacio groaned in pain. "That's our money, not Anson's."

"Keep your mouth shut, Iggy," Lyle whispered, wrapping the buggy reins around the short brake handle.

On the horses, Sheriff Deluna looked over at Stone and adjusted his flop hat brim. She glanced down at his empty holster and noticed that his loincloth had slipped a little to one side, exposing him.

"Are you ever going to come back to your senses?" she asked quietly, not even expecting an answer from Stone as he reached down and adjusted the loincloth to cover his lap against the burning sun.

"I'm . . . trying," he whispered with much effort.

Deluna stared at him, stunned for a moment. Then she saw the Cadys standing beside their horses, Iggy with his splinted upper arm stuck out to the side.

"All right, get down from there," Lyle said sharply. "You've been riding our horses long enough."

Stepping down, Deluna helped the half-conscious Stone over to the buggy and up into the seat. She looked around as the Cadys mounted their horses and rode up front beside Anson.

"All right, men," Anson called out loudly enough for all the riders to hear him. "This is what we've been waiting for. Roland, you and Charlie take the buggy out of sight. I don't trust the woman sheriff far as I can throw her." He glared back at Deluna as he spoke. Then he turned to the Cadys and said, "I see you both have bandannas. Pull them up over your mouths."

"What?" Lyle said in disbelief. Ignacio just stared, his broken arm out to the side.

Anson's rifle swung up at him from across his lap.

"You heard me. Now, don't make me say it again. I'll kill you, bribe money or not."

"Can I smack them, Bo?" Ape asked. The Cadys looked at him, again in disbelief.

"Not now, Ape," said Anson. He raised a hand and waved the riders forward. "Let's go, men. I want us to be moving along the trail when the colonel finds us."

Lyle and Ignacio gave each other a puzzled look. But they kept quiet and nudged their horses forward beside Bo Anson and Ape Boyd.

An hour later, the colonel saw Bo Anson and the newly hired riders moving along the trail toward him, and he hurried his detectives and rail guards forward the last quarter of a mile. As Colonel Hinler and his men drew closer to Anson and the new riders, Anson saw one of the detectives riding beside the colonel leading Foley's horse by its reins.

"Everybody stay cool and calm," Anson said to the

riders bunching up behind him. "This might get touchy right off."

Ape hefted his rifle in his hand and said, "Want me to—"

"No, Ape," Bo said, cutting the big man off before he could even ask. "I said stay cool and calm. Just keep doing what I told you to do." He gestured a nod at the Cadys. "Keep them quiet."

Ape settled, and stared hard at the two brothers as they swayed in their saddles. They looked just as Anson had wanted them to. Each of them now had a large purple gun barrel welt across their foreheads, their bandannas tied tightly to cover their mouths. Their hands had been tied in front of them. Ape led their horses on a short rope.

"Here we go, men," Anson said quietly to Ape and the others. "You all know what to do." He watched the colonel stop his horse ten feet in front of him, his detectives behind him. A wide, harsh grin came to Hinler's face as he looked at the battered faces and tied hands of the Cady brothers.

"By Godfrey!" he said to Anson. "I see you've snared a couple of the scoundrels."

Oh yeah, we're good, Anson assured himself.

"That's right, Colonel," he said. "We don't miss a thing. This desert is ours."

At the sight of the colonel and his men, Lyle Cady grew hopeful. He struggled to speak, but the bandanna muffled his voice to a series of grunts.

"No more out of you," Ape said, swiping the barrel of his Starr sidelong across Lyle's jaw. Lyle's head bounced backward as if on hinges. He slumped back down in his saddle.

"What was that man saying?" the colonel asked.

"It makes no never mind," Anson said. "Probably cussing you and your whole family. They're some real heathens, this Bard Gang."

"Indeed," said the colonel. "Well, we'll see how much cussing he does hanging from a limb." He looked all around the barren terrain as if searching for a hanging tree. Seeing none, he grumbled to himself and then looked back at Anson. "Good work, Bo," he said. He looked around at the new faces. "I take it these are the men from across the border you spoke of?"

"They are," said Anson. "Men," he called out over his shoulder, "meet Colonel Hinler, the man I've been boasting about these past days."

The colonel gave a nod to the men. The men touched their hat brims in return.

"You'll learn everybody's name in time, Colonel," Anson said. "I figured you'll want all the men to get to know each other straightaway." He waved the new men forward. "Go introduce yourselves, boys. These men will be your trail pards while you're riding for the colonel."

The colonel turned his horse a little as the new men filed past him. Ape remained beside Anson, the Cady brothers' horses in hand. Lyle's eyes opened a little, but he dared not say a word, seeing Ape snarl at him under his breath.

"Have you happened to see a rider I sent out to find you?" the colonel asked Anson pointedly. "That's his horse back there." He nodded back at his detectives as the new men spread out and rode in close to them, some touching their hat brims, others extending their hands in friendship. "We found the animal a while ago, shortly after hearing a gunshot." He studied Anson closely.

Anson eyed Foley's horse as he took out a fresh wad of chewing tobacco and poked it back against his jaw.

"Interesting," he said, positioning the wad into place with his tongue. "We heard a gunshot too . . . the same one you heard, I'm thinking."

"Most probable," the colonel said. He looked all around the trail, the downward slope over rock and brush, pockets of towering rock stands—endless possibilities for an ambush. "The man is a fool. Most likely his gun went off, he fell and his horse left him. I hate losing him, though. He's a fool, but he's *my* fool, if you know what I mean."

"I do indeed, and I wouldn't worry too much, Colonel," Anson consoled him. "I'm certain you'll be joining him real soon." He smiled at his private little joke.

"I hope so," said the colonel. "Even fools like him are hard to find in this line of work." He paused, then changed the subject, saying, "We're headed back to Gun Hill, Bo."

"Oh, really?" said Anson. "I've been telling these men we were heading across the border, going to kill us some ol' guerrilla riders."

"There will be plenty of time for that in the coming days," the colonel said. "First we're going back to Gun Hill to resupply."

"Might I ask why, Colonel?" said Anson. As he spoke he raised his hat from his head and ran a bandanna across his moist, gritty brow.

The colonel turned rigid in his saddle. His face took on a stern expression.

"No, you may not ask," he said. "Don't get too big for your britches, Bo."

Anson glanced at Ape and the Cadys, Lyle with his eyes barely open and sitting as silent as stone. Then he turned his eyes back to Hinler.

"My apologies, Colonel," he said quietly. He placed his hat back down atop his head and spat tobacco. Turning his horse slightly, his cocked rifle lying across his lap, he lined the barrel up with the colonel's chest. "I won't do it again," he said resolutely. He pulled the trigger; the bullet lifted the colonel backward from his saddle and tossed him away like some broken rag doll.

"Tell that *fool* of yours howdy when you join him," he said, staring down at the colonel's twisted body lying bloody in a puff of dust. Ape laughed beside him; the Cadys' eyes had flown open wide at the sound of the rifle blast.

A heavy barrage of gunfire followed in the wake of Anson's shot. As he looked up from the dead colonel, his men had made similar moves on the detectives. Their rifle shots at close quarters lifted the unsuspecting detectives from their saddles. Those preferring revolvers rode their horses back and forth among the fallen detectives, killing those still mounted and finishing off any wounded on the ground. Anson backed his horse a step, sat with a twisted smile and spat a stream.

"And that's *that*," he said. "Some of you strap the colonel across his saddle. We're taking him to Gun Hill with us—with *heavy hearts*, I might add." He looked around at the Cadys and said, "Now that we've got some time, we'll talk about that bribe money. I want to know if it's worth fooling with—how much cash does it take to bribe a territorial judge?"

The Cadys struggled, trying to speak against the tight bandannas around their mouths.

"Ape, pull down their gags," Anson said to Boyd. "Let's hear what these *Cady brothers* have to say."

Chapter 14

―――――

"*Yee-hii!* Kill the hell out of them railroad sons a' bitches!" Mexican Charlie Summez shouted, laughing out loud. The sound of gunfire rose over the hill separating the main trail from the smaller lower path where the buggy sat with the two sheriffs aboard it. He turned to Roland Crispe and said, "I wish I had a bottle so's I could drink to a job well done."

Crispe looked him up and down. "How do you know that's not the colonel's detectives *killing the hell* out of our gunmen?"

"Watch your language, Roland," said Mexican Charlie. "I can read the thunder. Our men started the shooting and they ain't letting up none." Gunfire continued to roar, waning some but still strong and steady.

Roland smiled and nodded.

"In that case, I'd drink to it too," he said.

"I'm only sorry I wasn't in on it," said Charlie, "instead of having to sit here eyeballing these two *lawmen.*"

"*Lawmen?*" Crispe nodded at the buggy and sized the woman up. Deluna didn't like the look in his eyes.

"If you think that's a lawman sitting there, you need to be eyeballing through a pair of spectacles."

"You know what I mean, Roland," Mexican Charlie said. "What am I supposed to call her, a law-*woman*?" He shook his head. "That's the trouble with these gals today. They jump into a man's work and confuse every damn thing—don't even know what to call them. Makes my head hurt sometimes."

"Yeah, well, let's get on back," Crispe said. "Bo said we can ride in as soon as the shooting dies down some." He started to turn his horse alongside the buggy. Let's go, *law-woman*," he said to Sheriff Deluna, mimicking Mexican Charlie. "Get this rig rolling."

But instead of unwrapping the reins, the woman stood straight up from the driver's seat. She had been sitting watching, studying, searching for any chance to make an escape. She knew the single worn-out bay pulling a two-horse rig wouldn't stand a chance getting away from two mounted riders. But she had to do something and do it fast before they got back to the rest of the men.

"I must relieve myself," she said, as if struggling to maintain her dignity under the circumstance.

"Like hell," said Roland. "Sit down and unwrap the reins and let's go. Relieve yourself when we get around the trail."

"No, I'm going before we leave," Deluna said. She stepped down from the buggy and started to walk away.

"I'll be damned. Do you believe this?" Crispe said, surprised by Deluna's defiance, he and Charlie glancing at each other.

"See what I mean?" Mexican Charlie said. He shook his head and let out a breath. "The world's gone plumb to hell. In France I hear they've got men doing things to them that no man should do—"

"Get back in this rig, woman!" Crispe shouted, interrupting Mexican Charlie. But Deluna walked on with rigid determination toward a stand of rock and brush ten yards away.

"She ain't *listening* to you, Roland," Charlie said in sheer wonderment.

"Damn it, *that's it*!" Crispe said. "I'm smacking her around some!" He gigged his horse forward sharply.

The sheriff walked on, hearing Crispe's horse pounding up behind her. She heard the hooves sliding to a halt, dust billowing around her. She felt Crispe's arm reach down around her and yank her up onto his lap almost effortlessly.

"I'll teach you to ignore me, *law-woman*!" he shouted. He slapped her head back and forth with his gloved hands. But they were glancing blows and she took them, her hand slipping down into her boot well.

Mexican Charlie watched, rocking in his saddle with laughter at the sight.

"You teach her, Roland. Give it to her good!" he shouted, seeing the horse slow to a walk in the rising dust. He saw the woman fall from Crispe's lap and land on all fours in the dirt. Sunlight glinted off some metal object in her right hand. Dust began to settle around her. "What the hell . . . ?" he commented, seeing Crispe's horse stop and start to turn.

Charlie didn't know what was going on over there, but he knew something was wrong. He instinctively threw his hand around the butt of his holstered Remington. As he raised the revolver he saw Crispe topple sidelong from his saddle as the turning horse now stopped, facing him.

"Holy Joseph!" said Mexican Charlie, seeing the blood down Roland Crispe's front, the bone handle of a knife standing out of his chest—stuck deep from the looks of it. He swung his gun toward the woman. "You *murdering bitch*!" he raged. He tried to take aim, but before he could get his shot lined up, he saw the woman kneeling down on one knee, holding Crispe's gun out at arm's length in both hands.

Uh-oh!

She had him; he knew it, seeing her head tilted to one side staring at him down the gun sights. Blue-orange fire blossomed around her. Shot after shot pounded Charlie in his chest. The first shot lifted him backward, his faded Mexican poncho flaring out around him. The second shot nailed him only two inches from the first. Blood spewed from both wounds. The third shot hit him up under his chin as his body fell backward. The shot blew his hat off and sent a portion of blood, bone and brain matter streaking from the top of his head.

Sheriff Deluna stood slowly, the smoking gun still up and out, moving back and forth between the two gunmen lying dead in the dirt. Feeling the weight of the gun, she bent both elbows and held it up in front of her. She reached her left hand over and gathered the reins to Crispe's horse. The animal hadn't flinched at the sound of gunfire.

"Good boy," she said. She hurriedly led the animal forward and stopped at the buggy. Mexican Charlie's horse milled in the same spot, blood streaked and splattered on its rump. "Sheriff Stone, wake up, help me," she said, raising her voice to the head-bowed sheriff. "We've got to get out of here!"

Stone had heard the shooting and already started to stir. As Deluna grabbed a handful of chest hair and shook him, he awakened fully.

"I'm awake!" he said, trying hard to shake the cobwebs from his brain. He looked around, at the two horses, at the woman, the gun smoking in her hand, then at the two dead gunmen lying sprawled in the dirt.

"Good—good shooting," he stammered. He scrambled shakily out of the buggy. "Yes, I know . . . we've got to get going." But he only seemed to stagger about shakily in place.

Deluna handed him the reins to Crispe's horse. When he took them she lowered the gun and watched him fumble with uncertainty. She hurried over, gun in hand, got the other horse by its reins and ran back with it. Stone was still standing looking confused.

"Sheriff, I need your help," she said. "Do you even know what's going on?"

"Yes, yes. Now I do," he said. He seemed to snap out of his stupor a little. He grabbed the reins to both horses and started to lead them to the front of the buggy.

Deluna grabbed his arm and jerked him and the horses to a halt.

"What are you *doing*?" she demanded.

"Tu-turning the . . . bay loose," Stone stammered, his voice trembling, sounding pressured. "Hitching these two horses to the buggy?"

"Wake up!" Sheriff Deluna cried out. "We're not taking the buggy!" She swung a hard roundhouse slap across his face. The blow stung his jaw, staggered him backward a step. But Stone shook his head and looked at her.

"I'm—I'm sorry," he said. "You're right. I'm good now." He handed her the horse's reins, hurried over near Mexican Charlie's body and grabbed the Remington up off the ground. He looked himself up and down as if puzzled by his sparse wearing apparel. He looked at Charlie's bloody poncho, then glanced at Deluna as if needing her permission.

"Grab it, and let's go!" Sheriff Deluna said. "They're going to be coming anytime." Firing from across the hills had fallen to only sporadic shots that silenced the wounded and dying.

"All right, I'm ready, let's go," Stone said. He slipped the revolver into his empty holster. Even as they leaped up into the saddles, he couldn't help looking himself up and down once again. He wanted to know why he was wearing a loincloth. But he saw the impatient look on the woman's face and decided not to ask right then.

"Okay, don't shoot yourself," Deluna said, nodding at the holstered Remington, the rifle standing in the saddle boot.

"I won't. I learned my lesson *two toes ago*," Stone said, forcing the shakiness from his voice.

"I know you won't," Deluna reassured him. She looked at him and nodded favorably, the slight trace of a smile on her lips. They turned the horses and raced away deeper into the hills, opposite the gunmen.

On the trail back to Resting just before dark, the Ranger had spotted a long line of black smoke streaking upward and drifting on the horizon. Knowing the smoke spelled trouble, he'd hurried on through the night. He stopped only long enough to rest his horse for a few minutes and give the animal a short drink of tepid water from the deep crown of his sombrero.

In the first purple-silver light of morning, he rode onto the streets of the badly burnt town. Along one side of the wide dirt street, the devastation was complete. The wind had swept the fire from end to end of the town and taken out everything: every business, shop, home, barn and toolshed. A church lay in smoldering ashes. Charred remnants of timbers and framing stood blackened in the growing morning light.

Across the street the homes and businesses were smudged, blackened and singed, yet they had escaped the spreading rage of the flames. Torches that had been thrown by Anson's men had burned out in sandy alleyway dirt, or had been trampled out by townsmen as soon as Anson and his marauders rode away. As they rode away, they'd taken any cashboxes left in stores, any ammunition, any guns that happened to suit them and enough trail supplies and coffee to last them a long time. Anson had threatened to shoot any man caught trying to carry whiskey out onto the trail with him.

Inside the badly smudged and blackened cantina, two outlaws who had been sent deeper into Mexico to gather fresh horses stood looking out the smoky window at the Ranger riding in. One of them, Doyle Hickey, tossed back another drink of rye and let out a whiskey hiss. Out front a string of a dozen bareback horses stood bunched up, the end of their lead rope tied to a hitch rail.

"That's him all right," he said in a low half growl. "Wonder if Bo knew it was my birthday coming up, and this is a present." He chuckled at his dark little joke.

A Montana gunman named Jim Purser eased closer and stood beside him. He took the bottle from Hickey's hand, swirled its contents and raised a long swig.

"Bo ain't big on birthdays is what I'm guessing. I'm just a little put out that he didn't wait for us to get back to Bexnar before ripping out of there and burning this dung hill." He grinned through a dusty black beard stubble lining his leathery face. "I like fires too, don't you?"

Hickey reached around without looking and took the bottle of rye back from him. "Not as much as I'd like shooting this Ranger's belly open, see what he et this morning." He grinned, a little drunk first thing in the morning. Both of them watched as the Ranger looked over at the string of horses, rode to the hitch rail and stepped down, rifle in hand. The two watched him give the horses a closer look.

"Ain't it just like a law dog?" said Purser. "Half the damn town lying in smoke and he's curious about these horses."

"It does look peculiar, you have to admit," Hickey said. "These horses are the only ones left here that ain't tail- and mane-singed."

"That ain't our fault," said Purser, the two still watching Sam as a townsman walked up to him. Both gunmen stopped talking, listening close, trying to make out the conversation.

"Thank goodness you're here, Ranger Burrack. This has been a mess from beginning to end." He held out a smudged hand. "I'm Silas Radler. I often serve as temporary deputy when our sheriff is away—which she is right now." He gestured a hand, taking in the half-burnt town. "You can see what's been done to us—a mounted raid. White men, I might add."

"Any idea who they are?" Sam asked. He'd already caught a glimpse of the two men standing inside the cantina window.

"Oh yes. Half the town recognized them. They're a bunch of border trash who've drifted into Bexnar," Radler said, pointing at the hill line between Resting and Bexnar, the Mexican border town. "Two Mexicans who live here said the leader is a gun-killer named Bo Anson. *Malas noticias*, they said he is."

"Bad news," Sam translated, turning back to the horses, giving them a closer look. "Where are Sheriff Deluna and Stone?" he asked.

"Sheppard Stone wandered off drunk, is what we heard," said Radler. "Sheriff Deluna went out to deliver a baby. We haven't seen her since. The gunmen released a prisoner that Stone was supposed to be guarding. The prisoner rode off with them, carrying an anvil shackled to his leg." He shook his head. "I have to say, I'm most concerned something has happened to our sheriff."

Sam didn't answer. Instead he ran a hand down one of the horses' withers, inspecting it, taking note of how many were there. A dozen horses? Was that how many men would need fresh horses?

"My dun's worn out. I'm going to need a rested horse to go look for her," he said. "These are some fine-looking animals." He rubbed the horse's withers a moment longer and said, "Maybe I can swap my dun out."

"Pull your hand off that cayuse, Ranger," said Doyle Hickey, stepping out of the cantina. "These horses ain't for sale."

Sam looked up, feigning surprise, as if he hadn't known he was being watched. Behind Hickey, Purser stepped out; the two spread apart a few feet, their hands hanging close to their holstered revolvers. Sam recognized the nameless faces from the posters he'd seen. He'd met Doyle Hickey before. The other he would know soon enough. He also knew their connection to Bo Anson, thanks to Sheriff Deluna's posters.

"Too bad," Sam said. "I'm paying top dollar." He studied the two men, seeing a whiskey glow on their faces. They stared at him stone-faced.

"I said they *ain't for sale*, lawman," said Hickey. "Don't you hear good?"

Sam ignored him. He saw them both stiffen as he casually lifted his Colt from its holster. But they settled as he raised the Colt to clamp it under his left arm and lifted his empty holster to get to his trouser pocket. His right hand pulled out some folded bills and spread the edges a little for the gunmen to see.

"Cash?" he said. "American greenback?" He stared at them, his rifle in his left hand, his Colt clamped up under his left arm. Finally he saw the trace of a smile come to Purser's lips. Probably thinking how bold and dandy that would be, Sam decided, selling what might be a stolen horse to an unsuspecting lawman.

"Lawman, I said these horses ain't—"

"Go on, Doyle, sell the man a horse," said Purser, cutting Hickey off. "We've got plenty."

"Huh-uh, put your money away," Hickey said, having none of it.

"I tried," Sam said, looking disappointed. He tipped the empty holster up and shoved the bills back into his pocket. When the holster fell back into place, he reached over and took the Colt from under his arm. But instead of dropping it into the holster, he held on to it, the tip of the barrel pointed loosely at the two. He tipped the rifle just enough in his left hand to aim it at their bellies. Both the Colt and the Winchester cocked at once. The two gunmen looked dumbfounded, caught off guard, seeing both gun barrels aimed at them.

"I'm through horse talking," Sam said in a flat, even

tone. "Skin your shooters out real slow and let them fall."

The two gunmen knew they'd been taken by the Ranger. They stared, smoldering, neither one wanting to feel the bite of the bullets they knew were coming if they didn't do as they were told. Still, Hickey wasn't having it.

"You've got some damn gall, Ranger—" he said. Before he could continue, the Ranger cut him off.

"Let them fall or *fall with them*, Doyle Hickey," he said grimly, seeing the look of defeat had already come into Purser's eyes.

Hickey stiffened and said, "You know me, Ranger?"

"Not as well as I'm going to," Sam said. He was through talking, through warning. His next move would be the pull of both triggers.

Hickey saw it too. But it didn't seem to matter to him.

"To hell with this!" he shouted, his hand grabbing his gun butt.

"Doyle, wait!" shouted Purser. But it was too late. The Ranger fired both guns at once. The shot from his Colt slammed Hickey in his chest and sent him flying backward in a red mist. His Winchester bucked as the bullet punched Purser high in his right shoulder and spun him like a broken child's toy. Both men went down. Luckily the townsman Radler had seen the seriousness of the situation and backed out of the way just in time.

"Are—are you all right, Ranger?" he said shakily, in spite of hearing no gunfire except for Sam's.

"I'm all right," Sam said, both rifle and Colt smoking in his hands. Hickey lay lifeless in a dark pool of blood, and Purser writhed in pain, clutching his shoulder. Sam nodded toward the wounded outlaw.

"Let's get this one inside," he said to Radler. "See what he knows about Bo Anson and his men."

Chapter 15

Inside the cantina where the air smelled of stale whiskey and mescal laced with wood smoke, Silas Radler
and the Ranger helped the wounded gunman to a table
and lowered him into a chair. Radler looked all around
the empty cantina as if at a loss for what to do next.
Behind the bar a short, stocky bartender stood staring,
having only cleaned the floor moments earlier.

"My, my," Radler said, "this is the sort of thing our
sheriff always handles so well. We have no doctor
here."

"I'm bleeding bad here," said Purser, frightened,
clearly in pain. "And I wasn't even going for my gun!" He
gripped his bloody shoulder. "Hey, am I arrested?"

"Not yet, but keep talking," Sam warned.

"Sometimes our barber helps out doctoring," said
Radler, touching a finger to his lips in contemplation.

"I don't need a damn haircut! I'm shot!" Purser
shouted. He tried to stand up and attack the townsman
with a bloody fist. Sam intercepted him and sat him
back down.

"Take it easy," he said. "Carrying on just makes the

bleeding worse." He stepped over to the bar with an outstretched hand.

The staring bartender reached down and came up with a short stack of bar towels, handing them over as if surrendering something of great value.

Sam stepped back to the table and dropped the towels on it. Radler stood watching wide-eyed. The bartender shook his head and sipped his morning coffee from a thick mug.

"Go get your barber," Sam said to the townsman. "I'll press a towel on this wound until he gets here."

"Right away," Radler said, turning and hurrying out the door. As his boots pounded across the plank walkway, Sam picked up a towel, stuck it up under Purser's bloody shirt and pressed it firmly over the gaping shoulder wound.

"Breathe deep and try to steel down some," he said to the shaken gunman. "Is this the first time you've been shot?"

The gunman, agitated and nervous, stared angrily up at the Ranger.

"It's none of your damn business how many times I have or haven't been shot!" he snapped.

"All right, then," Sam said coolly. He turned toward the bartender and said, "I'm obliged if you'd pour me a cup of that good-smelling coffee, barkeep."

"Coming up," the bartender said, eyeing the blood that had dripped onto his freshly swept floor.

Sam drew his hand away from the gunman's shoulder, letting the bloody bar towel sag. He turned toward the bar as the bartender poured steaming coffee into a mug.

"What the hell, Ranger?" said Purser, seeing blood spring anew from the bullet hole. "I need some help here!"

"I'm not butting into your business anymore," Sam said, picking up the mug of coffee, hiking a boot on the battered iron bar rail. He tipped the mug as in salute. "Feel free to bleed on out. I'm just going to have some coffee, watch you take care of yourself."

"Damn it, Ranger!" Purser shouted, his eyes stricken with terror. "Don't let me die! I need help!" Blood poured freely down his chest. He swallowed hard and said, "Okay, listen . . . yes, this is the first time I've been shot—*satisfied*? Anything else you want to know?" He raised his trembling bloody hand, not knowing what to do for himself.

Sam noted the sarcasm in his voice. He sipped the coffee and looked at the bartender.

"Good coffee," he said, tipping the raised cup in his direction.

"*Gracias*," the bartender said. The two of them looked back at the frightened gunman. "Are you going to bleed him out all over my floor?" he asked flatly.

"That's up to him," Sam said.

"Because if you are, I'm hoping you'll—"

"All right, I'm sorry!" Purser shouted, half sobbing, his sarcasm gone. "Don't let me die. I'll tell you anything you want to know. Help me here!"

The Ranger walked over, coffee mug in hand, and stood over the wounded gunman.

"Are you sure?" he said quietly. "I don't want to meddle in your business."

"I'm sure, just ask me," Purser said, staring help-lessly at the blood flowing down from under the soaked bar towel.

Sam set the steaming mug down, adjusted the bloody bar towel and pressed on it, his other hand atop Purser's shoulder holding him forward.

"To start with, what's your name?" he said.

"James E. Purser," came the quick reply. "Call me Jim . . . or Jack. Hell, call me Edward if it suits you." He settled down as he saw the flow of blood slow immediately under the pressure of the Ranger's hand.

"Where'd you steal the horses?" Sam asked matter-of-factly, watching himself press the towel onto the gaping wound.

"Who says we stole them?" Purser replied.

Sam looked at him and relaxed the pressure; fresh blood surged in the towel.

"We picked them up here and there, all along the border—that is, *across the border*, I should say," he added quickly. Realizing the Ranger had no reason to arrest him yet, he decided to be careful with what he said. He felt the pressure return on the wound. He breathed easier. "It's not like stealing—Mexes do it to us, we do it to them. Mostly we all just keep switching horses around. No harm in it, right?"

"Depends on who catches you," said Sam. He paused and then said, "And you ride for Bo Anson." It wasn't a question; it was stated as a fact.

Purser started to deny it; Sam saw it in his eyes. He let up on the pressure, just a little.

"Okay, yes, I ride for him some, me and him both."

He nodded in the direction of Doyle Hickey's body. "Everybody rides for everybody out here."

"A dozen fresh horses?" Sam said. "How many men ride with this bunch?"

"I don't know," Purser replied, "seven or eight right now. Some are always drifting in, drifting out. . . ."

Sam let it go, seeing no solid forthright answer coming to anything he asked. Besides, Purser might be right, the numbers were always changing with these border gangs.

"What are you getting ready to rob?" he asked bluntly.

"I don't know about no robberies," Purser said, "and that's the damn truth. We were just told to get horses, so we did. We're supposed to catch up to Bo on the trail."

"Who's *we*?" Sam asked.

"Some ol' boys from here and there," said Purser. "Gunmen," he added.

"The ones who've been lying up over in Bexnar?" Sam asked.

"Yeah, them, maybe . . . and some others," Purser said, looking curious as to how the Ranger knew so much. "Who told you?"

Sam didn't answer. Instead he took the outlaw's free hand, laid it on the bloody towel and pressed it there.

"Keep it tight," he said. He backed up a step and took a sip of coffee with his bloody hand, watching Purser closely.

"Hey . . . ," Purser said, seeing that he could do the same for himself that the Ranger was doing. "I can do this? This ain't nothing." He almost grinned, glancing up at the Ranger as the sound of boots pounded up to the open doorway.

"It's something I figure you'll need to know, *James E. Purser*," Sam said as if committing the name to memory, "the kind of company you're keeping."

"What I *need to know*, Ranger," Purser said, "is how soon can I get out of this burnt-down pissant town?"

"You didn't go for your gun. I can't prove any horse theft," Sam said.

Purser grinned and said, "I was what you call *in the wrong place at the wrong time*."

"When you can ride, you'd do well to clear out of here," the Ranger warned. "Folks can get tense when their town's been burned down around them."

"Don't worry, Ranger," Purser said. "If you hadn't shot me I'd already be gone."

It was afternoon when the Ranger touched the brim of his sombrero to Silas Radler and a few smudged and haggard townsfolk and turned his copper dun onto Resting's wide dirt street. Taking three days' worth of food and four canteens of water with him, he headed out of town following Sheriff Deluna's buggy tracks out across the sand flats. He'd been given directions to the place she'd ridden out to in order to assist in the childbirth. But something told him she wouldn't be there.

The buggy wheel tracks had already faded a little in the loose sand, yet they remained true to their destination. He followed them to a line of low hills and saw where they had wound upward out of sight. Higher up on the hillside he saw a small timber and adobe cabin sitting perched on a rocky ledge. Rather than go farther up, he looked around and saw what he decided to be the buggy's return tracks reaching back down ten yards to his right. He nudged his dun in that direction.

He followed the tracks the next half hour and soon saw where the rig had swung off the trail and set out across the flats. Stepping down from his dun, he noted the hoofprints of many horses filled the sandy dirt at this point. Yet only the sets of two horses' prints cut a layer atop the winding wheels. *Following her*, he told himself, finishing his own thoughts.

He looked all around the desolate terrain, picturing the two horses on Sheriff Deluna's trail—late at night, her taking to the sand flats to get away. He put the picture away, stepped back atop the dun and rode on. He followed the buggy prints farther out onto the flats and came upon the woman's battered sombrero lying upturned on its side in the sand. Stepping down, he picked it up and looked all around again as he retied the two loose ends of the hat string.

"We're gaining a little at every turn," he said quietly to the dun.

Farther on he came to a spot where the buggy had sat long enough to deepen its wheel ruts into the sand. All around it he saw where hooves and boots lapped over a single set of smaller boots that led off across the sand. He followed those smaller boot prints to the rock stand at the water hole. There he saw blood spots, more boot prints, large and small, and amid them one large bare footprint that stood out above all else. It had two toes missing.

Sam let out a breath, getting a strange picture. Someone was shot here, he decided, from all the dried blood on the ground. He only hoped it wasn't Sheriff Deluna. Or Sheriff Stone, if the missing-toe footprint belonged to him—and what were the odds of it *not*? he asked himself. He turned and stepped back up on the dun and rode on, unaware of the eye watching him through the telescope from the cover of rock and pine in the distant hills overlooking the flats and the water hole.

"Yep, that's him," said Max Bard, seeing the Ranger and the dun move away among the glaring sand and wavering heat. Bard lowered his old Confederate telescope, closed it and put it away. He rubbed his eyes, then looked around at Holbert Lee Cross, Pete Worley and the others. Then he looked at Rudy Bowlinger, who fidgeted in his saddle, the anvil still chained to his ankle. Close behind Bowlinger sat Parker Fish, Russell Gant and Dewey Lucas.

"Was Burrack trailing you to us too, Rudy," Bard asked, "but maybe something else caught his attention?"

Bowlinger heard the accusation in Bard's voice. He looked all around nervously at the eyes riveted on him. On the ground lay a man in a ragged black suit and a torn and bloody duster. His hat was missing; his holster was empty on his hip. His breath came fast, labored. But there was no fear in his dark eyes.

"I swear, Max," Bowlinger said, "I had no idea I was being followed. I figured there was none of the detectives still out searching when Bo Anson turned me loose. I wouldn't get myself followed to our hideout! You've got to believe me. I'd die first. I'd swallowed one of my bullets."

"Settle down, Rudy," said Holbert Lee Cross. "If Max didn't believe you, you'd already be dead."

Max gave Cross a look.

"Crosscut's right, Rudy," he said. "Anyway, this wounded man might be one of the colonel's detectives, but it wasn't the colonel who put him on your trail. It was Bo Anson."

Bowlinger looked stunned. He gave the man on the ground a hard stare, bewildered.

"Bo sent him tracking me?" he said in disbelief, looking down at the wounded man. "But Bo set me free. Said to tell you he was doing what you and him talked about doing."

"Bo Anson is a snake," said Bard. "He wants to know where our hideout is just as bad as the colonel. Might figure on taking the railroad bounty on us. Why do you think he left that anvil on you to slow you down?"

"I—I never thought about that," Bowlinger said. "I figured Bo left me chained to it just to be a turd, the way he's prone to be sometimes."

Max looked down at the man on the ground. Thirty yards back a dead horse lay in the sand where the man had run the animal to death with Bard and his men closing in on him.

"Lucky we spotted him trailing you in, Rudy," Max said. He said to the detective, "You've led us a long way, made a good run. Now it's over." As he spoke, he lifted his rifle one-handed, cocked and pointed down at the man. "Who put you on Rudy's trail," he asked quietly, "Bo Anson or the colonel?"

The man let out a breath, knowing he was dead regardless of how he answered. He'd gotten too close, seen too much trail in the direction of the hideout just across the border.

"Bo Anson," he said. "I've been riding for the colonel and Curtis Siedell for peanuts. Anson and I have been keeping tabs on the reward money on you fellas. It's gotten high. You can't blame us."

"What's your name?" Max asked.

"Mallard Trent," the detective said.

"Mallard Trent, the tracker?" Max asked. "Used to ride for General Crook?"

"Yeah, that's me," the man said. He let out a deep breath. "I was big hoss riding for Crook. Look where I'm ending up." He shook his head. "Soon as we collected the railroad bounty, we were all set to start robbing Siedell's operations ourselves. I've got all kinds of information about his business, his comings and goings. Fat lot of good it's going to do me now."

Bard leveled the rifle a little, but he looked at Cross and Worley and saw them give him a slight shrug.

"You gave us a hell of a run, Trent," he said down to the detective. "Learned to ride like that fighting the Apache, I expect?"

Trent stared up at him, sensing a fine crack opening in what he'd considered his sealed fate.

"Yeah, I expect," he said. He continued to stare, barely daring to breathe as he saw the wheels turning in Bard's mind.

"I heard the general's a son of a bitch to ride for," Bard said. Checking him out, Trent decided.

"I never rode for a blue-leg general who wasn't," Trent said.

"So you say?" Bard motioned him to his feet with his rifle barrel. Trent stood up, noting that Bard's finger was off the trigger. "Let me ask you something, Mallard Trent," he said, eyeing him closely. "Was that blue-leg remark something you said just because you know us ol' boys are all guerrilla rebels? You figured maybe saying it might save your life?" His stare hardened. But it seemed not to bother Trent. The detective reached a hand back and dusted the seat of his trousers.

"I don't know," he said. He paused for a moment, then said, "If it was . . . did it work?"

Max looked at Cross and Worley and gave a short little chuckle. Seeing their approval, he turned back to Trent and lowered the rifle and said, "Yeah, why the hell not?"

The men gave a short round of laughter; Bard uncocked the rifle and laid it back across his lap.

"Ride up front with me, Trent," he said. "Let's talk about Curtis Siedell some."

Trent looked all around.

"I'd like to oblige, but I'm without a horse," he said.

"Help Rudy get that chain off his ankle. He'll likely double up with you until we get somewhere."

Bowlinger eased his horse over, dropped the anvil off his lap and watched the length of chain play out. He climbed down behind the anvil as soon as it hit the ground.

"I'm glad to be getting shed of this heavy bastard," he said.

As Max Bard backed his horse away and sat watching, Cross and Worley sidled to him.

"If we're taking Trent into our fold, I figure we're never going back to our old hideout again?" Cross said.

"That's right," said Bard. "It was time to give that place up anyway." He watched as Bowlinger handed Trent a rifle. Trent laid Bowlinger's chain out across a rock, stood back a couple of feet and took aim.

A shot rang out and the chain jumped up from the rock, landing in two pieces.

"Where are we headed now?" Cross asked, seeing Bowlinger grab up the shorter piece of chain still attached to his ankle. The freed outlaw danced all around on the ground.

"We're headed back to Gun Hill, robbing King Curtis's railroad like we set out to do." Bard added, "We're going to kill Bo Anson before he gets any bigger, and we're going to have to kill this Ranger before he gets any closer." He looked at Cross and Worley and gave a thin, flat smile. "Always somebody that needs killing," he said.

"Don't forget King Curtis himself," said Worley, eyeing the colonel's stallion Bard was mounted on.

"I haven't forgot him, Kid," Bard said. "We're just biding our time, waiting for him to stick his head up." He turned his horse toward the trail and nudged it forward. "That's where Bo might be able to help us out a little. He's after Siedell and nothing will stop him." He smiled. "We'll let him flush him out for us."

"No chance we might be able to trust Bo a little?" Worley asked.

"No way, Kid," said Bard. "Bo is stone crazy. He gets on a mad tangent and decides he wants everything— the only thing can stop him is a bullet in his head."

Part 3

Part 3

Chapter 16

It was midafternoon when the Ranger heard two rifle shots from up in the hills above the sand flats. He'd been riding the flats for the past hour, following the hoofprints of three horses that lay stretched out before him leading right up in the direction of the shots. The sheriff's battered sombrero hung from his saddle horn by its repaired string.

"Let's go, Copper," Sam said down to the dun, raising its pace to a gallop at the touch of his boots to its sides. The dun closed the last half mile quickly, the sand flats billowing behind them, only tapering its pace back down when the flats sloped upward onto the rocky hillside. The Ranger touched back on the reins and slowed the horse even more, searching the ground beneath them for the hoofprints that were now going to be more difficult to follow.

With the dun climbing upward on a stone path, Sam reined the animal back and forth, leaning down its side, searching for the hoofprints, for scrapes and markings on an unyielding surface. Nothing. But as he straightened in his saddle and nudged the dun forward, he saw rock and dust kick up from the ground a few yards off the path to his right. Behind the kick of dust came the sound of a rifle far up on the hillside. Jerking the dun to a halt, he leaped down from his saddle, rifle in hand, and pulled the dun to safety behind a tall cactus. High on the hillside he saw the glint of a rifle being turned deliberately back and forth in the afternoon sunlight. Then he saw and heard another shot come from the same position. This time the kick of dirt was farther away to his right than the first shot.

Again he saw the repeated back-and-forth glint of metal in the sunlight.

All right, I get it.

He took off his sombrero, held it out to the side and waved it up and down. A moment passed and he saw the signal again. "Here goes," he said to the dun. Leaving the animal in the cover of the cactus, he stepped out into full view of the high ridgeline from where the shots had come. After a tense second the glint of metal came again. This time the signaling didn't stop even as he pulled the dun from behind cover and led it up to the right of the rocky path toward the flashing signal.

"All right, I'm coming," he said under his breath.

"He's coming," Sheriff Colleen Deluna said over her shoulder, as if having heard the Ranger from her position high atop the ridge. Near exhaustion, she lowered the scoped rifle from her eye and leaned back in relief against the stand of rock behind her. She looked over at Sheriff Stone, who lay leaning back against a rock in the sandy clearing.

Sheriff Deluna could tell he was still trembling, yet not as badly as he had been earlier in the day. The dusty striped poncho he wore was dark with sweat. His bare foot was scarred and bruised from traveling through brush and rock.

"Did you hear me, Stone?" she said. "The Ranger caught my signal. He's on his way up." Her voice sounded strained and weary, from the heat, the lack of water.

"G-good," Stone stammered in spite of his tremors having waned considerably. "I— I hate for h-him to see me like this. I'm going to catch hell for wh-what I done, letting everybody down." He sat up and hugged himself tight with both arms. A near-empty canteen lay in the dirt beside him. They had been under pursuit, rationing the last of their water to a short sip every now and then throughout the long day.

Sheriff Deluna looked from Stone over to the body of their pursuer, one of Bo Anson's men, Hugh Kirchdorf, who lay sprawled in a dark pool of dried blood. He had followed them and shot at them repeatedly from afar. Stone had taken a chance. He'd put himself in the open, waited for the right near miss, then fallen to the ground and waited. When the rifleman checked on his marksmanship, Stone rose and killed him before Deluna got a shot off.

"I wouldn't say that, Sheriff. I'm grateful you killed this long shooter before he could kill us," she said, sounding hard-edged even as tired as she was. She turned the big rifle back and forth in her hands as she spoke, inspecting the long-distance brass scope. Then she stood, walked to Stone and reached her hand down .

to help him to his feet. But Stone ignored her offer, feeling ashamed. Instead he struggled and pushed himself up, bringing the canteen with him. Handing Deluna the last drink of water, he dusted his bare legs and smoothed the poncho down his front.

Using each other for support, the two walked to the place where they had tied their horses and led the animals by their reins down the steep rocky path. A half hour later, they met the Ranger leading his dun up the path toward them.

Upon seeing him, the two sheriffs sank down onto the rocks along the edge of the trail. Sam, noting their condition, hurried to them with two full canteens in his hands. He uncapped the canteens and helped them both drink until they'd sated their thirst. Then the two leaned forward. Stone removed his flop hat and the Ranger poured a stream of the tepid water over their heads.

"Thank God, we . . . saw you from up there, Ranger," Sheriff Deluna said, catching her breath as she washed her face with both hands. "Bo Anson held us prisoner. . . . We got loose. But he sent a long shooter. We've been run ragged all day and night . . . couldn't get to any water holes." She gave a tired nod up the trail where the body lay. "Sheriff Stone killed him . . . earlier today. We were resting up, walking out of here tonight."

Sam looked at Stone. His wet head, his poncho, his loincloth, missing a boot. Seeing the Ranger's eyes on him, Stone lowered the flop hat back onto his head and looked away. His hands trembled. He clamped them together.

"I expect you heard what happened to me," he said.

"Yes, I heard," Sam said. "I heard you got drunk and wandered off with an old Indian who sells cocaine and whiskey."

"A medicine man," Stone said, half-sullen.

Sam wasn't letting him off the hook all the way, not yet.

"A medicine man?" he said. "What kind of medicine was he—?"

"There's something for you to see, Ranger," Sheriff Deluna said to Sam, changing the subject. She gestured toward her horse where she had stuck the scoped rifle under her bedroll. "It's a rifle with a brass scope on it."

Sam stood and walked to her horse, pulled the rifle out and looked it over.

"Looks the same," he said. "There's not that many of these scopes in use. Think this was the man who ambushed us?"

"No, it wasn't," said Deluna. "This man was in Bexnar at the time. He wasn't riding with Anson until afterward."

Sam gave her a questioning look.

"I recognized him from his wanted poster," Deluna said. His name is—*was* Hugh Kirchdorf." She nodded at the scoped rifle in Sam's hands and said, "You can keep that for evidence."

"Obliged," said Sam. He walked back to the two sheriffs with the rifle in his hands and said to Deluna, "I left a wounded prisoner with your temporary deputy, Silas Radler. He and another gunman had a string of a dozen horses they'd gathered across the border. He said the number of Anson's men is always changing."

He gazed at Sheriff Deluna knowingly. But it was Sheriff Stone who replied.

"Sounds like he's . . . putting something big together," he said in a weak voice. "I know a little about Bo Anson. He's the kind who hates riding small."

Deluna and Sam looked at each other, a little surprised to hear from Stone.

"What do you suppose it could be?" Sam asked, encouraging the sheriff to take part.

Stone fell silent for a moment.

"I'm telling you both right now . . . I'm sorry. Sorry I let you down, sorry I've acted like a fool, sorry I let you down—"

"You already said that," Sam corrected him.

But Stone continued. "That I've been drunk, acting loco—"

"Let's get away from all that, Stone," Sam said, wanting him to know they were out for the same thing, to uphold the law. "Stay with Bo Anson. What do you figure he's up to?"

Stone appeared to have a hard time considering the matter. Finally he let out a breath, giving up.

"That's anybody's guess," he said. "But he's at the center of everything going on, whatever it is." He looked away again.

Sam stood looking at Stone for a moment, deciding whether or not to trust him again.

"What are you going to do, Ranger?" Sheriff Deluna asked, raising the canteen for another drink.

Sam hefted the rifle in his hands.

"I want the long shooter," he said. "I want the men

you're holding posters on. I'm riding to Gun Hill, soon as I get the two of you back to town."

Deluna shook her head as she lowered the canteen.

"I'm riding to Gun Hill with you," she said. "They burned my town, took Stone and me prisoner. I'm not letting it go."

"Your town needs you there, Sheriff," Sam reminded her.

"I know that," Deluna said, capping the canteen, pushing up onto her feet. "We best get to Gun Hill and get this done right away."

Seeing her stand, Stone pushed up beside her and stood looking at the Ranger.

"Count me in," he said.

Sam looked him up and down, sizing him up.

"Gun Hill is well named," Stone said, for no apparent reason.

"Yes, it is," Sam said. He paused, then said, "Are you going to be able to do your job, Sheriff?"

"If I'm not, there's a graveyard in Gun Hill," Stone said in a grim tone. "It's as good a place as any. . . ." He left his words unfinished.

Gun Hill

From the platform of his private Pullman car, Curtis Siedell stood up from a green canvas folding chair and looked out at the riders headed into town, leaving a cloud of roiling dust in their wake. On either side of him a bodyguard stood in suit, tie, derby hat and long

tan riding duster. They both stepped forward with repeating rifles at port arms, flanking him. On his right a
Texan gunman named Virgil Pennick, on his left a
younger man, Arnold Inman.

"Summon the men around us, Arnold," Siedell said
in a low, even tone. He stared straight ahead, evening
sunlight landing on his right shoulder. "We'll want to
make a fine show of strength for the colonel." He raised
a thick unlit cigar in his hand and put it in his mouth.

"Yes, sir," said Inman. He stepped over to the side of
the platform, leaned out and gave a hand signal, summoning one of Siedell's leaders who stood smoking a
cigarette outside the car in front of the plush Pullman.
The man, Jacob Bead, nodded and crushed out his cigarette under his boot; he leaned and called out into the
car, "All right, men, form up out here. There's riders
coming."

On the platform of his Pullman car, Siedell turned to
Pennick as boots pounded down the iron steps from
the next car.

"Virgil, get the meat chopper set up on its stand," he
said, gesturing a nod upward toward the top of the car.
"I think Colonel Hinler will appreciate seeing it."

"Yes, sir, right away," said Pennick. He turned, yet
hesitated for a second. "But I need to say, sir, I don't see
the colonel among these men."

"Hmm . . . ," said Siedell, studying the riders closely.
"They are wearing our uniform dusters for the most
part, are they not?"

"They are, sir," said Pennick. "But I don't see the colonel. I don't even see any faces I recognize."

"Puzzling," said Siedell. "I'll have to see what the colonel's up to."

"Yes, sir," said Pennick, stepping down off the platform quickly and trotting back to where the shape of a Gatling gun and tripod sat on the ground covered by a canvas tarpaulin. Along the wide wooden dock, freight handlers stopped working and watched as the armed men spilled out of the private car and assembled around the rear of the Pullman. Bo Anson also watched the armed men as he and his men drew closer from the far end of the street.

He chuckled under his breath and spoke to Ape Boyd riding beside him.

"Feels good, don't it, having folks turn out when you ride into a town?" he said sidelong.

"I'd sooner ride in shooting," Ape replied. "I don't take to warm receptions much—never did."

"All in good time, Ape," said Anson. "Just keep watching for my signal."

Counting a few more of his men who had fallen in with him along the trail as they'd planned, their ranks had now grown to seventeen, gunmen and murderers all. Just the kind of men he needed, Anson told himself, drawing his horse down to a halt thirty feet from the rear Pullman platform. Ape Boyd stopped his horse beside him, leading a horse with the colonel's body tied down under a dusty blanket.

The rest of Anson's men drew their horses down and bunched up behind him and Boyd on either side. All of them wore tan riding dusters. Most of them wore derby hats. Rifles stood in their laps. Bandoliers hung from their saddle horns. A large furry dog sprang out from under a boardwalk and ran forward barking and snapping at the horses' hooves. A sharp kick from a big sweaty bay sent the dog flipping, rolling and scrambling away, leaving a painful yelp lingering in the air behind it.

"Hope that wasn't your dog, Mr. Siedell," Anson called out as Siedell and his men stared at the unusual sight.

"It is not," Siedell said regally, dismissing the matter. "I take it you're Bo Anson? The colonel telegraphed about you. Welcome to my rail-spur operation." He spread a hand to take in the station, freight dock and entire town.

"*Gracias*, Mr. Siedell," said Anson. "The colonel told me you needed more men—sent me to round some up." He nodded at the men on either side.

Siedell eyed the men over, noting that he'd never seen a harder, tougher-looking bunch of gunmen. There were no familiar faces among them, which he found curious.

"Very good." He nodded. "And where is the colonel?" he asked. "I want to show him my new Pullman ornament." He gestured up to where three men were busily mounting the canvas-covered Gatling gun.

Even with the canvas hiding it, Anson could tell what was underneath. Seeing the print of the Gatling gun alone gave him pause. He knew that one man firing and one loading the big gun could wreak havoc on him and his gunmen. This was no place to launch an attack on Siedell. Anson decided to let the matter simmer a little while longer—get Siedell out of town on the desert. Once there he could take the man captive and demand whatever amount he wanted from Siedell's businesses.

"I'm afraid I have some bad news about the colonel, Mr. Siedell," he said. He motioned for Ape to throw the blanket off Colonel Hinler's body. "The sons a' bitches killed him only last evening, before me and these men got there to stop it." He reached up, pulled off his hat and clasped it to his chest. "All we want now is the chance to kill them low, no-good dogs."

Siedell looked at the colonel's body lying strapped down over the saddle.

"You're going to get that chance, Bo Anson," he said. "I'm sending you and your men right back out there come morning."

"You do that, Mr. Siedell," said Anson. "And you've got my word we'll catch every one of them."

"Let's make something perfectly clear, Bo," Siedell said, already calling him by his first name, Anson noted. "I do not want Max Bard and his band of cut-throats simply *caught*. I want them killed, to the man."

Anson stared at him for a moment, nodding.

"That right there," he said, pointing a finger at Siedell, "is exactly what I've been hoping to hear." He straightened in his saddle. "We'll be ready to go come morning. Nothing would please us more than you riding side by side with us."

Siedell cocked his head a little to one side, visibly not pleased with Anson's words.

"You forget yourself, Anson," he said. He gestured his cigar toward all the men around his Pullman, at the

Gatling gun atop the car. "When I travel I go with my
entire army. We all may meet you and your contingent
on the trail. But you're new here. Do not assume yourself to be my right-hand man." He looked around at his
detectives. They gazed flatly at Anson and his gunmen.

Bo Anson's face reddened.

"No, sir, Mr. Siedell," he said, keeping a cordial tone
even as anger raged in his chest. "Please excuse me. I
only want to do the best job we can for you."

"I understand," Siedell said, but there was an edge
of superiority in his voice. "Now take these men over
there where I can summon you when you're needed."
He pointed out at a wide, barren sandlot at the far edge
of town. "I'll have some elk stew sent over. I'll come
and meet each of you later. That will be all," he added.

Summoned? When he was needed . . . ?

Anson only sat staring for a moment, keeping his
rage and humiliation from spilling over to his gun
hand.

"Elk stew sounds just fine, sir," Anson managed to
say tightly without betraying his rage.

Chapter 17

———

Curtis Siedell took the horse carrying the colonel's body and watched as the gunmen rode toward a barren stretch of ground at the far end of town and swung down from their saddles. He smiled to himself and drew on his fresh cigar as Arnold Inman held a long sulfur match to the end of it.

"Thank you, Arnold," he said through the smoke looming around his head. He continued to stare where Anson and the gunmen stepped down to make camp. "Did Virgil get the meat chopper set up?"

"He did, sir," Inman said, shaking out the match. "He was only waiting on word from you to take off the canvas cover."

"Good, let's leave it mounted for the time being," Siedell said. He nodded his agreement at two men who stepped out and led the colonel's body off the street.

"Covered or uncovered, sir?" said Inman.

"Covered, of course," said Siedell. "Too much dust here. I would have only uncovered it for the colonel. But leave it mounted for now and make sure the ammunition crate is full."

"Yes, sir," Inman said, giving Siedell a curious look. "I'll see to it right away."

Siedell remained staring out at Anson and his men as Inman hurried around the side of the Pullman car and climbed the iron rungs leading up to the roof.

At the sandy ground where the gunmen began setting up camp, Ape Boyd stood staring back at Siedell, a hundred and fifty yards between them.

"What are you looking at, you pillow-assed poltroon, son of a dripping—" Ape snarled under his breath.

"That's enough, Ape," Anson said, cutting the wild-eyed gunman off.

"All right," Ape growled. "But I don't know why you didn't let me shoot holes in him while I had him in pistol range."

"Because then *you too* would be dead, Ape," Anson said, knowing the futility of trying to reason with Ape Boyd.

"Yeah, so?" Ape said, turning his stare away from Siedell, looking around at Anson.

Anson shook his head and took a patient breath.

"I want you alive, Ape," he said. "Don't worry, you'll get all the killing you crave, as soon as I get things set up just right here." As he spoke, some of his men gathered around him, their bedrolls under their arms, rifles in hand.

"Holt, you worked the rails," he said to one of the gunmen who'd joined him on the trail. "How much fuel do you say is in the wood bin?"

"Enough to run easy for three days, maybe," said

Gus Holt, who stood staring back at the big black steam engine and its three-car train.

"How about running hard?" Anson asked.

"A day, a day and a half," Holt said. "Run any harder than that, you'd likely blow the boiler."

Anson nodded and said, "How often they have to run that boiler just to keep the water ready?"

"In the heat of the day every two or three hours," Holt said with authority. "Likely they'll stoke it up and let it idle all night, though, keep the water boiling enough to get them going if they needed to."

"I see." Anson nodded and looked back at the station.

Lou Stiles, another gunman who'd joined him along the trail, gestured down at the bedroll he held clamped under his arm. Saddlebags draped his shoulder.

"Before I throw down here, Bo," he said, "are you sure we're here for the night?"

Anson stared at him for a moment.

"Throw down, Stiles—and all the rest of you," he said, looking around at the other gunmen. He raised a finger for emphasis. "But always be ready to drag up and leave when you're riding with me."

Bedrolls hit the ground with muffled flops. Lou Stiles grumbled to himself under his breath, "That's about the sort of answer I expected." He kicked his bedroll out and pitched his saddlebags down on it.

At the rear of the gathered gunmen, Lyle and Ignacio Cady sat down stiffly in the dirt, having no bedroll, no saddlebags. They looked around at the gunmen rolling out their blankets.

"We're in a dire state of want," Lyle said. "Anson strikes me as not giving a damn about the bribe money."

"He strikes me as not giving a damn about us," said Ignacio. He wrapped his forearms around his shins and leaned his head on his raised knees. "If we get a chance tonight, I say we skin out of here while we can."

"He'll kill us if he catches us, Iggy," Lyle warned.

"Why?" Ignacio asked in a blunt voice.

"I don't know *why*," said Lyle. "Because he's *crazy*, I guess. He just will." He lay on his side in the dirt and drew himself up in a ball, his arms crossed on his chest. "If we live through this, I say we ought to go kill Edsel Centrila, for putting us here."

"Put Edsel Centrila out of your mind," Ignacio said with resignation. "We're not going to live through this." He stared intently at his brother. "Look around us, Lyle. These are mostly new faces. Anson's gunmen don't appear to last long."

"Jesus, Iggy, you're right," said Lyle, looking all around in the evening light. "You and I are lucky we've made it this far."

After midnight, three of Anson's men walked crouched and shadowy among the sleeping figures on the ground near the low-burning campfire. Hands reached out and shook the sleepers by their shoulders until they awakened and sat up on their bedrolls.

"The hell is this?" asked a bleary-eyed gunman named Chris Jackson. Instinctively he jerked a long-barreled revolver from under his head.

"Get up. We're leaving," another gunman named

Randy Meeks whispered close to him. "Wake the man next to you." As an afterthought, he said as he turned away, "Loosen your trigger finger—it's going to get bloody tonight."

"All *right!*" Jackson whispered in reply, excited at the prospect of a gunfight. He sprang up into a crouch himself and kicked the man lying rolled up in the blanket next to him. "Get up, Marvin! We've got gun work to do," he growled under his breath.

As the men awakened, staying low, gathering their guns and bedrolls, Bo Anson, Ape Boyd and three other men hurried along on the ground beside the freight dock, guns and knives in hand. Making their way under the cover of darkness, they hurried toward the idling steam engine and stopped and looked up at the glow of a cigarette perched like a firefly atop the big engine.

"Ape, he's all yours," Anson said sidelong. "You'll only get one chance, so cut deep and fast."

"I'll cut his damn head *off*, if you want me to, Bo," Ape said, barely keeping his voice down to a whisper.

"Shh, keep quiet," Anson warned. "Now get going." He and the other two men watched as Ape disappeared along the side of the dock. A moment later, they saw him climb upward almost in a crawl and make his way over to the idling engine. He ascended its iron rungs to the top. They waited, almost holding their breath, until they saw the small ball of cigarette fire fall and break into sparks down the black-shadowed side of the locomotive.

"Ape got him," Anson whispered to the two men

beside him. "Here we go." As the three slipped along the side of the dock, on the Pullman platform one of Siedell's guards stood up and stared out into the darkness, his senses piqued.

"What you looking at, Felix?" another guard asked, sitting sprawled in a folding chair, his boots propped up on the iron handrail. He held a tin cup of coffee in his gloved hand. A rifle leaned against his side.

"Thought I saw something out there, Herb," said Felix Otto. He kept searching the darkness as he spoke.

"You're jumpy as a damn cat," Herbert Shiller said with a little chuff. "Sit down and have some of this coffee before the pot gets cold on us."

"I'm just doing my job," Otto said, still searching the dark as he backed up to his folding chair and sat down. He laid his rifle across his knees and relaxed a little. "I could have sworn I saw something moving around."

"Might've been a coyote," said Shiller. "They get bold and brazen when there's been elk gutted and skint for dinner." He patted a hand on his belly. "Can't say that I blame them."

"If I am *jumpy as a cat*," said Otto, "I think we all have good reason to be. Did you get a good look at those new gunmen—I mean *detectives*—who rode in here?"

"I saw them," said Shiller with a short little grin, "but I didn't let the sight of them ruin my day."

"Hell, neither did I," said Otto. "But I would feel better if they had rode on a few miles instead of bedding down right next to us."

"Best get used to them," said Shiller. "That's the kind of gunmen Mr. Siedell wants riding for him until he gets shed of Max Bard and his men." He paused and drew a Colt from its holster and twirled it on his finger. "Besides, we ain't exactly schoolboys ourselves, are we?"

Otto relaxed a little and gave a low chuckle.

"Hell no, I expect we ain't at that," he said, patting his repeating rifle on his knees.

Inside the plush Pullman car, Curtis Siedell lay on his bed with a cigar glowing in the dark. At his left side a young local woman named Violet Kerns lay naked outside the bedcovers. Siedell's left hand lay on the small of the woman's back. His fingers tapped lightly, idly as he stared up in thought and blew smoke at the car's ornate ceiling.

When a scuffling of boots sounded on the rear platform, he cocked an eye toward the door and listened closely, smoke looming around his head. After a moment, all was quiet, and he started to go back to his thoughts. But a tapping on the door caused him to sit up and listen again. He stood up and wrapped his robe around his nakedness.

"Yes, Otto, what is it?" he said, a little annoyed, knowing it had to be Felix Otto, certain that Herb Shiller would never interrupt him while he had a woman in his bed.

When he heard no response from the other side of the door, he walked over to it, cursing under his breath.

"This better be important, damn it," he growled. He swung the door open and saw no one standing there, just the two guards sitting upright in the folding chairs. He gave them a questioning stare when they didn't even look around at him. "Are you two asleep?" he asked angrily.

Still no answer . . . ?

"I better not see either of you—" His words stopped short when he saw Shiller's hand fall limp at his side and dangle there.

"My God!" he said, seeing blood run down Shiller's fingertips and pool on the platform floor.

"Uh-uh-uh," Bo Anson said, stepping around from beside the door, clamping his boot down to keep Siedell from slamming it shut. "It's just me," he said coolly. "Waiting to be *summoned*, King Curtis." He held a cocked Colt only inches from Siedell's face. As Anson took a step forward, Siedell stiffened.

"What the devil are you doing, Anson?" Siedell said, trying to sound in command, even though he fully realized he wasn't.

"You didn't come to see us," Anson said, still stepping forward as Siedell stepped backward. "We figured we'd come see you." He glanced at the naked woman lying asleep on the bed.

"I hope we didn't interrupt anything." He grinned. Behind him the other two men stepped inside and closed the door. On the bed the woman stirred only slightly and mumbled, but never awakened.

"Nobody saw nothing," said one of the new gunmen named Frank Castor.

"Good," Anson said. "Holt, you and Harvey get up the engine. Make us ready to back out of here. There's a switch track a hundred yards out. Back us into it when we get there, and cut the other car loose."

"You got it, Bo," said Holt. He and a gunman named Harvey Clausen hurried away through the front door of the Pullman.

Anson looked all round at Siedell's plush private car with admiration.

"My, my," he said as if in awe. On a silver tray stood a selection of whiskey, brandy, wine, an open leather bag of brownish Mexican cocaine. "It's almost a shame killing a man who has so much to live for."

"I don't know what you're up to, Anson," said Siedell, "but it's not going to work. My men will chop you to pieces. Did you see what I have mounted overhead?"

"I saw the Gatling gun," said Anson. He reached his rifle barrel up and tapped it three times on the ceiling. Immediately Ape replied with three taps of his rifle butt. "But that's my little meat chopper now."

"What is it you want?" Siedell said, sounding less unyielding now that he saw Bo Anson and his men were building an upper hand on him. "Has Max Bard put you up to this?"

"Huh-uh," said Anson, "although we did once talk about taking over your operation, see how long we could run it before anybody realized you were dead." He shook his head. "No, this is all my idea. I'm even going to kill Max and his men and collect the reward you've got on their heads—the reward says redeem-

able at any rail station belonging to Siedell Enterprises."
He grinned.

"Jesus, you're out of your mind, Anson," said Siedell, seeing a gleam of madness in his eyes as he spun
out his delusional plans.

"You say that now," Anson said, "but wait until you
see me opening the strongbox full of cash your home
office pays to get you back with all your fingers and
toes—most of them anyway."

"Listen to me, Anson," said Siedell, "if it's money
you want, how much? It's my enterprises. I can have
cash sent to me at any bank in this country—whatever
amount I ask for. Just take me to one, I'll show you. We
don't have to be uncivilized about this."

"I like being *uncivilized*," said Anson, giving Siedell
a sharp poke with his gun barrel. "I want the ransom
delivered where I say, not in some damn bank with riflemen on every roof. I'm going to collect ransom on
you, reward money on Max Bard, maybe even rob a
couple of your new rail spurs while I'm at it. So sit
yourself down and watch what happens next."

Just then a blast of steam resounded from the engine; the train lurched back a foot and started moving
slowly. Both Anson and Siedell had to steady themselves. On the bed, the woman looked up drunkenly at
the two and rubbed her eyes.

"Oh, Mr. Diddles," she said playfully, "you've in-
vited a friend?"

"We're not friends," Anson said, wagging the gun in
his hand for her to see. "Go back to sleep." He shoved

Siedell toward the rear door. "Stand right here, *Mr. Diddles*." He reached down and clamped a handcuff around Siedell's wrist. He clamped the other end to his own. "You make one false move when we're out on the platform, I'll blow your head off."

Chapter 18

In the darkness, Siedell's men who'd been asleep in the next car had been awakened by the train lurching and the blast of steam. They quickly shook sleep from their eyes and stuck their heads out the windows, looking back and forth. "The train's moving!" one called out in surprise. More of his men came running from the boardwalk of a nearby rail shack.

Four men ran alongside the engine, still able to keep up with it as it slowly gained momentum. Above the roar and throb and hissing steam, one called out to the engineer, who stood in an open window with his hand on the throttle. "Leonard, where are you going?" he shouted up.

The engineer, Leonard Loew, stared down stiffly at him from the loud engine. The running men didn't notice the look of fear in the engineer's eyes.

"Mr. Siedell said move it," he called back to them, "so I'm moving it."

Satisfied, the four men slowed to a halt, unable to see that behind Loew stood Gus Holt with a gun to the back of the man's head.

"I wish King Curtis would tell us things sooner," one of the men said.

"Let him hear you call him King Curtis, he'll tell you things sure enough," another man replied. The four stood watching as the train continued backing away from the station.

"What's that?" one asked, nodding toward the dark object lying alongside the empty tracks as the train rolled on.

Without reply the four trotted toward the object. In the grainy purple light, they stopped again, this time looking down at a man's body, less its head, lying on the rocky ground. A few feet away lay the head of Jacob Bead with a stunned expression frozen on his grim face.

"Oh my God!" one of the men said. They all looked up and saw an unrecognizable figure standing in the darkness atop the engine behind the Gatling gun. "We're being . . . *what*? Robbed?" one asked the other three with uncertainty.

Seeing what was going on, one shouted, "Come on, the train's being stolen!" He started running toward the train as it made its way in reverse toward the switching track. At the car next to the Pullman, men were still hanging out the windows watching the station grow smaller behind them. Some had jumped down while they could, but now the engine had started gathering speed, making escape more difficult.

Inside the Pullman car, Bo Anson could hear shouting back and forth. Men's boots pounded hard and fast alongside the car. The boots quickly fell away, replaced by more running boots as the train rolled past.

"Let's go, before the shooting starts, Siedell," Anson said, turning the rear door handle and swinging the door open. He shoved Siedell out in front of him as a shield. "Talk loud, make them hear you," he demanded.

Siedell stepped over the two dead guards lying on the small platform, Anson at his back with his cocked revolver at the base of his skull.

He leaned out of the car and shouted down at his men running alongside the train, "Don't do anything rash. This man will kill me!"

His words caused most of the men to fall down from a run and slow to a halt as he went past them. They stood watching, their guns slumped in their hands.

"What now?" one man asked as the train swerved onto the length of the switching tracks.

"Over here, damn it!" shouted Arnold Inman from the open doors of the livery barn. "Get your horses and let's get after that train!" Behind him in the light of the oil lanterns, men busily saddled and bridled their horses. Others checked their revolvers, their rifles. Some were still stepping into their boots. Yet even as the men prepared themselves, over a hundred yards down the rails the train slowed almost to a halt and uncoupled the car carrying the detectives.

The four men turned and ran toward the livery barn, following Inman's tone of authority. They heard gunfire behind them as the men aboard the detectives' car jumped down from the slowing train. They immediately ran alongside the Pullman and started firing.

"They don't listen to you very well, do they, King Curtis?" Anson said, back inside the car now, bullets thumping against the wooden sides. The gunfire sent Violet sitting straight up in bed, grabbing a sheet on her way and holding it in front of herself.

"They won't stop, Anson. They'll keep following you," Siedell said. "These men are professional detectives, not some desert riffraff."

"Too bad for them." Anson jerked him by his cuffed hand over to a side gun-port window. As Siedell looked out through the small slot, Ape and his Gatling gun started firing on the men from overhead, chopping them down and leaving them dead in his wake. Empty shells bounced atop the Pullman car and rained down its sides.

"Damn you!" shouted Siedell. He tried to turn and grab Anson by his throat, but Anson stopped him with a blow from his gun barrel across his forehead.

Siedell staggered, dazed. Anson grabbed him by his lapel and shook him hard.

"Don't you pass out on me, King Curtis!" he shouted. "We've got a hard ride ahead!" He laughed in jubilation. Then he settled himself and asked, "How far does this rail spur go?"

Siedell, his mind addled by the gun barrel, tried to shake his head to clear it.

"You p-planned all this . . . without knowing how far we can go?" he asked as if finding Anson's methods faulty.

"Never mind how I planned it," Anson said. "I ask the questions here, not you." He shook the gun in Siedell's face. "Tell me how far, and don't lie about it."

"Thirty miles—a little more," Siedell said. "It's my

longest spur. It goes past two mining compounds and ends at Gnat."

"My man tells me we have enough wood to make it that far running hard," Anson said.

"I don't know—probably," Siedell said. "I own this railroad. I'm not the fireman—"

"Hey, over there, you two," Violet cut in on them from the bed, above the gunfire, the bullets thumping the outside walls. "Are we about through here, then? Should I go ahead, clean up and get dressed?" she asked drunkenly.

The slowed train gave a hard bump as outside, between cars, one of the three men Anson brought along uncoupled the detectives' car from the Pullman.

"No, don't *get dressed*," said Anson. "Get the hell *out of here* before the train speeds up again."

Violet stood up with the sheet around her and gave Siedell a piercing look.

"What about my money?" she asked bluntly.

"*Jesus*, Violet, I'll have it sent to you," Siedell said. "Please get out while there's time."

"Huh-uh, I don't think so," she said, shaking her head. "I want my money."

"Violet, I'm being kidnapped here," said Siedell, trying to make her understand.

But Violet would have none of it.

"All the more reason . . . ," she said, extending her hand and wiggling her fingers toward Siedell as the train began regaining speed. "I never should have trusted you. I should have gotten paid first—"

Her words cut short as a bullet from Anson's gun

thumped into the mattress and sent up a swirl of feathers. Violet jumped and cursed at Anson.

"Get out of here, woman!" he shouted, and fired again. Another puff of feathers kicked up as Violet ran from the Pullman car, cursing loudly. Still issuing a stream of vulgarity over her shoulder as she crossed the bloody platform, she leaped out and down to the ground, the sheet billowing in the air behind her. As she hit the ground, more detectives ran to her; back at the livery barn mounted men rode quickly toward the train. But they held their fire, following Arnold Inman's orders.

"Well, then, we're on our way," Anson said with a grin as the train increased its speed into the black-purple night. Behind them the gunfire had stopped altogether; so had the Gatling gun above them. He reached down and unlocked the handcuffs and pitched them aside. "Now, we can have a drink and behave like gentlemen," he said to Siedell, his revolver slumping only a little. "Or we can spend the trip me slicing pieces off you and throwing them out the window."

Siedell stepped warily over to the silver tray.

"What's your pleasure, Bo?" he said. "Or do you prefer I call you Mr. Anson?"

"Rye," Anson said, nodding at the tray. "You can call me whatever suits you. Just don't try nothing stupid that'll get you killed." He glanced out the side window through the gun port and saw lantern light growing smaller behind them. Yet he still saw riders' black silhouettes against the purple night. The horses were doing their best, but he knew the animals couldn't keep

up with them for very long. Behind Siedell's riders, he
knew his men would be coming, pacing their animals,
taking their time. Caught between the Gatling gun and
his gunmen, the detectives and their worn-out horses
wouldn't stand a chance.

The Ranger first sighted Max Bard and his men as they
moved two at a time across a narrow stream deep in a
pine-filled valley. He watched the riders slip across the
stream, long-rider style, he told himself, two of them
riding double. He gazed out and down through his
battered telescope. After what he considered a long
period of time, he saw the last of the men had made it
across. Still he waited. A full three minutes later a
single rider came forward from the pine cover and
crossed stealthily, looking back over his shoulder.

That's all of them, he told himself. He closed the scope
and scooted backward across the flat he lay on. Out of
sight from the valley below, he stood up and dusted his
trouser knees and the front of his shirt.

"It's Bard and his guerrillas," he said to the two
sheriffs who sat atop their horses, the woman holding
the reins to Sam's copper dun. "Looks like they're following Anson and his men the same as us. They
must've just got onto his trail from the other side of
these hills. We might have to deal with them first if the
opportunity presents itself." He looked back and forth
between the two as if asking for their thoughts.

"I say take what comes to us first," said Sheriff
Deluna. "They're all the same element. Besides, it's not
every day that you run into Max Bard and his gang.

When you do see them, like as not they're headed to rob something."

Sam looked at Sheriff Stone.

"She's right. Let's take them down while they're within reach," Stone said, sounding better than he had for the past two days.

Deluna turned in her saddle and looked him up and down with a question.

"I'm up to it, Sheriff Deluna, if that's what you're wondering," Stone said. Sam noted the faded trousers and shirt he'd given Stone to wear, both items coming from down deep in his saddlebags. He was still missing a boot, but with any luck Sam figured he'd shoot his way into one somewhere.

"I'm just checking on you, Sheriff," Deluna said. "I know you've got the guts for it. I've seen your gun work."

"Then what's your concern, Sheriff?" Stone asked quietly. "That we'll get into a gunfight and I'll run off howling at the moon?" He offered the trace of a grin, which told Deluna and the Ranger that he was back to himself.

"All right," the Ranger said, getting back to business. "The new rail spur from Gun Hill ends twelve miles ahead. It might be that Bard and his men are headed there to rob it—make up for what they missed last time." He took the reins from Deluna and stepped atop the dun. "If we can skirt this hillside and get ahead of them, there's a blind pass up ahead, with another stream running through it. They didn't stop for water here. They'll have to stop there. It's a good place for us to set up a trap."

Sam turned his copper dun and put it forward, the two sheriffs flanking him. They rode hard, gaining ground on Bard's gang by taking the higher, more treacherous trails. These were trails that had evolved from ancient game paths, routes worn into rocky ground by centuries of elk, deer and the four-footed predators who'd stalked them.

By early afternoon the three had ridden back down a steep gravelly path leading to the main trail. There, beside a rolling stream that pooled against a half circle of tall chimney stone, they watered their horses to keep the animals from growing restless and nickering at the wrong time at the scent of the cool stream. With the horses watered, the three checked the animals' hooves and forelegs and led them out of sight and waited.

No more than a half hour had passed when a drift of dust rose above the sound of horses' hooves moving at a light and steady pace. The Ranger watched as a single rider came into sight, slowed his horse and scouted along the edge of the water hole. Before the rider reached the spot around the half-circling edge where Sam and the sheriffs had watered their mounts, Max Bard and the rest of his gang rode up off the trail through a maze of rock and stopped.

Before the guerrillas could get down from their saddles, the scout stopped his horse sharply where hoofprints of the Ranger's and the sheriffs' mounts stood in the soft wet ground. As the scout leaned a little in his saddle and stared down, Sam whispered to himself, "He's seen us," and he cocked his rifle around the edge of a large rock.

"Max! It's an ambush!" shouted the scout, already jerking his horse around and batting his boots to its sides. But he didn't get ten feet before a shot from Deluna's rifle felled him, horse and all, in a tumbling entanglement of man, horse, rock and dirt.

As the first shot rang out, Sam stepped into sight long enough to draw a bead on Max Bard's chest at a distance too close to miss. Bard and his men, having spread out on the way in to the water's edge, now turned quickly as one, guns coming up, firing at the sound of Deluna's rifle shot. As Sam squeezed the trigger on Max Bard, he saw Bard look his way and quickly raise his rifle toward him.

As both lawman and outlaw drew their beads, Parker Fish's horse sprang into Sam's sights. The shot intended for Bard hit Fish high in his right side and sent him sprawling from his saddle onto the ground. Bard pulled his shot and grabbed Fish as the wounded gunman struggled to his feet. With Fish behind him, Bard spurred his horse away.

Bullets from Bard's men pinged and thumped and ricocheted off rock and pine where the Ranger and the two sheriffs had positioned themselves a few yards apart above the water hole. Even as the gunmen fired they rode back the way they'd ridden in. Sam tried to get Bard in his sights again, but Bard was already gone. As the men rode away in Bard's wake, another gunman caught a bullet through his neck. Leaning deep in his saddle, the wounded man lost control of his mount and crashed headlong into a young supple pine as the spooked animal swerved from beneath him. The pine bowed with the impact of the man's weight and launched him twenty feet backward, flailing in the air.

Seeing the last of the men ride down out of sight, Sam stood up and looked around warily. So did Deluna and Stone. All three stood with their guns smoking in their hands. To their left the sound of horses' hooves fell away down the hillside.

"Anybody hit?" Sam asked. Both sheriffs shook their heads as Sam looked at them in turn.

Stone called out, "Three down. Two dead and one looking badly wounded." He nodded at the two bodies lying strewn on the ground in pools of blood. One of the dead men's horses had settled and stood knee deep in the water drinking. Sam took close note of the dusty, sweaty animal. The outlaws' horses were worn and thirsty. This was not the time to let up on the gang, he told himself. This was time to press them hard.

"Three's a good start," Deluna said, stepping from behind cover, down through the rocks and brush. "Too bad Bard's not lying here somewhere."

Sam and Stone followed suit, stepping down toward the water hole. At the water's edge Deluna stood reloading her rifle. She also noted the thirsty horse standing in the water hole drinking. So did Stone. The three of them gave each other a knowing look.

"I'll get our horses," Sam said. "While we've got them on the run, we need to stay right on them."

Chapter 19

Max Bard and his men didn't stop until they reached a lower trail crossing a stretch of sand flats that led toward the mining town of Gnat. They had missed their chance to water their horses. Bard realized it had been a mistake not stopping at the stream they'd crossed in the pine valley. But it was too late to do anything about it now. The horses were tired and thirsty. They would have to push the animals on to the little mining town. At the same time they had to hold off the three ambushers who would now be dogging them hard, knowing their horses would soon be giving out on them.

"You figure it was the Ranger?" Cross asked Bard, all of them bunched up behind a boulder at the edge of the sand flats.

"No *figuring* to it," Bard replied, gazing back along the uphill trail. "I saw him plain as day—saw his sombrero."

"Anybody can wear a sombrero," said Fish, gripping the bullet hole high up in his side under his arm.

Bard just looked at him as Worley, Cross and Rudy Bowlinger took a closer look at his wound. Mallard Trent stood off to the side, a newly rolled cigarette between his lips. He held the reins to the horse he shared with Bowlinger.

"It's the *Ranger*, Parker," Bard said, leaving no room for further discussion. "Him and whoever's with him sprung a trap on us. I fell for it when I never should have let it happen."

"Gant was scouting," said Worley. "Maybe he should have said something sooner."

"Gant was still scouting the water hole," said Bard. "We should have waited until he signaled us in. These horses were so thirsty I didn't hold us back."

Cross stared off along the trail and chuffed under his breath.

"While you're busy blaming yourself, try this on. You or I should've made sure we stopped and watered these cayuses back in the valley."

"That's right, one of us should have," Bard said, his voice taking on a sharp edge. "I don't like losing men."

"Nobody does," said Cross, "but that's the game we're in." He looked over at Parker Fish and said testily, "Are you going to make it? Because if you're not we can't be blowing a horse out carrying you."

"Pardon the hell out of me for getting shot, Holbert Lee," Fish said in a pained voice. "Hell yes, I'm going to make it."

Bard looked all around at the men, Worley and Bowlinger working quick, tearing a larger opening in Fish's shirt around the bullet hole. Bowlinger stuffed a wadded bandanna inside the shirt and Fish clamped his upper arm on it.

"There, that's all I needed," he said. "Anybody thinks I ain't going to make it doesn't know spit about ol' *Fish* here." He gave a weak pained grin and struggled up onto his feet. Dark blood oozed from his lips. He tried to lick it away, but there was too much of it.

"Let's get at it," he said.

"*Jesus,*" Cross whispered to himself. His hand streaked up with his revolver in it and bucked once as a bullet tore through Fish's heart and sent him backward to the ground.

The men froze, staring, stunned. The horses stirred but settled quickly.

"Anybody got anything to say about it?" Cross said flatly. "You all saw he wasn't going to make it. I'd've wanted him to do the same thing for me without me having to ask."

Bard let out a tight breath and looked down at Fish's body, his bloody chest, his wide-open eyes staring at the white-hot sky.

"Drag him out of sight," he said. "Let's get the hell out of here." He turned and stepped up into his saddle as Bowlinger and Worley took Fish by his limp arms and pulled him across the rocky ground. Trent grabbed the reins to Fish's horse and swung up into the saddle, still holding Bowlinger's horse for him.

Cross replaced the spent cartridge in his smoking gun and shoved the warm barrel back into his holster. He stepped up into his saddle and reined his horse over beside Bard.

"That's something for us to remember when we get Burrack in our sights," he said. The two nudged their horses forward, the other three gunmen mounting quickly and following behind them.

They rode on.

In the afternoon as they reached the crest of a rocky rise, they looked a short ways down onto Gnat, seeing the new rails running along the rear edge of the small mining town. On the other side of Gnat, a high hillside stood honeycombed with darkened mine shaft openings that looked out above the distant sand flats.

"All right," Bard said, "let's get watered and get out of here in a hurry."

"I say we stick tight right here," said Bowlinger, no longer riding double. "Kill the Ranger and whoever's with him. Like as not it's that female law dog and that drunken wolf-man, Stone." He held his horse back as if refusing to go any farther while the others passed him down a narrow trail into town.

"You stick tight here, Rudy," Cross said, moving his thirsty horse past him. "Go ahead, kill the Ranger and catch up to us."

"You think I'm scared?" Bowlinger called out to him.

"Ride down and water your horse, Rudy," Bard demanded back over his shoulder. "When the time's right we'll take care of the Ranger, not a minute before."

On their way down toward the town, they heard the roar of the locomotive; they saw the roiling black smoke as the big engine rose on the sand flats and came boring over the barren desert against the afternoon sky. The riders stopped for a moment and settled their horses to the jarring earth beneath their hooves. They stared as the engine pulling a single Pullman car barreled closer.

"Trent," said Max Bard, "ain't that Curtis Siedell's private car?"

"Yes, it is," said Mallard Trent, his horse sitting beside Bard, the five riders lined abreast. "We heard talk that Siedell was coming. I figured it to be just rumors. But it looks like he's here."

"Talk about a stroke of luck!" Bard reined his horse sidelong to the coming train as he pulled up a telescope, stretched it out and raised it to his eye. "Wouldn't you say this thing is coming awfully fast?"

"Looks like it to me," Trent said.

"Hell yes, it's coming too fast," Cross put in. "One wrong move it'll plow that platform down and grind this town into the dirt."

They watched tensely as the train rumbled alongside the platform and kept going. Freight handlers dived out of the way as the platform quaked and bucked underfoot. A mailbag hanging for pickup exploded as the engine, rocking back and forth on the rails, clipped it and sent its contents spraying out in all directions.

"It's not stopping," Bard said, watching through the telescope.

"It's not even slowing down!" said Worley.

They kept their excited horses settled as the train rolled on past them and continued out onto the flat.

"How far do these rails go?" Bard asked Trent.

"Three or four miles," Trent said. "They always leave a few miles of tracks to add to later on."

Bard turned to the others. "I've got to know if Siedell's in that Pullman car."

"He's in it," Trent said confidently.

"What makes you think he is?" Bowlinger asked as they put their horses forward down toward the straight line of rails.

"Because it doesn't go anywhere without him," Trent said before Max Bard could answer. "Siedell never lets it out of his sight."

Bard stared after the train as it rumbled on, growing smaller, sinking over a sand rise.

"Holbert Lee," he said, "you three go into Gnat. Water your horses—or get some fresh ones, whichever is quicker. Trent, you come with me."

"Whoa," said Bowlinger. "What about the Ranger?"

"If he shows up, shoot him," said Bard.

"Oh, shoot him, just like that," said Bowlinger.

"A while ago that's all you wanted to do, Rudy," said Bard. He looked at Cross and saw the concerned look on his face. "Don't worry, I'll be all right. The colonel's stallion's got plenty of run left in him." He rubbed the big stallion's damp withers and looked at Trent and nodded at the horse beneath him. "What about Fish's horse?"

"It'll do," Trent said. "If it don't, I'll find myself another one."

The two booted their mounts and rode away as the train sank out of sight over the edge of a sandy rise.

When the end of the tracks came into sight out on the desert floor, Curtis Siedell leaned out over the platform's handrail and stared ahead through the softened glare of afternoon sunlight. He saw a single rider seated atop his horse holding the lead rope to a string of saddled horses. Behind Siedell, Bo Anson chuckled and puffed on a cigar he'd helped himself to from the businessman's private supply.

Siedell's left hand was cuffed to the handrail. He'd been allowed to get dressed and pull his boots on before walking up the engine and back.

Anson reached around and unlocked the cuffs. He spoke above the rumble and roar of the locomotive as Siedell turned to face him, also with a cigar in hand.

"As you can see, I already knew how far it was to the end of the line," Anson said. "I just wanted to know if you'd lie to me." He grinned as he nodded in the direction of the rider and the string of horses. "I've had my plans laid from the get-go."

"And if I had lied to you?" Siedell asked.

"Instead of us smoking cigars together, I might have put one or two out in your ears," Anson said, still with the grin. "But it didn't go that way, and I'm as glad as you are about that."

As the locomotive began to slow down, Anson motioned Siedell toward the Pullman car door with his cocked revolver. Siedell walked inside the car and stopped, waiting to hear what Anson's next order would be.

"Get your duster and hat on," Anson said. "We're heading through some uphill country tonight." As he spoke, the single-car train slowed more. A slight screech of metal brakes came from under the engine.

"May I ask where?" said Siedell.

"No, you *may* not," Anson said, mocking him. Then he gave a dark chuckle and wagged his gun barrel toward the line of hills ahead to their right, along the border. "Up there," he said. "We're going to get high up and out of sight—wait for the message to get to your flunkies that we've got a wire around your neck. We'll tell them we'll start twisting it tight if they don't come up with what we want."

"Which is . . . ?" Siedell let his words trail. The train slowed more, coasting along on its own now.

"Never you mind, King Curtis," said Anson.

"Damn it, man," Siedell said. "I keep telling you I hold the purse strings. Tell me how much, we'll settle this thing and go on about our business!"

"I'm not just doing this for the money, King Curtis," said Anson. "I want everybody to know what I did. I want folks to know that while your people were getting ransom money together, two men showed up with the bodies of Bard and his pals draped over their saddles." His eyes gleamed with madness. "Won't that be dandy?" he said. "Nobody will know it was me collecting their reward until it's all over—too late to do anything about it."

Siedell only stared at him, not knowing what to say.

They both turned at the sound of Ape Boyd stepping in through the front door, a telescope in his thick hand. The train slowed down to a crawl.

"Jim Purser made it here with the horses," Ape said. "Looks like somebody winged him. Want me to go on and kill him?" he added bluntly.

"No, Ape, for God sakes," said Anson. "Jim did what he was supposed to do. Why would we kill him?"

Ape shrugged and eyed Siedell up and down as his next possible target.

"Just thought I'd ask," he said. "I looked back along the rails. Nobody's caught up with us yet. And I broke down the big gun. I'm ready to carry it down and load it on a horse."

"Good, then," said Anson. "Get Holt and the others ready." He glanced at Siedell. "Tell them our little train ride is just about over—"

Before he got the words out of his mouth, one of the men, Dan Brody, stepped inside the car.

"Bo," he cut in, sounding urgent. "We've got two men following us, riding hard. Holt and Jenkins are keeping an eye on them."

"Detectives? They've caught up to us so soon?" Anson said. He gave Siedell a curious look.

"That's impossible," Siedell said confidently. "Horses don't stand a chance against iron and steam."

"It's not detectives," said Brody. "Holt said it's Max Bard, and some fella he's never seen."

Anson looked concerned, but only for a second. Then his face split with laughter.

"This is too perfect," he said. "I thought I'd have to lure Max Bard here—get word to him that I have you under lock and key." He shook his head as he laughed. "How did he know? Do you hombres smell each other coming?"

"Want me to go kill them?" Ape asked, getting excited all over again.

"No, Ape, not just yet," said Anson. "Go load up and let's get moving. I'll give Max just a quick whiff of his ol' pal here when we ride away. That'll draw him up to where I want him." He looked at Siedell and asked, "Does that sound like a good idea to you, King Curtis?"

Anson saw Siedell look a little frightened for the first time since the whole bloody business had started.

"Listen to me, Anson. I don't want Max Bard around me," he said, his voice different now, sounding more serious than before. "If he gets near me he'll kill me. Then you'll get no ransom, maybe no reward money either, if he gets away after I'm dead."

"Take it easy, King Curtis," Anson said. "This has all been thought out and is going as planned, except for ol' Max showing up so soon. I still don't understand that." He shook his head as if in amazement and continued, saying, "I'm not letting anything happen to you, unless you try to get feisty on me and I have to put a bullet in your head."

"I'm not going to try anything stupid, Anson. See to it that you don't either."

See to it . . . ?

Anson gave him a hard, sharp stare.

"I'm sorry," Siedell said quickly, wanting to take the sting out of his prior statement. "But this changes things for me. As far as I'm concerned you can consider me your partner until Max Bard is dead."

Anson kept his temper in check.

"He will be real soon, King Curtis," he said. "You can count on it."

Chapter 20

At the same rise where Max Bard and his remaining men had stopped their horses an hour earlier, Sam and the two sheriffs reined their horses down and looked at the hoofprints that had led them there. The tracks they'd followed had split up. Two riders had taken off down toward the rails on the sand flats below. Three more sets headed off and down toward Gnat in the opposite direction. On a warm afternoon breeze the smell of wood smoke wafted up from along the tracks.

"They split up right here. Why?" Stone queried the Ranger and Deluna. "Two of them rode off following a train?" he asked with a puzzled look on his face. He now wore Parker Fish's boots, having followed the dried blood and found Fish's body in the rocks.

Sam sat staring off in the direction of Gun Hill. He saw a heavy drift of dust looming upward on the distant horizon.

"Good question," he said quietly. "The answer might be riding this way." He reached back under his bedroll and pulled out his telescope. Deluna and Stone also studied the rising dust.

"That's a lot of horses coming," Deluna said in a wary tone.

"Can you make them out yet, Ranger?" Stone asked Sam.

"I can," Sam replied, gazing out through the lens. "From the black suits and tan dusters, I make five of them out to be detectives." He paused and then said, "Detectives in some big trouble."

"Trouble?" Stone asked.

"Their horses are blown," Sam said, still studying the situation closely. "They're leading them, trying to rest them some."

"That's a lot of dust for five men leading tired horses," Deluna offered.

"It's not their dust," Sam said, still looking. "The dust belongs to a bunch of riders farther back behind them." He took the lens from his eyes and handed it to her. She looked out and found the riders and almost gasped.

"The detectives are going to get ridden down and slaughtered," she said. "We can't let that happen." She lowered the lens and looked at Stone and the Ranger.

"Come on," Sam said, already turning his dun toward Gnat's town limits below them. "If these five don't get fresh horses and extra guns real quick, they're dead."

The three rode hard down the sand rise and across a short stretch of ground into the small mining town. On the street, townspeople stood looking off at the heavy dust drifting across the sand flats. Seeing the badges on Sam's and Sheriff Deluna's chests, the people drew close while the three reined their horses down outside the gates of a livery barn corral.

"Is there something we can do to help, Ranger?" one townsman asked, knowing the Ranger and the woman sheriff being there must have something to do with the coming riders. They eyed Stone as if he might have been the Ranger's prisoner.

"This is Sheriff Deluna from Resting and Sheriff Stone from Big Silver. I'm Ranger Burrack," he said quickly. "We need fresh horses for some detectives who are about to get killed out there." As he spoke he leaped down from his saddle and threw the corral gate open, Deluna and Stone right beside him.

An elderly livery hostler hurried forward from the barn, hearing the Ranger.

"Take what you need, Ranger," he called out. "Is that Apache coming out there?"

"No," Sam said. "Outlaws."

"Just as bad these days," the liveryman said. "There goes some right now. I knew when I saw them." He pointed Sam's attention east of town where Cross, Worley and Rudy Bowlinger raced away upward toward a pine- and rock-covered hillside.

"They came here for fresh horses," Sam said, "and now they've got them."

"I wouldn't have sold them horses except they were pushy as hell about it," the old man said.

Sam knew they had no time to think about the Bard Gang right now. He walked past the livery tender and began stringing horses with a coil of rope he took from around a corral post.

"Keep tabs, mister," he said to the livery tender. "We'll be back to settle up with you."

"Obliged if you do, Ranger," the liveryman said. "These are all good horses, straight here from across the border—not stolen though, *no, sir!*" he added quickly, realizing he was talking to a lawman.

"I understand," Sam said, hurrying, getting the string of horses ready to go. He pulled a knife from his boot well, sliced through the rope and threw the rest of the coil to Deluna and Stone. "Each of you take a couple of separate strings in case we lose some."

"Good idea," Stone said. As he let out some rope and ran it around a horse's neck, a young boy tugged at his trousers. Stone looked down at him.

"My pa says you can turn yourself into a wildcat and you kill chickens," the boy said.

"*A wildcat?*" Stone said in disbelief. "Your pa's crazy, son! I used to turn into *a wolf* and *kill sheep*. But I quit doing it. Tell your pa I said so." He looked up from the boy and around at the faces staring at him. "Did you all hear me? *I quit,*" he said in a raised voice. He kept working with the rope as he spoke, slicing a length off the coil for himself and pitching the remaining coil to Deluna.

On the flats the five detectives tried pulling their thirsty, worn-out horses a little faster. But the horses had nothing more to give. Seeing the large cloud of dust, and having heard the sporadic gunfire behind each time another of their ranks had given up and fallen behind, the detectives knew what awaited them if they fell back. So they struggled on. These were younger detectives, less experienced men who'd only recently joined Siedell's security force.

"Somebody . . . ought to be bullwhipped," a young man named Riley Soots panted, "thinking we could . . . keep up with a train on horseback." His wire-rim spectacles were coated with thick sand dust.

"Save your breath, Soots," said a slightly older detective named Dallas Carson. He looked back at the dust. "I expect a bullwhipping wouldn't mean nothing . . . to the man who gave that order right now." He jerked his horse along by its reins, seeing the outline of the riders move into sight ahead of the rising dust.

"Jesus! Here they come," another young detective cried out, seeing the figures closing in on them.

"Take these horses down! Get behind them!" shouted Carson. "It's our only chance!" As he spoke, the first bullet from an outlaw's rifle streaked past, followed by the sound of it. Carson twisted his horse's head as he tapped its foreleg with his boot. The tired horse staggered down onto its knees, then rolled over onto its side.

"Gather up into a circle," Carson shouted in a parched and weary voice. "Hurry now, men!"

As more shots zinged past them, the detectives did as they were told. With their horses' bodies providing cover, they heard the gunfire grow heavier, the bullets right above their heads whining sharply through the dry desert air. Carson counted fourteen rifle cartridges in a leather pouch he'd hung over his shoulder. He knew the other men were no better fixed for ammunition than himself.

"Hold your fire until they are right upon us, men!" he shouted, looking all around their small circle. He jerked a small pair of binoculars from his coat pocket and wiped dust from them. To the rear, he saw another rise of dust, more riders pounding toward them.

"They have us surrounded!" he shouted. But then, raising the binoculars to his eyes, he found the figures in the circling lens and caught the glint of the badge on the Ranger's chest, the silver-gray sombrero. "Wait, these are not Anson's men. It's that Ranger, Burrack, from Nogales. He's bringing help—they're bringing us horses!" But even as the men heard the good news, the firing from Anson's men grew heavier. A horse let out a loud grunt, then fell limp as a bullet struck its neck just below its head. Another horse screamed in pain as a bullet sliced through its saddle and bored into its back. One by one, the rest of the horses whinnied in pain.

Even through the heavy gunfire, the Ranger and the two sheriffs heard the sound of the dying animals ahead of them. The three pounded on toward the hapless detectives.

"Move to my right, start firing," he called out, handing Deluna the two-horse string he led beside him. Both Stone and Deluna knew they were out of range, especially Stone with only his big Colt; but they did as the Ranger told them to do, both of them also leading fresh horses beside them.

As the sheriffs swerved their horses to the Ranger's right and began firing, Sam slid his dun down to a halt and quickly drew the scoped rifle from under his bed-

roll. With a firm tap of his knees and a twist of the tightened reins in his hands, he brought the animal down
onto its side. He stepped off the horse expertly at the
last second and dropped down behind it. As heavy firing continued, he leveled the scoped rifle out across the
dun's side. He took a second to rub a gloved hand over
the dun's flank; then he took aim through the scope and
locked on to one of the riders at the front of the outlaws.

The man, Marvin Poole, flew from his saddle in a
spray of blood. The riders near him veered away as
Poole's blood stung and splattered their faces. One of
the veering riders, Randy Meeks, had barely got his horse
straightened when the Ranger's second bullet raised an
identical spray that sent him down, horse and all. Man
and animal rolled in a tangle of limbs, reins and leather
as dust billowed around them. Seeing their two side-
kicks fall within seconds of each other, the remaining
gunmen dropped back, reining their horses down and
circling away.

"To hell with all this," Lyle Cady shouted at his
brother, Ignacio. "If they want to shoot us, they'll have
to shoot us in the back." The two turned their horses
and rode straight away from the other gunmen. "To
hell with Stone and the bribe money. Don't stop till
we're out of the territory!"

Seeing the two racing away across the sand, other
gunmen broke away and took off. A gunman named
Frank Castor, whom Anson had put in charge of the
riders, had to shout above the gunfire from the pinned-
down detectives and the three riders farther back who
had come to their aid.

"Split up. There's only five left!" he said. "We did what Bo wanted! Get out of here!"

Even as Castor shouted, one of the men flew side-long from his saddle, a bullet painting the dusty air with a spiraling ribbon of blood. The remaining men had seen enough. Ducked low in their saddles, they jerked their horses around and pounded away, Castor right alongside them, holding his hat down on his head. He only glanced back once, past the detectives, at the black dot of man and horse lying prone in the distance.

Wise decision . . .

Sam raised himself onto his knees behind the dun and waved a hand back and forth, signaling Stone and Deluna to stop shooting. As they stopped, and in turn as the detectives' gunfire waned, they all watched Anson's men ride farther way in their own billowing dust. The detectives were too spent and thirsty to celebrate their victory; they slumped onto their dead horses and for a moment lay as still as stone.

Sam rubbed the copper dun's side again, in appreciation. Then he stood, reins and rifle in hand, and nudged his boot to the dun's rump.

"Let's go, Copper," he said. He threw his leg over the saddle as the horse stood up under him.

After he met Stone and Deluna on the way, the three rode to where the detectives were starting to stand up and look all around, in disbelief that they were still alive.

"Man, are we glad to see you, Ranger!" said Dallas Carson, dusting himself off. His horse was one of the few left alive, yet the worn-out animal took two tries at rising onto its hooves as Castor tugged its reins. "We were goners, sure enough."

Sheriff Deluna rode in close and handed a full canteen down to him. Carson took it, uncapped it with a shaky hand and took a long swig.

"Obliged, ma'am," he said, out of breath. "Best water I've tasted in my life." He wiped a sleeve across his parched lips and passed the canteen off to eager hands.

"How'd you detectives manage to get yourselves dogged so hard out here?" Sam asked, gazing back in the direction of Gun Hill.

"We got ourselves in a tight spot trying to catch up to Curtis Siedell's train," Carson said.

"You can't keep up with a train, Detective," Stone said, looking the man up and down.

"I know that," said Carson. "But they captured Siedell at gunpoint. We had to try—not knowing we had gunmen ready to ride us down as soon as we spent out our horses." He looked back in the direction the riders had fled in. "Bo Anson had this whole thing planned. With us dead, he'd have nobody to stop him"—he looked up at Sam and the sheriffs—"except you three, I reckon. He wasn't counting on the law getting into this. Railroads deliver their own justice."

"Not this time," Sam said. He gave Deluna a nod; she took Stone's horse string, her own and the string Sam had handed her, and stepped forward and gave the horses to Carson.

"I don't know what to say," Carson said, his head lowered a little. "We've still got to catch up to Siedell.

Knowing Anson, he might cut his throat just for the fun of it."

"He's not going to harm Siedell," Sam said, "not for a while anyway. He didn't go to all this trouble for nothing. He'll try to get his hands on Siedell's money first."

"I figured that too," said Carson. "I'm just talking about the worst that can happen, dealing with a man like Anson."

Sam considered it for a moment. He hadn't seen Max Bard among the riders galloping away from Gnat's livery barn on fresh horses. Bard had to be the one who'd split off and followed the train as it sped through town.

"Sheriffs," he said to both Stone and Deluna, "I'd be obliged if you'll stay here and help these men back to town."

"Wait a minute, Ranger," said Stone, seeing Sam ready to turn the dun back in the direction of Siedell's train. "Where are you going?"

Sam just gave him a look, as if saying he should know without asking. Deluna sat watching, listening.

"I'll go," Stone offered. "I'm back on my game."

"I know you are, Sheriff," Sam said. "But we're a long way from your graze. This is Ranger jurisdiction."

"You're pulling jurisdiction on me?" Stone said.

"I've seen how you handle that Colt, Sheriff," Deluna cut in quickly. "Stay here with me, in case these gunmen come back."

"They won't be coming back—" Carson said before catching himself. Seeing the look Deluna gave him, he added, "I mean they could, though, any minute."

Stone looked back and forth between Sam and the woman sheriff.

"I know when I'm being *had*," he said, letting out a breath. He gave the Ranger a nod. "Be safe."

Sam returned the nod. With a touch on the reins, he rode away across the loose sand.

After escorting the detectives back to Gnat without incident, the two sheriffs liveried their horses and took rooms in an adobe hostel off the main street of town. Sheriff Deluna excused herself after a meal of red beans, goat meat and flatbread, and went off to her room for the night. Stone, left to his own company, retired to his room, but in spite of his fatigue and his efforts to sleep, he found himself leaning on his elbows staring out an open window toward the lights of a cantina.

After a while he realized how badly he wanted a drink—no, *needed* a drink, he corrected himself. He thought about the Ranger, still out there on the trail, and realized how badly he wished he was out there himself. Out there was real life, law work, he reminded himself. *Here . . . ?* He gazed all around the empty streets, then around his empty, quiet room. He bit the inside of his dry lip in contemplation.

This was nothing, he told himself scornfully, just a quiet place where old men went to die. He gazed off in the direction of the trail the Ranger had ridden away on. *To hell with this.*

What seemed like only a moment later, he found himself atop his horse, leaning down from his saddle in the alley behind the cantina, taking three tall bottles of rye from the Mexican he'd sent inside to buy them for him. He gave the old Mexican a small gold coin for his trouble, then reached back and put two bottles in his saddlebags, resting the third in his lap.

"If you need help drinking them," the Mexican said, nodding at the bottles. He grinned in the darkness.

"*Gracias*," Stone said. "*Yo voy a beber solo.*"

"Ah, you drink alone," the Mexican translated in his border English. "But perhaps this one time—"

"*Cuando bebo me convierto en un lobo*," Stone said, cutting him short. He stared down at the Mexican to make sure he understood.

"*A wolf?*" the Mexican said, his eyes turning wary as he took a step backward.

"*Sí*, a wolf," Stone said with the same flat stare.

"*Por favor*," said the old man, raising a hand as he stepped farther way. "Go with God."

Stone turned his horse and a spare horse beside him and rode out of Gnat at full gallop. The Ranger had a head start on him, but he could close that gap by morning.

Chapter 21

—

Darkness had set in by the time Bo Anson and his men started leading their valuable prisoner up a thin trail, and it was well after midnight when they made it to the crest of the hill line and followed an even thinner path along a craggy ravine to a secluded mining shack. A three-quarter moon stood centered in a purple starlit sky, guiding their way once they left the lower shadowed hillside. A thousand yards back Ape Boyd and Dan Brody set up the Gatling gun to cover the trail.

At the shack, Anson, Purser, Holt and Sal Jenkins stepped down from their saddles, the first silver-gray hint of morning streaking on the eastern curve of the horizon. Jenkins held the reins to Curtis Siedell's horse.

"There, King Curtis, that wasn't so bad, was it?" Sal said to Siedell as the handcuffed businessman stepped down from his saddle beside him. "For an ol' guerrilla rider like yourself, this ride oughta be a walk in the park—"

"Stop goading him, Sal," said Anson, cutting Jenkins off. "Get yourself inside and build us a cook fire. We could all use some coffee." He and Holt took down supplies from one of the spare horses as Purser tied the string to a hitch rail.

"Right away, Bo," said Jenkins. He gave Siedell a shove from behind. "You heard him, King Curtis. Get inside, before I take a sharp stick to you." His tone sounded like that of a harsh schoolmaster threatening a child.

Siedell stumbled forward in the moonlight to the front porch of the shack and stood beside the closed door waiting for Jenkins to open it for him.

"Ha," said Jenkins, "your hands are cuffed, but your arms ain't broke." He stopped and stood facing Siedell a foot away. "Open the damn door your—"

His words stopped short as Siedell's cocked knee shot up into his crotch and raised him up on pigeon toes, letting out a pained, gasping squeak. With his hands cupped to his smashed testicles, Jenkins jack-knifed at the waist just in time for Siedell to grab his hair with both cuffed hands and slam him headlong into the thick plank door. The impact of skull on pine jarred the entire shack. Dust rose from the timbers.

Jenkins sprang backward off the door, off the porch and onto the hard ground at Anson's and Holt's feet. The two looked down at him, Anson shaking his head. He looked up at Siedell, who stood beside the door, which had swung open on its own. Seeing Siedell's attack as a test, Anson spoke to Holt over his shoulder.

"Gus, cut a finger off," he ordered Holt as he stepped up onto the porch and faced Siedell.

Siedell bristled but stood silent.

"Cut a *finger off*?" Holt said as if he hadn't heard

Anson correctly. He stepped up onto the porch beside Anson.

Anson stared at Siedell and said to Holt, "*Yes*, cut one off. Cut another one off every time he tries another stunt like that."

"You've watched this man goad me this whole ride," Siedell said, nodding toward Sal Jenkins. "I'm your prisoner, but I won't be mistreated."

"Holt . . . ?" Anson said.

Holt fumbled at his boot well for his knife. From the dirt Jenkins stumbled forward onto the porch, stiffly bowed in pain.

"Let me . . . do it!" he gasped, a hand still pressed to his crotch, a string of spittle bobbing from his lip. He lurched at Siedell, but Siedell sidestepped him. Jenkins stumbled through the open door; the darkness swallowed him up. The three men stood watching and listening as the hapless gunman crashed and yelped and tumbled about inside the shack.

When the banging sound of metal cookware and the thump and breaking of wooden furnishings settled into silence, Anson raised a finger at Siedell in warning.

"This time I let it go," he said. "Do anything like that again, I swear I'll kill you, ransom money or not."

Siedell stared at him. Anson was right; he had been testing him, seeing where he stood, what he could get by with.

"Then tell your gunnies I won't be manhandled," Siedell said.

Anson let out a breath, dismissing the matter.

"Get inside," he said, gesturing him into the dark

shack with his gun barrel. "Let's see if this idiot's killed himself."

As the three walked inside, Holt struck a match and looked around for a lantern. Finding one, he shook it, found it contained oil and lit it. As Holt raised the lantern Jenkins groaned and stood up against the wall, his face and shoulder covered with blood. He staggered forward, wiping a hand over his bloody brow, but he found no sympathy or concern from Anson.

"Get out of here, Sal, before I beat you myself," he said, giving Jenkins a shove. "You and Jim get down the trail a ways, take cover in the rocks. Max Bard will be coming. When you hear Ape's Gatling gun, be ready in case Bard gets past it."

Wiping his face, Jenkins staggered out the door and down onto the ground where Purser stood at the hitch rail looking the spare horses over.

"We're going back along the trail," Jenkins mumbled.

"What the hell happened in there?" Purser asked, seeing the gunman's bloody face. "Sounded like you jumped a bear."

"I'll jump his gawdamned bear," Jenkins cursed in his strained voice. He jerked a rifle from his saddle boot and stomped off along the moonlit trail. Purser shook his head, grabbed his rifle and walked along behind him.

In the darkness before dawn the Ranger and the copper dun climbed the hill trail. The trail was a narrow black ribbon that meandered along the rugged hillside, appearing in and out of sight slowly before his eyes. He kept the dun moving forward steadily but carefully, knowing that to veer to his right off that black ribbon would send him and the animal plunging to their deaths.

But you know what you're doing.

He rubbed the dun's withers with a gloved hand, hearing only the soft clop of hooves in the black-purple silence.

To his advantage he needed no torchlight to keep himself from losing the hoofprints of Max Bard and his partner's horses. He had spotted Max Bard and the other rider in the last hour of twilight the night before and followed them, knowing they were all headed to the same place. Bard rode with a torch flickering in the darkness, not realizing, or perhaps not caring, that he was seen or being followed.

Sam watched the firelight and kept a hundred yards or more between himself and the two outlaws at all times, knowing how much the sound of a horse's hooves carried in the still night air. When he lost sight of the torch for a longer than usual time, he stopped the dun and sat as quiet as a ghost, studying the darkness before him and listening for the slightest sound.

Suddenly the sight of rapid gunfire and the rattling explosions of the Gatling gun split the night. The Ranger flung himself from the saddle, grabbed the dun's reins and hurried off the trail to his left against the stone shelter of the upreaching hillside.

All around him bullets zipped, thumped, ricocheted and splintered pine saplings. But Sam knew the shooting was not directed at him. Someone up there had spotted Bard and the other rider. Whatever reason Bard had for following Anson, Sam didn't know. Whatever reason Anson had for opening fire on Bard was equally puzzling. But all of that aside, Curtis Siedell was up there—held for ransom, Sam told himself.

He crept forward into the blue-orange gunfire, leading the dun, keeping both himself and the horse against the sheltering stonework while the Gatling gun swept back and forth, spitting out what seemed to be an endless stream of lead and flame.

As he and the dun gained ground up the trail, the big gun stopped as suddenly as it had started. Reloading, Sam told himself. Yet as he and the horse continued moving forward again along the inner wall of the trail, he saw return rifle fire streak in the direction of the Gatling gun from not more than thirty yards in front of him. Bard and the other gunman, he told himself. Taking close note of the rifles' positions, he turned to the dun and pulled the animal even closer to. the stonework than before.

This is as far as you go, he said silently to the copper dun.

He tied the dun's reins around a stand of rock, rubbed its withers and moved away in the darkness, needing to gain as much ground as he could before the Gatling gun started again. By the time the reload was complete, he'd moved in closer under the fire. He found himself safer up close where the terrain fell away. From there he heard the bullets ping off rock and crackle and thump into pine limbs on the next hillside far back along the trail.

As the big gun swept off to the right, Sam saw the return rifle fire kick up dirt fifteen yards from him. When the rifles fell silent and the Gatling gunfire swept back across the hillside, he lay low to the ground and inched forward as bullets whistled above him.

When the Gatling gun once again stopped to reload, he saw Bard and the other rifleman spring forward in the grainy morning mist, over the rocks and hill foliage toward the Gatling's position. He also rose from his crouch and bounded along behind them. This time when the two dropped to the ground and he did the same, he heard a voice call out from the trail.

"You and your pard come on up and get yourselves a bellyful of lead, Max," the deep voice said.

"Don't worry, Ape," Bard called back. "I'm coming. I'll step over your dead carcass on my way to kill Curtis Siedell."

Ape let out a dark laugh.

"Get to it, Max!" he shouted, his words falling away under the blasts of the big gun as he cranked its handle. Lying flat, Sam searched the upper trail above the gun position and saw the glow of tiny embers racing skyward, skittering in a black swirl of chimney smoke. That was where he would find Curtis Siedell, he told himself as the Gatling gun swept past. That was where he needed to be. He lay poised and ready. When the Gatling gunfire moved away from him, he sprang to his feet in the silver-gray light and raced up through tangles of brush and rock toward the trail leading to the shack.

"There's that damn Ranger!" Bard said to Trent, seeing Sam's sombrero, his flapping duster moving away from them up the steep hillside. He raised his rifle toward the Ranger, but then he stopped and held his shot when Sam dropped out of sight among a stand of rock. "I'm not letting him get to Siedell before I do," he added. Even as the big gun started making another sweep of destruction, Bard sprang to his feet and ran up the steep slope. But on his way, his foot slipped on a loose stone. He lost his footing while all around him bullets streaked past like angry hornets.

"Jesus!" Trent shouted, seeing Bard was in trouble, watching him tumble backward down the hill amid the heavy gunfire. "Stay down, Max. I'm coming!" But Bard wasn't listening to him.

Trent sprang up in a crouch, fired three rapid shots at the big gun, then ran upward and dived into Bard as the addled gunman tried to stagger back onto his feet. Bullets whipped the hillside and whined past them both so close that Trent felt their hot breath as he pinned Bard down.

"My—my rifle . . . ," Bard said in a failing voice, reaching all around on the ground.

"Forget the rifle!" said Trent, pulling Bard against him. The two tumbled and rolled and slid back down the hill almost to the same spot where they'd started.

Trent, seeing that Bard had struck his head on the rocky ground and knocked himself out cold, grabbed him by both shoulders and dragged him over behind a rock. He could hear Ape Boyd screaming with wild mindless laughter as the gun hammered the rock and the ground all around them.

"To hell with this," Trent said to Bard, who lay unconscious, blood running down his neck from a large welt on the side of his head. "We're getting out of here."

When the heavy firing stopped, Trent mistakenly thought it was time for the Gatling gun to reload. He stood up quickly, holding Bard over his shoulder. But the minute he started to hurry away down the steep hillside, the gun roared to life again. The impact of the bullets hammering the ground at his feet sent Trent and Bard tumbling once again down the hill. Trent let out a yell as they crashed through brush and slid down loose gravel.

"I got them both!" Ape laughed and shouted. "I sent Max Bard straight to hell!" His voice echoed all along the surrounding hills and valleys.

Dan Brody stood tense beside him, trying to listen down the hillside for any signs of life. Ape continued laughing and whooping, the Gatling gun quiet in his hands.

"Jesus, Ape, shut the hell up," Brody said testily. "All I can hear is your mouth."

Ape fell silent, but stared sidelong at him.

"You told me to shut up?" he said as if having a hard time believing it.

"Yeah, but I didn't mean nothing by it," said Brody. "You were carrying on so, I couldn't hear what was going on down there."

Still staring hard at him, Ape said, "They're both dead, that's what's going on down there. I just killed Max Bard the way Bo told me to." He paused and said, "You saw them fall, didn't you?"

Dan Brody settled some.

"Yeah, I saw them fall, but that doesn't mean they're dead," he replied.

"They're dead," said Ape with dismissal. "Go look if you don't believe me."

"I'll just do that, to make sure," Brody said. "You keep me covered."

"You've got it, pard," said Ape, still elated at having seen the two men crumple in the fire of the big gun. "Watch your step going down there."

"Obliged, I will," said Brody. He stepped off the trail and started down the hillside. Before he'd gone thirty feet, Ape opened fire on him with the Gatling gun. Brody's back exploded and flew away in bloody pieces. The impact sent him flying forward, almost torn in two.

"You don't tell me to shut up, fool," Ape said down to the empty hillside, smoke curling up from the hot gun barrel.

The Ranger had heard the voices shout back and forth; he'd heard the laughter and the victory shout following the last long burst of gunfire. Then he'd heard silence for a moment, until it was shattered by a sudden shorter burst of gunfire. *That's it—kill each other*, he said to himself, speculating, glancing over his shoulder into the darkness as he pulled himself onto the trail and headed toward the smoking chimney.

Chapter 22

On the trail, moonlight was giving way to grainy morning. The Ranger moved quickly but quietly toward the black silhouette of the smoking chimney fifty yards in front of him. Behind him the Gatling gun had been silent for the past few minutes while he put more space between it and himself. Winchester in hand, he froze and then dropped down over the rocky edge when he heard a voice call out to him from less than sixty feet away.

"Ape . . . Dan Brody, is that y'all?" the voice said in the dim predawn light.

Sam lay as still as stone. From the same spot another voice came out of the darkness.

"Y'all best let us know it's you, pards," the second voice said. "Bo's tight as a steel hatband—wants us to shoot first and ask questions later out here."

Sam stayed down and silent. He heard the voices speak to each other in a lower tone.

"Don't be fooling around, now," one of the voices warned in the fading darkness. The two figures stood up from behind a waist-high rock, gray apparitions ris-

ing from some lower world. They looked all around.
Sam knew they weren't going to back off and decide
there was no one out here. Morning was coming; he
had to make his move.

Get ready, he told himself.

The other voice called out, "Jim's right, we've got no
time for foolishness—"

But the voice halted as the Ranger rose onto a knee,
took quick aim and sent a bullet through the figure's
chest.

As the man fell away Sam levered a fresh round and
swung the rifle at the gunman beside him. But the other
man dropped out of sight and fired from behind the
rock. The shot whizzed past the Ranger and raced
away in the darkness. Realizing that the Gatling gun
could join into whatever shooting fracas he found himself in, Sam stayed below the darker edge of the trail
and moved along thirty feet in the grainy light without
returning fire. From behind the rock two more shots
blossomed.

At a place where a dark rock shadow blacked out a
wide stretch of the gray trail, Sam stayed in a low
crouch and waited for a moment before venturing
through rock and brush toward the rifleman's position.
Leaving his rifle leaning against a rock, he moved along
silently with both hands free.

Climbing along the hillside on all fours like a
stalking cat, he wondered what had happened to the
Gatling gun, hoping it wasn't going to start firing any
second. If it did he had little chance of getting away
from both it and the rifleman here on the upper side of

the trail. Luckily the big gun didn't make its presence felt.

So much for luck.

He stopped on the hillside fifteen feet above the rifleman and stared down at him. As he kept his eyes on the man, he reached his right hand down and pulled a bowie-style game knife up from its sheath. With the knife poised and ready, he crawled a few feet farther down until he felt the steep ground slip under him. As a stream of dirt and gravel streamed down, the gunman turned around and looked up, and Sam leaped out and down on him.

The gunman tried to swing his rifle up, but the Ranger knocked the barrel to the side as a shot exploded. Knowing the silence was broken, Sam swung the hard blunt end of the knife's hilt around and slammed it against the side of the man's head. The gunman melted to the ground, knocked out cold.

Sam grabbed the smoking rifle and dropped down behind the large rock. He levered a fresh round into the rifle chamber and waited expectantly for the sound of the Gatling gun.

Nothing, he told himself after a tense, silent moment.

On the ground the rifleman groaned and batted his eyes. Sam recognized his face even in the shadowy light. He saw the bullet hole in the shoulder of his shirt, the lump of bandage on the wound under it.

"Jim Purser," he said barely above a whisper. "How are you healing?"

"Huh? Okay, I guess," Purser said dreamily. But he batted his eyes some more at the sound of his name and the inquiry about his shoulder wound. He opened his eyes, saw the big knife still in the Ranger's hand and opened them even wider in fear. "It's you!" He scooted back a foot on his rump and elbows. "Don't kill me!" he cried out.

"Shut up, Purser," Sam warned him in his lowered voice. "Get that gun started up again, I'll feed you to it."

"All right, Ranger, I'll shut up!" Purser said, lowering his voice. He held his open hands up as if to fend off the big steel blade in the Ranger's hand. "Don't kill me!"

The Ranger realized the man's fear of the knife and deliberately kept it in sight. He also noted no Gatling gunfire. He reached out and slipped Purser's revolver from its holster and pitched it aside.

"How many are in the shack?" he asked, nodding toward the chimney smoke. He remembered how hard it was to get a straight answer from this man when he'd questioned him before in Resting.

"Should be three in there, Ranger," Purser said, giving it up freely this time, his nervous eyes glancing back and forth at the big knife. "There's Bo Anson, a fellow named Gus Holt and Curtis Siedell. That's all I know of, so help me God. If any showed up after I came out here—"

"Take it easy, Purser," Sam said. "Who's manning that Gatling gun? How much ammunition do they have for it?"

"There's plenty of bullets from what I saw. The fellas manning it are Dan Brody and April Boyd—April goes by *Ape*. Which so would I if I was him. Bo's holding

Siedell for ransom. Said he's going to kill Max Bard, Holbert Lee Cross, Kid Domino, the whole bunch of them for all that reward money."

Sam looked at him curiously. After a moment of consideration he said, "Ransom money and reward money, huh?" Then he just shook his head.

"Yeah, I know," Purser said as if reading his thoughts. "He's crazy as a loon if you ask me." He shrugged a little. "I didn't see until after I brought the string of horses. Bo only tells you a little at a time, until it's too late to turn back." A trickle of blood ran down from the fierce knot where the knife hilt had struck him. He paused and glanced toward the knife again, as if trying to think of more information to give. Finally he shook his head. "I swear that's all I know about anything, Ranger. If I come up with something else—"

"You're coming with me," Sam said, cutting him off.

"I'm being arrested?" Purser said, sounding a little relieved at the prospect.

"We'll see," Sam said. "If the Gatling gun starts, or you let anybody in the shack know I'm coming, I'm not going to waste a bullet on you." He jiggled the knife in his hand for emphasis.

"I won't, Ranger. You've got my word," said Purser in a serious tone.

Sam stood up and pulled Purser to his feet. Purser staggered a little from the hard knock on his head. Sam nudged him along the trail, keeping watch for the big gun. Sam stopped for his rifle where he'd left it, and nodded Purser on toward the chimney smoke. He slipped the knife back down into his boot well.

When they stood in the cover of rock and pine across a clearing from the shack, they both sank behind a large stone, Sam with his rifle ready in his hands. Two horses stood close to the shack, picking at clumps of wild grass. They looked rested now, but still dirty and hard ridden from the day before. Another looked around the corner at them and chuffed. Two more stood in a corral whose gate had been left open.

Not a good sign . . .

"Bo Anson," he called out, "it's Ranger Sam Burrack. Send Curtis Siedell out unharmed. Don't make me come and get him."

Jesus! Purser gave him a taken-aback look, not used to hearing anyone speak that way to Bo Anson.

Sam waited; he had little doubt his order would be followed. His hope was to get Siedell out alive by any advantage he could take. He was certain this was going to end up bloody, but he had to see it through the right way all the same.

After a long tense moment Sam looked at Purser, who had a puzzled expression on his face.

"I—I don't think anybody's in there," Purser said.

"Neither do I," said Sam. He pulled Purser up in front of him and gave him a slight push toward the shack. "If I walk into a trap that you're in on, you're the first one going down," he warned.

When they walked onto the plank porch, Sam flattened against the wall beside the door, reached over with his left hand and shoved it open. Purser stood on the other side of the door with a worried look on his face.

Sam stepped into the open doorway, his Colt out at

arm's length, cocked and ready. He relaxed when he saw the shack was empty.

"Nobody home," he said quietly under his breath.

"Damn Bo's hiding. I can't believe he done me this way," Purser said. "I haven't even been paid for those horses yet." He shook his head in regret. "And they're all *real* good horses."

"Believe it, Purser," Sam said. "I warned you about the bunch you're keeping company with. Do you believe it yet?"

"I wasn't looking to join a men's choir, Ranger," Purser offered. "It might be that Bo got so busy, he forgot about me being here."

Sam lowered the Colt and gave him a skeptical look.

"That was going to be my next guess," he said.

"Really?" Purser said.

Sam didn't answer. He looked all around the shack and let out a breath. An empty ammunition crate stood on a wooden table.

"Where are they headed?" he asked.

"Ranger, I swear I don't have any idea!" Purser said quickly, nervously. "Had I known they weren't here, I would've told you first thing when you had that pigsticker pointed at me. Big knives give me the shivering shits—that's the truth. I'd sooner get shot any day—"

"Think *real hard*, Purser," Sam said, letting his shoulder drop a little as if ready to reach down to his boot.

"All right, I *am*!" Purser said.

Seeing it was going nowhere, Sam said, "You had a dozen horses when you left Resting. How many did you bring up here?"

"All twelve," said Purser. "That's how many Bo asked for. That's how many I brought him."

Sam considered it. He scanned the empty shack again, seeing what looked like a shiny new oil tin. He picked up the tin, felt a film of oil under his thumb and shook it.

Empty. . . . Looking around again, he saw no oil lanterns or lamps. On the floor he saw a smudged broken lamp globe.

"How many supplies did they have?" he asked.

"I brought along enough grub and horse feed to last a small group a week or two," Purser said, "but it'll last a lot longer than that if they stick an elk or a few rabbits into the mix."

Sam motioned him toward the door with the barrel of his big Colt. Purser walked onto the porch.

"What's on the other side of this hill?" Sam asked, stepping back over into the doorway, looking out at the long hill line.

"I don't know," Purser said. "I heard Bo mention some old played-out mines over there, go back to the days of the Spaniards. Maybe some old pueblo dwellers—Mayans from the old days."

Sam looked at him, running possibilities through his mind. He stepped out of the doorway and motioned Purser off the porch. Purser walked down and looked at Sam expectantly.

"How much water did you bring with the supplies?" Sam asked.

Purser gave a shrug.

"None, except my own couple of canteens," he said. "Bo never asked me to bring any."

Sam nodded as if coming to a conclusion. He looked down at layer upon layer of hoof and boot prints on the ground, unable to untangle them. He shook his head a little.

"Let's grab a couple of those horses and get out of here, Purser," he said.

"Wait, where am I going, Ranger?"

"With me," Sam said.

"Why? Are you arresting me after all?" he asked.

"No," Sam said. "But I can either take you with me or shoot you and leave you here. Make up your mind, quick."

"Let's get those horses," Purser said without hesitation.

In the midmorning sunlight the Ranger and Jim Purser rode two of the loose horses down to where Sam had left the copper dun hitched out of sight from the trail. Purser had found a worn saddle and bridle lying in the corner of the shack. Sam had ridden bareback with a rope hackamore and a short length of lead rope. When Sam stepped down from the horse's back, he handed Purser the lead rope.

"Keep this horse as a spare," he said. "We might need him where we're headed."

"Oh? Where's that?" Purser asked, watching Sam step up into the saddle and turn the dun toward the trail.

"We're headed over to the old Spanish mines," Sam said. "I've got a hunch that's where Anson is headed."

"A *hunch*?" Purser said. He gave the Ranger a doubtful look.

Sam looked away toward a deep rock pass in the distant hill line.

"It's more than a hunch," he said, not about to tell Purser any more than he felt he should. "We'll get to that pass and see if we find tracks there." He paused, then said, "You brought Anson some fine-looking riding stock. Is that what he asked for?"

Purser looked at him curiously.

"He never said," Purser replied. "He must've figured they'd be good horses."

"If he wanted them for a robbery he wouldn't have just *figured* they would be *good horses*. He would have made sure you knew they had to be the best," Sam said, the two of them riding along the rocky trail.

Purser fell silent, considering it, leading the spare horse alongside him.

As they rode on, the Ranger checked the rocky ground beneath them at every minor turn or fork in the trail. After the better part of an hour, the tangle of hoofprints had fallen away gradually until a fresher set of tracks showed clearly above all the older ones. The fresh tracks led them to the mouth of the deep rocky pass that wound through the stone hillside.

They rode for the better part of an hour across rugged terrain and reached a standing pool fed by runoff water from the stone cliffs to their left. As they watered themselves and the animals, Sam looked to their right at a low stone dam where water seeped over the top and snaked away along the hillside. Studying the fresh hoofprints along the pool's edge, he saw that the riders had taken that direction.

So far so good.

He took down his canteens from his saddle horn and filled them while the dun drank beside the other two horses. When the horses were watered, Sam adjusted the dun's cinch and swung into the saddle. He waited until Purser was in front of him with the spare horse in tow. Then he raised his rifle from its boot, laid it across his lap and nudged his dun along behind him.

Chapter 23

Following the hoofprints along an ancient upward trail running along the hillside, Sam and Purser stopped at the sight of the single rider rounding in and out of view down the trail toward them.

"Recognize him?" Sam asked.

"Yeah, it's one of Anson's men—name of Gus Holt," Purser replied.

Sidestepping their horses off behind a boulder, they sat and waited quietly as hooves clacked on the hard, stony surface. As the rider drew closer, Purser's mount made a slight chuffing sound, but Purser reached down and patted the horse's withers to keep the animal quiet. He saw the Ranger give him a look.

"I don't owe these jakes a thing, Ranger," he whispered. "After the way they treated me, Anson and his men can go to hell."

Sam only nodded and waited.

When the rider rounded the boulder and came into sight, the Ranger stepped his dun out, his Colt raised and cocked, ready to fire.

"Stop right there, *Gus Holt*. Don't try it," he said, seeing the man grab for a Remington revolver at the sound of his name.

The gunman didn't heed the warning. He reined his horse down hard and yanked the Remington up, cocking it on the upswing, moving fast. But not fast enough. The Ranger's big Colt bucked once in his hand and sent the gunman flying back off his saddle. The man's gun flew from his hand as he back-flipped off the horse's rump in a mist of blood and landed facedown on the trail. The startled horse reared a little, ran forward a few steps, then circled and stooped. Sam sat for a few seconds with his smoking Colt still out at arm's length, making sure the fight was over.

Purser stepped his horse out from the cover of the sunken boulder and looked down at Holt on the ground, blood running out of his chest in a puddle beneath him.

"That's what you get, you son of a bitch," he said to the body on the ground. He swung down from his saddle and started to step closer.

"Stay back," Sam said. He dropped the spent shell from his Colt, replaced it with a fresh round and closed the gate. Gun in hand, he swung down from his saddle and picked up the Remington, shoving it behind his gun belt. He stooped and rolled Holt onto his back and saw a letter sticking up from the pocket of his flared-open lapel. Purser eased in closer now that the Ranger had Holt's Remington in his belt.

Sam unfolded the letter and read it.

"Here it is, in Curtis Siedell's own handwriting," he said. "Siedell's instructing that two hundred thousand dollars be delivered out here by two of his rail detectives."

"Two hundred thousand dollars!" Purser said, stunned at such a high figure.

"Let's drag him off the trail," Sam said, grabbing Holt by the front of his riding duster. Purser stepped in and took the dead man by his wrists.

"Why'd you ask the quality of horses I brought Bo?" Purser said as they dragged Holt off the trail into some rocks and brush.

"He only has three men with him, counting Siedell," Sam said, thinking of no reason not to tell him. "He's riding over here among the pueblo hill dwellers. He can't just ride into their lair without offering them something."

"The horses?" Purser said, putting that much of it together. He paused and said, "But the hill dwellers don't have much use for horses. They mostly travel on foot."

"They'll ride horses all summer long if they've got them," Sam said. "Come winter they butcher them and dry the meat."

"So the horses were food gifts for the hill dwellers," Purser reasoned.

"That's what I figure," Sam said. "These people have no use for money. But for something as useful as horses, they'd give Anson the run of the hillside. Like as not they've already spotted us and told him we're here."

Purser looked higher up along the rocky hillside, at a flat cliff hewed level by hand, and black openings like dark eyes looking out across the lower earth.

"Don't look for them," said Sam. "You won't see them unless they want you to."

"I don't want to think about getting killed and scalped in my sleep," Purser said, but he stopped scanning along the hillside.

"They're peaceful enough," Sam said, straightening and dusting his hands. "Anyway, here I come, *peaceful* or not."

"If you don't mind my asking, Ranger," Purser said as they walked back to their horses, "what do you care about freeing King Curtis Siedell? He's a no-good son of a bitch." He swung up atop his saddle and gathered the lead rope to the spare horse.

"I care nothing for Siedell," Sam said. "But he has a right to all protection provided by law. Like it or not, I'm part of that protection—I swore an oath to it." He swung up atop the dun and turned it to the trail. "Anyway, I didn't come looking for Curtis Siedell, or Max Bard or Bo Anson. I was on my way to Yuma on some other business. All this just fell in my lap. Now I've got to finish it."

Atop a terraced cliff higher up and farther along the row of black abandoned mine entrances, Bo Anson looked down through his telescope. He watched the Ranger and Jim Purser in the circle of the lens as they rode into sight around a turn on the lower trail. Beside him a hill dweller stood with his slim, weathered arm extended, pointing out the two riders.

"Take your arm down before I break it over my knee," Ape Boyd said to the old Indian with a hard stare.

"Leave him alone, Ape," said a gunman named Bird Harkins, one of the men Bo Anson had sent ahead a week earlier to secure them a place among the hill dwellers. "Cole and me won these filthy savages over. We don't need you coming in undoing everything."

George Cole, sitting beside him, nodded in agreement.

"Bird's right," he put in. "That ragged old bummer is held high among these *hole livers*. Leave him alone."

"It's *hill dwellers*," Harkins corrected him quietly.

"What's the difference?" said Cole. "This old turd don't know what I'm calling him anyway." He gave the old Indian a wide smile and nodded. "Ain't that right, *old turd*?"

The old Indian only stared with a blank expression. He hadn't told any of them he understood their language. He watched and listened, and kept his arm up a few seconds longer before dropping it to his side.

Ape glared at Harkins.

"That's twice you've butted in, tried to tell me what to do. Do it again, I'll kill you," he growled.

"Save all your threats, Ape," said Harkins. "I ain't easily impressed. Besides, somebody had to say something, you pissing off the cliff like that. What about the poor Indians walking on the next level down?"

"What about them?" Ape said. "Let them think all their rain-dancing paid off—"

"That's enough, all of you!" Bo Anson roared, jerking the telescope from his eye. "We've got that damn Ranger riding up on us. Jim Purser is with him."

"How'd they find us?" Harkins asked, surprised.

Anson just stared at him without reply.

"They followed your tracks, you raving idiot," Siedell cut in, getting his fill of the outlaws—finding them a far different breed than the guerrillas he'd ridden with back when he and Max Bard's gang rode side by side.

The men appeared to not even hear Siedell amid what he considered their mindless banter.

"Jim Purser . . . *damn*," Cole said to Anson. "Has the Ranger got him cuffed?"

"Doesn't look like it to me," Anson replied. "You and Bird get down the switchback somewhere and kill them before they get up here."

"Bo!" said Ape, as if stricken by a great idea. "What about I just go get the big gun, carry it down and chop them to pieces?"

Listening, Siedell just bowed his head and shook it slowly in disgust.

"Jesus," he whispered under his breath.

"No, Ape, the big gun stays up there, to cover me," Anson said, lifting his eyes upward toward the top of the cliff line above them. "I want it in your hands, in case these two bite the dirt."

Harkins and Cole looked at each other as they stood up and picked up their rifles.

"We're not going down, Bo," Harkins said with confidence. He glared at Ape and added, "And we don't need no *Gatling gun* to send one Ranger on the road to hell."

"Yeah, Ape," Cole taunted as they headed for the open front of the ancient chiseled-out Spanish mine, "maybe you'll have us a pot of coffee boiled when we get back—we'll tell you all about it."

"Son of a bitch . . . ," Ape snarled as the two walked out and down along the footpath. The Indian looked at Anson, got a nod from him and turned and walked away behind them.

Against the stone wall Curtis Siedell sat handcuffed, his boots and hat missing. He slumped even more now that he knew the Ranger was coming up the path. Any hope of him convincing Anson to take him somewhere to a bank and get the ransom money was gone now. With the Ranger here, a gun battle was coming. He'd seen his share of battles years ago. His only hope now was to stay down and stay alive.

"Get up on top, Ape," Anson said. "Make sure the tripod will let you aim that Gatling down along this path before the Ranger gets here. Stay up there and be ready for him."

When Ape left at a trot toward the Gatling gun set up atop the cliff line, Anson turned, picked up a rifle and looked over at Siedell.

"And now here we are, just a couple of ol' long-rider outlaws turned *businessmen*." He gave a thin smile behind his thick mustache and a week's worth of beard stubble. "Would you call this an *emergence* of sorts or an out-and-out *takeover*?"

"I call it me struggling all my life to make my fortune, and having a thieving, murdering scoundrel come take it from me," said Siedell.

"Ain't that how big business and outlawing both work?" Anson grinned. "You spend part of your life stealing what you can, and the rest keeping the next thief from stealing it from you?"

"Wise thinking, Bo," Siedell said, keeping the contempt and sarcasm from seeping into his words. "If I had my hat on I'd tip it to you."

"You're taking it awfully well, King Curtis," Anson said, "me gutting you for two hundred thousand dollars." He eyed Siedell with suspicion.

"What choice do I have?" said Siedell. "If you kill the Ranger, I'll have to suck up my loss and take it like a gentleman. As long as I'm alive, I'll figure a way to make back my losses."

"Should I have asked for more?" Anson said.

"No, two hundred about clears my table," Siedell replied. "My people would refuse to send any more than that amount."

He wasn't about to tell Anson that giving up two hundred thousand wouldn't hurt him. He'd cut the pay of his employees and up the price of shipping on his rails, and get that money back in no time—a lot less work than what Anson had gone through to take him prisoner and set all this up. What low-class thieves like Anson didn't realize, Siedell reminded himself, was that the only thievery worth committing was the kind where the laws of commerce protected its own.

Damn fool . . .

"You do realize that my detectives will not hand over the money unless they see I'm alive, and they're able to secure my release, don't you?"

"That is understandable," said Anson, liking this kind of talk, businessman to businessman. He pointed at

Siedell for emphasis and said, "You realize that if it comes down to me and that Ranger and holding a gun to your head to get myself out of here, you're a dead man."

"Yes, of course," said Siedell. "Let's hope that doesn't happen."

"Yeah, I thought you'd feel that way," Anson said. He stooped, picked up a pair of boots and pitched them both over at Siedell's bare feet. "Pull them on. Where we're headed I want you to be able to keep up." As he spoke he picked up a torch leaning against a rock. He pulled a long wooden match from his shirt pocket.

Siedell nodded, picked up the boots one at a time and pulled them up over his bare feet. No sooner had he gotten the boots on than he flinched at the sound of a rifle shooting from down on the lower hillside.

"Hurry yourself up, King Curtis," said Anson. He wagged his rifle barrel toward a black mine shaft entrance that led through the stone wall off to their right. "It sounds like the fight has commenced. This will take us down onto the trail. I'll catch the Ranger by surprise."

"Down there?" Siedell said, looking at the shaft opening with apprehension. "We'll be lucky if we don't get ate up by rattlesnakes."

"Snakes, huh?" Bo Anson gave a flat, mirthless grin as he struck the match and lit the head of the torch. "Just think of it as a family reunion," he said. "Now get moving." Outside on the lower trail, another shot resounded.

Chapter 24

The Ranger and Jim Purser both pulled their horses back and swung them off the trail when the rifle shot zinged past their heads and kicked up dirt on the hard trail behind their horses' hooves. Before the shooter could get a fresh round levered and get another shot off, Sam swung his dun off the trail, Purser right beside him. With only enough short rock cover for themselves, they shooed their horses and the spare away and ducked down.

On a ledge only fifty feet above the trail in front of them, a second shot rang out. They hugged the ground as the bullet chipped fragments of rock into the air. A puff of gray smoke billowed atop the cliff, revealing the shooter's position.

"Stay here, Purser. Don't try to leave," Sam said, rising into a low crouch.

"*Leave?*" Purser said, his voice shaky. "Where *else* am I going to go, Ranger?"

Sam didn't answer. He took off his tall sombrero and rose just enough to look around and find another low rock closer to the trail. He knew once he sprang into sight, there was no turning back. He'd have to be ready to turn a dangerous move into an opportunity. As he waited, another shot rang out.

Here goes. . . . He leaped up, running forward, his rifle against his chest in a flat port arms, the barrel pointed toward the cliff where more gray smoke drifted sidelong on the air. Atop the cliff the rifleman sprang up, seeing his running target. But as he took aim, certain the Ranger would keep racing toward cover, to his surprise, Sam came to a fast, sliding stop, his rifle springing up to his shoulder, his head cocked over to his right, taking quick aim.

The shooter, having given his running target some lead, the way a hunter would give lead to a fleeing elk, suddenly realized his rifle sights had jumped ahead of the halted Ranger by three yards. *Uh-oh, this is no elk!* He jerked his rifle sights back onto his target just in time to catch the Ranger's bullet in the center of his chest. Sam saw the man fall away as a shot from his rifle exploded and thumped into the ground five feet to the Ranger's right.

Sam ran on to the rock and dived behind it as another rifle reached out over the cliff and fired down at him.

Two riflemen up there? Looking up, he saw a man hurrying upward, hand and foot, along a steep, rocky path to the next terraced level ten feet higher up. Sam started to take aim, but before he could he saw the man's boots go out of sight up over the edge.

"Get up here, Purser. You're covered, but hurry," he called back over his shoulder.

"Yes, I will, Ranger," Purser called out sharply. He sprang up and raced forward, sliding down into the dirt beside the Ranger.

"There's another one up there," Sam said.

"I know," Purser said. "I saw him take off."

Sam looked all around, farther along the trail and up the side of the rocky hill right behind them.

"These old Spanish mule-cart trails are going to stay switchbacks until they get up to the mine paths," he said.

"I thought you've never been here," Purser said.

"I haven't," Sam said. "But I've been to some just like it. The Spaniards laid all these old mining sites out the same way." He nodded up the bare stone hillside to where the open mines appeared to glare down on them. "A man could die quick searching from one mine opening to the next with a Gatling gun breathing fire down on him." He paused, then said, "It's up there somewhere, watching, just waiting for us."

"What are we going to do?" Purser asked with a pale worried look on his face. "We leave the horses here, the Indians will have them and be gone before we can get back down and stop them."

"We're going on up the switchbacks until we get to the first mine," Sam said. "I'm leaving you and the horses there while I find the big gun." He studied Purser closely, seeing the wheels starting to turn in his mind.

"All right, I got that," Purser agreed, nodding. But he paused and then asked, "What if the gun starts shooting at us while we're headed up the switchbacks? What will we do then?"

"We'll get out of its way," Sam said flatly.

* * *

Anson and Siedell had traveled down through the mine shaft to a fork where another shaft led them out onto the switchbacks three levels down the hillside. When they stepped out onto the trail, Anson spotted the Ranger and Purser leading their horses up the trail toward him. Pulling Siedell back out of sight into the mine shaft opening, Anson peeped around an edge of stone and watched the two walk inside the first dark opening a quarter of a mile downhill from him. He glanced up atop the hillside to where he knew Ape was waiting with the Gatling gun ready to fire.

"It's all going my way." He chuckled to himself.

Inside the first mine shaft, Sam and Purser tied their horses' reins around the iron wheel spoke of an ancient upturned ore cart.

"All right, Ranger," said Purser, sounding more than happy to be left behind with two saddled horses at his disposal, "good luck up there. I'll be waiting right here— rooting for you, you can count on it."

"I know I can," Sam said. He reached out and snapped a handcuff around Purser's wrist. As Purser stared in stunned surprise, Sam snapped the other cuff around the same iron wheel spoke the horses were hitched to.

"Hey, what the—" Purser said. He jerked his cuffed hand back and forth as if testing the cuffs. "You can't leave me handcuffed here. What about all these Indians? They'll cut my throat and take these horses."

"These hill dwellers are peaceful folks," Sam said. "But you're right about them taking the horses." As he spoke he pulled the big Remington from his gun belt and stuck it down into Purser's empty holster. Purser looked down at the gun, started to put his hand on the butt. "Touch that Remmy while I'm still here and you'll feel life make a sudden stop," Sam warned.

Purser pulled his hand up from the gun butt as if it were red hot.

"What if you don't come back, Ranger?" he said.

"I'll be back," Sam said, "especially knowing you'll be right here 'rooting' for me." Facing Purser, he backed out of the shaft opening, rifle in hand, and started walking up the trail. He kept close to the stone facing of the hillside, moving steadily but cautiously from one shaft opening to the next, expecting at any moment to hear the Gatling gun exploding and see its rapid flashes light up the blackness.

At the entrance to the mine shaft where Anson and Siedell stood out of sight, Anson gave his handcuffed prisoner a shove farther back inside. Siedell stumbled backward and sat down hard on a large rock.

"You stay right there until I finish this," Anson said. The blackened torch that he had extinguished leaned smoking against a wall. Anson knew Siedell had no matches, and he knew the man wouldn't attempt to go back inside the black meandering mine shaft without a light in his hand. "Make any noise, I'll start carving off fingers and toes," he warned.

Siedell sat staring, seething at Anson for having put hands on him.

*　　*　　*

Sam had only made his way up past the next two mine openings when suddenly Bo Anson jumped onto the trail in front of him. Anson fanned three rapid shots and jumped back out of sight fast as Sam's Colt streaked up from its holster. Instead of swinging his rifle up into play, Sam kept his Colt cocked, raised and ready, and started to hurry along the trail toward the gun smoke Anson left hanging in the air. Yet something stopped him in his tracks. Why had Anson done that, jumped out and revealed his position? It was a careless, stupid move, fanning three shots— *Uh-oh!* Three shots were a signal.

He stopped himself in midthought and dived off the trail into the nearest shaft opening as bullets kicked up dirt and rock all around him. From atop the cliff fifty yards above him, the Gatling gun's operator had heard Anson's signal and brought the big gun to life. Sam, realizing he had no cover other than the mine shaft opening he'd left a dozen yards behind him, tried to ball down behind a short rock and wait it out. He'd have to make a run for it, back to the mine shaft opening, when the gun stopped to reload.

But even as he considered his position, a rifleman straight across from the next hill line sent a bullet pinging off the rock he lay behind. Sam couldn't get a shot off without chips of rock and dirt pelting his face from the Gatling gun's fire. Across from him the rifleman fired again. Pinned down, Sam knew it was only a matter of time until the two guns chopped him to pieces. But in a second, the big gun fell silent above him.

What now?

In the silent pause, Sam heard two pistol shots ring out from the direction of the Gatling gun. He heard a pained yell as he glanced up and saw a man sailing down off the top of the cliff. Every few feet the flailing man bounced off the stone wall and narrow terraced cart paths on his way down. Even as the man fell, Sam wasted no time. He took aim across the hill line. As the rifleman rose enough to get another shot off, Sam's rifle bucked against his shoulder and sent the man flying backward out of sight, a red mist hanging in the air behind him.

Sam watched as Anson sprang out of the mine's opening so he could see the silent gun's position.

"Give it up, Anson," Sam called out, emerging into sight, chips of rock and dirt peppered all over him.

But Anson only spun toward him.

"Go to hell, Ranger!" he shouted; he fired a wild shot and raced back inside the shaft. But only a second later he came staggering backward and turned a full circle on the trail, blood running down from his black-smudged forehead. He tried to raise his gun toward Siedell, who stalked out of the shaft toward him, gripping the stub of the broken torch handle in both hands, ready for another swing.

Before Anson could fire, a bullet from Sam's rifle lifted him off his feet and sent him flying out over the edge of the terraced trail. Siedell stood staring at the Ranger as if not believing his ordeal was over. Sam lowered his rifle and stared up at the top of the cliff where Sheriff Sheppard Stone stood with his rifle butt propped on his hip.

"Coming down, Ranger," Stone called out.

Sam looked at Curtis Siedell. Siedell tossed the broken torch, looked down at Ape's body lying in the trail and spat on it. He looked back up at the Ranger and said in an arrogant tone, "Any reason you couldn't have gotten here sooner?"

"None that I can think of," Sam said coolly. He had started to lower his rifle when a voice behind him said, "Go on and drop it, Ranger. You're all through here."

Sam saw Siedell's face turn pale at the sound of the voice. Turning around slowly, rifle still in hand, Sam saw Max Bard and Mallard Trent facing him, Bard with his long revolver out at arm's length, cocked and ready.

"I won't tell you again, Ranger," said Bard. "None of your gun tricks, and no talking. Make a move on me and you're dead."

Sam could tell he meant it.

Letting the Winchester fall to the ground, Sam took a step back in silence, letting his arms drop to his sides. He kept his right hand away from his Colt, giving no sign of being poised to reach for it. He knew that Bard had no interest in killing anybody here other than Curtis Siedell—and that intense vengeful hatred was going to have to be his downfall, Sam decided.

"I've got you, you rotten son of a bitch," Bard said, stepping forward slowly, his eyes now riveted on Siedell. "I can't tell you how long I have waited to open your belly and watch you suck air like a fish!"

There it is, Sam noted, watching as Bard took another slow step. His hard stare at Siedell seemed to have shut out everyone else around him. Sam saw his gun hand tighten on the big revolver. *Here it comes.*

Before Bard's finger pressed the trigger, Sam shouted, "Bard!" The vengeful gunman swung his revolver just enough toward Sam to take his aim off Siedell. That was what Sam needed. His Colt streaked up from his holster, firing on the upswing. His first shot sent Bard staggering backward, Bard's gun flying from his hand. The second shot sent him over the edge of the terraced trail onto the rocky hillside. Almost before Bard fell out of sight, Sam swung his Colt toward Mallard Trent and saw him raise his hands chest high away from his gun.

"Don't shoot," said Trent. "I'm not one of his men. I was riding with him until I saw a chance to get away." He nodded at Siedell. "I work for Curtis Siedell. Just ask him."

"He works for me, Ranger. He's a tracker," Siedell said. As he spoke he took out his last cigar from inside his coat and stuck it between his teeth. "You're through here. Obliged for your help, but you can go now. Trent and I have things under control. We're quite capable...."

Sam just stared at him.

Having heard the two pistol shots, Sheriff Stone hurried down the hillside and slid through loose gravel onto the trail, his Colt out and cocked.

"Can't I turn my back for a minute without more shooting starting up?" he said to Sam, a wry half grin on his weathered face.

Sam looked at him, seeing he was sober, steadier, stronger looking, more sure of himself than before.

Seeing the look on Sam's face, Stone said, "That's

right, Ranger, not a drop." He uncocked his Colt and
held it up in his hand. "I bought three bottles on my
way out of Gnat. But I haven't opened any of them. I
thought about it. But it came to me—hell, I've been a
wolf all my life. I don't need rye to make me think I'm
one."

Sam watched him spin the Colt on his finger, lowering it and twirling it expertly into its holster.

"That's good," Sam said. He looked all around, understanding how Stone felt. There was something hollow
now. Something missing inside now that the shooting
had stopped and all that remained was to ride on to
Yuma. "I've got a man handcuffed inside a mine shaft
back there with the horse," he said. He turned and
started to walk away.

"What about these two?" Stone asked, jerking a nod
toward Siedell and Trent.

"Siedell says this fella works for him," Sam said. "I
figure they most likely deserve each other."

"All right." Stone nodded in agreement, falling in
behind the Ranger. "When we get to Yuma, do you
have to tell the judge about me, the drinking and all?"

"No, not if you tell him yourself," Sam replied without looking around at him. "I'll tell him I don't know of
anybody I'd sooner work with—tell him Sheriff Deluna
will say the same."

"Obliged, Ranger," Stone said quietly. "I'm telling him
about the bribery money, where it's at and how much it
is. Think he'll believe I wasn't holding on to it for myself?
The Cadys will say I was if they get a chance."

"Then he'll have to decide who he believes," Sam said. "Are you holding on to it for yourself?"

"No, I'm not," Stone said.

"Then there you have it," said Sam. "He'll hear the Cadys and know what they are. He'll hear you and know what you are. The truth ain't worth a tin nickel if you don't know who it's coming from."

"Yeah, that sounds about right," Stone said, satisfied. They walked on. "He's going to wonder what took us so long," he added as the two of them stopped before turning where Purser waited.

"He might wonder," Sam said. They faced the west, where the desert sun perched low, glowing red along the rim of the hill lines and the edge of the earth. "But he realizes a man never knows what to expect, crossing these badlands."

Turn the page for a look
at Arizona Ranger Sam Burrack's
next adventure in Ralph Cotton's

PAYBACK AT BIG SILVER

Available from Signet in October 2015.

Arizona Territory Ranger Sam Burrack sat waiting midtrail atop his copper-colored dun. Both man and animal stood perfectly still, statuelike in the crisp silver dawn. Their senses searched the silence along the winding trail leading off and upward along the rocky hills. A sliver of steam curled out of the dun's nostrils. The Ranger rested the butt of his Winchester rifle on his thigh, cocked and ready, its barrel pointing skyward. He'd removed his trail gloves and stuck them down in his gun belt. He held his hand in a firing grip around the small of the rifle stock, his finger outside of the trigger guard, resting along the cold metal gun chamber.

When the dun's ears pricked slightly toward the trail, the Ranger gave a trace of a smile and rubbed the horse's withers.

Not much longer . . .

The men he lay in wait for had robbed a mine payroll the day before—in fact had robbed two other payrolls over the past week. As the sound of horses' hooves overtook the morning silence, Sam wrapped his reins loosely around the dun's saddle horn, stepped down from the saddle and nudged the dun on its rump. The horse stepped away behind the cover of a tall rock as if trained to do so. Sam shifted his rifle to his left hand, drew his Colt and held it cocked down his right side. Looking up along the trail he counted four horsemen riding down, dust roiling behind their horses' hooves.

Riding into sight, the first horseman swung his horse quarterwise to the Ranger, and jerked it to a halt.

"*Whoa,* boys!" he called out to the others, caught by surprise at seeing the Ranger standing there, alone, armed, looking as if he might have been there all night, waiting.

Sam stood staring calmly, his duster open down the front showing his badge, should anyone be interested in seeing it.

"How the hell did you get around us, Ranger?" the first rider, a seasoned Missourian gunman named Bern Able, called out. As he spoke, the other three jerked their horses to a halt. They instinctively formed a half circle on the narrow trail.

"Simple," Sam said coolly. "You stopped. I kept riding."

"I'll be damned. . . ." Able gave a stiff grin through a long, unattended mustache. He looked all around the hill lines encircling them as if to see what route the Ranger had taken. "And that's all there was to it?" His hand rested on the butt of a Remington conversion strapped across his belly in a cross-draw holster. "I'll have to remember that."

The Ranger stood with his feet spread in a fighting

stance, his riding duster spread open down the front, his battered gray sombrero brim tilted down a little on his forehead—Sonora style—against the glare of rising sunlight in the east.

"I'll be taking that money now, Able," he said with resolve. He nodded at the bulging canvas bag hanging from the saddle horn of Able's pale speckled barb.

"*Taking's* what you'll have to do," said a younger Tex-Mexican outlaw named Brandon Suarez. His right hand rested on a holstered black-handled Colt with an eagle etched on its grip.

Sam only gave him a throwaway glance as if it went without saying that he would *take* the money. Then he looked back at Able, who still sat grinning, yet tensed, poised.

"Hush up, Brandon. We're talking here," Able said sidelong to Suarez without taking his eyes off the Ranger. "But he's right you know," he said to Sam. "I've never understood why you lawmen think a man will risk his life, get his hands on some hard-earned money and just turn around and give it all up to you." He shook his head in disgust. "I'd like to hear just how you see any fairness in it." He fixed a hard, sharp gaze on the Ranger.

"Yeah, me too," said Suarez.

"It would require a lot of explaining," Sam said quietly, almost patiently. "That's not why I'm here. . . ." As he spoke, his cocked Colt came up casually in an unthreatening manner and leveled at Able's chest twenty feet away. He slid a glance over the other two: a young but well-seasoned Wyoming cattle thief named Freddie Dobbs and a huge saloon bouncer from Maryland named Armand "Boomer" Phipps. He noted that Dobbs kept his hand well away from his holstered sidearm. Boomer Phipps, owing to his massive size, was not known to carry a gun.

"Well, ain't you slicker than pig piss . . . ?" said Able. Rather than looking taken aback at how coolly the Ranger had just gotten the upper hand, Able shrugged it off.

The other three just stared, not understanding why Able had allowed that to happen.

"See, Brandon . . . ?" he said as if undaunted. "That's his way of telling you to go to hell—that he don't give a damn how hard you work or what-all you go through to get the money. He figures his job is to take it back and make sure it goes to the square heads who wasn't fit to hang on to it in the first place. Right, Ranger?" He glared at Sam as if enraged by the unfairness of it.

"There you have it," Sam said with resolve. He saw the slightest clasp of Able's gun hand on the butt of the big Remington belly gun—the faintest move of his thumb toward the gun hammer.

Now . . . !

Sam's Colt bucked in his right hand before Able brought his belly gun out and up into play. Able flew backward as his blood splattered on Freddie Dobbs. Dobbs' horse whinnied and reared wildly. Sam fired the Winchester in his left hand, hoping the shot would distract Suarez. It did. The outlaw ducked a little as the rifle shot whistled past him. Before he could straighten and get a shot off, Sam swung his Colt toward him and fired. Suarez fell down the side of his spooked horse, blood spilling from his chest.

Even as his world faded around him, Suarez squeezed off a wild shot. Sam saw the round send Dobbs flying backward out of his saddle. He landed flat on his back. Sam swung the Colt toward Boomer Phipps, who sat unarmed and growling in his saddle like a mad dog.

"Hands in the air, Boomer," Sam called out. But even as he spoke, he had to holster his Colt quickly and grab Able's speckled barb by its reins as the animal tried to streak past him. He held on to the spooked horse's reins, his Winchester smoking in his left hand.

"Who says?" Boomer growled at him. He swung down from his saddle. Moving fast for a man his size, he charged at the Ranger as if unstoppable. "You're not going to shoot me. I'll break your head off!"

Sam knew he needed to lever a fresh round into the rifle chamber, but he had no time. Boomer Phipps charged hard and fast, a massive and deadly force pounding at him like a crazed grizzly. Sam let go of the barb's reins and drew the rifle far back over his right shoulder with both hands. With all his strength, he drove the rifle butt forward into Phipps' broad forehead. Phipps stopped as if he'd run into a brick wall. The impact of the huge outlaw sent the Ranger flying backward onto his rump.

Instead of going to the ground like any normal-sized man would, Phipps staggered backward two steps, caught himself and stood swaying, dazed but still on his feet. Sam came to his feet, levering a round into his rifle, and stood with his feet braced, ready to fire.

"Stay where you are, Boomer," he warned. "Don't make me kill you."

Phipps batted his eyes; he raised his arms and spread his big hands in a wrestling stance.

"You ain't going to *kill me*, Ranger," he said, still dazed. "I'm going to kill you!" He stalked forward one step, then another.

Sam leveled the cocked rifle and aimed it at the outlaw's broad chest. There was nothing more to say—nothing more to do. Sam started to squeeze the trigger. But before he made the killing shot at a distance of less than thirty feet, Phipps crumpled to his knees, growled aloud and pitched forward onto his chest, finally succumbing to the blow to his forehead. Even still he moaned and slung his big head back and forth, trying to clear it.

Sam lowered the rifle in both hands as Phipps groaned and wallowed in the dirt. Stepping over to the dun, Sam took a pair of handcuffs from his saddlebags and a coil of rope from his saddle horn. Walking back to the downed outlaw, he grabbed the reins to Able's barb again as the horse stepped nervously around on the narrow trail.

"Don't make me hit you again, Boomer," Sam said, stooping down, grabbing the outlaw's left arm and pulling it back behind him before Phipps knew what was happening.

"I dare . . . you to, law dog!" Phipps growled, sounding groggy and thick-tongued. He reached his other hand around behind him and flailed about for the Ranger. Sam managed to grab the big hand long enough to clasp the cuff around the other wrist.

Phipps, still a little dazed, struggled against the cuffs and wallowed until he managed to rise onto his knees.

"I'll twist your limbs off!" he shouted at Sam.

Sam stepped back, opened a loop in the rope and swung it down over the big man's shoulders, drawing it tight around his arms. Before Phipps could react, two more loops swung around him and tightened.

"There now, Boomer, settle yourself down," Sam said. "You're not going anywhere."

Phipps strained and struggled; Sam heard the rope creak with tension.

"Shoot me, Ranger. I dare you," he continued to taunt. "You won't shoot me. You're afraid to—!"

His words cut short as Sam stepped behind him, placed his right boot between his shoulders and shoved him forward. Phipps landed with a grunt and a solid thud. Sam wrapped three turns of rope around his thick knees and dogged the rope down.

"That ought to do it," he said quietly. Phipps struggled, but Sam could see he was wearing out.

"What about me . . . over here?" Freddie Dobbs called out in a weak voice. Sam saw him sitting up unsteadily on the ground. Blood ran freely from a bullet hole in his upper shoulder.

"I'm coming, Dobbs," Sam called out, dusting dirt from his hands. "Keep breathing in and out."

"That's . . . *real* funny," Dobbs rasped.

Sam helped the big outlaw to his feet and steadied him for a moment. Phipps' forehead carried a swollen welt the size and shape of the Ranger's rifle butt. Blood trickled down from the welt and dripped from his nose. Sam tugged on the short length of rope in his hand.

"Let's go, Boomer," he said.

The outlaw looked down groggily at his knees with the rope wrapped securely around them. He took a short six-inch step forward, swaying, his huge arms bound against his sides.

"How am I supposed to walk like this?" he asked.

"Real slow," the Ranger replied flatly.

S909

National bestselling author
RALPH COMPTON

"A writer in the tradition of Louis L'Amour and Zane Grey!" —*Huntsville Times*

Available wherever books are sold or at
penguin.com

No other series packs this much heat!

THE TRAILSMAN

**Available wherever books are sold or at
penguin.com**

S310